RITUAL MAGIC

THEA ATKINSON

Have you got your free ebook yet?

Be sure to visit http://theaatkinson.com to get your freebie.

CHAPTER ONE

THE GIRL WHO STOOD at the threshold of my shop wore a black eye swollen enough that I barely noticed the split in the corner of her mouth. My stomach clenched at the sight of her. She looked like a stray cat, beaten and mangy and terrified of a loving touch.

When she scanned the shop, clutching a single page of white resume paper, I knew why she was there, and I didn't care if she had a record for theft or drugs or if she was a crack-addicted prostitute. I planned to hire her right then and there.

I tried not to scurry out from behind my counter and ambush her, though the urge was pretty insistent. She gave me every indication that she'd take off like a shot if I did that. Instead, I busied myself with a few bars of spelled soap a customer had requisitioned as a special order. They'd been cut already into rustic shapes and I was tying the parchment around them, blotting each with a wax seal that held a single hair from her lover.

Love spells were tricky, but I figured since the two were already a pair, I couldn't do much harm if it did work, and if it was inert, I'd lost nothing in the attempt. With my attention carefully concentrated on the perfect dollop of wax, I barely heard the girl approach the counter until I sensed her lurking nearby.

A mouse, I thought. Not a cat. She was a mouse in an alley, beaten around a few times by the resident tom but still hanging in there. Good for her.

"Excuse me," she said. Her voice was like a rusty hinge, throaty with just a hint of abrasion. I wondered if she was a smoker.

I looked up, holding the sealer down on the gob of black wax. "I'm sorry," I said. "I didn't hear you come in. How can I help you?"

This close up, I could see how much the black eye had to hurt. It positively throbbed purple and yellow at the edges. It was all I could do not to wince as she shoved the paper at me with one hand. The other went behind her back. I had the feeling she was crossing her fingers back there, hoping for a stroke of luck.

"I want to apply for the job."

My gaze flicked to the sign I'd put in the window the day before. No one had applied for the job and I'd expected it to take a few weeks to find the right clerk. I couldn't afford a lot, which I expected to put a damper on the quality of applicants, but neither could I afford not to hire someone.

With the Cult of Blackburn still working in the shadows, I was getting too nervous to be in the shop alone all the time. I'd already been attacked by one of their goons and narrowly escaped his scythe. I'd passed out too many times playing around with the magic I'd seemingly acquired in recent weeks. And I'd apparently fugue-walked from the store to the scene of a triple homicide.

A gal had to know when enough was enough and call in the Calvary already.

I took the paper from her as gently as I could and laid it on the counter. "It's weird hours." Smoothing the resume out, I noticed she'd spilled coffee on it at some point. "Says here you've not worked since High School."

I didn't care, really, but neither did I want her to think I wasn't professional.

"I got married right out of High School," she said but didn't offer more than that.

I pretended to scan her resume as she fidgeted in clunky heels and chewed her lip. The furtive once over I gave it told me her name was Scarlett, and I stole quick peeks at her over the edge of the paper when I thought she wasn't paying attention.

She was a pretty thing with full lips and lush lashes, and beneath the facade of bruised and beaten mouse, I sensed a steely heart. I figured she had to have some of that iron in her backbone to survive whatever bastard in her life had done that to her.

"I could use someone in the morning, Scarlett," I suggested in a diffident tone, hoping she'd think I was giving it consideration but still wasn't quite sure. I knew the type. She'd want a chance to stand up for herself; she'd need a win that she earned, not charity. Oh, she'd take charity, but she needed the victory.

Her hands went down on the counter in eagerness. Her nails were chipped. A worker bee, I thought. "I can start right now if you like."

I flipped the corner of the paper down and scanned her more directly this time. I pressed my lips together primly, as though I wasn't really sure.

"I'll do anything," she said. "Put out stock. Sweep the floor. Wash windows. Hell, I'll even cook you dinner." She tittered at that and I couldn't stop the progress of the smile that spread across my mouth.

"Can you make curry and naan?"

"I make a mean chicken soup."

"But not curry."

She shrugged. "Sure I can make it. Remains to be seen if it's any good."

I came out from behind the counter because it seemed the most professional thing to do when you're going to shake someone's hand.

"No dinner needed. Just someone who's not afraid of a little bit of work." I stuck my hand out and she took it with a firmer grip than I expected.

"I'm not afraid of much," she said.

I almost balked when she said it. The comment was made probably because she knew I'd noticed the shape she was in and wanted to indicate she knew what she looked like, but I had a quick image of the things that I'd seen in the last couple months and wasn't sure I should expose her to that sort of danger. I mean, based on her shiner, she obviously had enough violence in her life.

But then she spun on her heel, a renewed vigor in her manner, and I knew I couldn't take the small victory away from her. I resisted the urge to warn her about the things that could go bump in the night, reasoning that she'd applied for a job in a psychic shop. She had to figure magic came with the territory.

"Are you any good at organizing things?" I said, planting my hand on the appointment book that had gone to complete chaos in the last two weeks. The one thing I'd hoped for when I'd hooked up with the police all those weeks ago, namely, gaining a reputation, had finally come to haunt me. I had more appointments than I could manage on top of the spell requests.

All well-to-do, older ladies and gents all looking for something they couldn't find in their usual day. I chalked that one up to Maureen, whom I'd never seen again after I'd puzzled out what sort of spirit was haunting her mother's death mask.

I looked up, expecting Scarlett to be hovering around the counter, waiting for me to shoo her away, but she was already re-organizing one of the candle shelves by the door. She peered up at me from between two pillar candles she was comparing side by side.

"I've got a bit of O.C.D," she said with a grin. "Lucky for you."

"Lucky for me," I mumbled as I caught sight of movement over her shoulder. Not that it was unusual to see anyone meandering around outside the shop. It was a tourist area, after all. I should be upset if I didn't see anyone milling around outside.

But my neck had started to prickle, and I wasn't about to ignore my intuition after all that had gone down since the beginning of summer. I grabbed the planner with both hands, intending to wander across the room to have a casual gander at what might be watching us from the corner of my shop door.

As I passed by Scarlett, I nudged her with the book. "Think you could clean up my mess in here?" I asked with a jerk of my chin toward the back room. "There's a desk out back and I'm afraid I've crossed and erased and crossed and rewritten things in here so much that I have no idea who is coming in when and I hate to call someone by the wrong name." I grinned encouragingly. "Not great for business."

She nodded with a quick waggle of her head and placed the candles side by side on the shelf so that they were nestled next to three half height pillars and formed an attractive grouping.

"Sure," she said and took the book with both hands.

I patted the pages as I looked over her shoulder. "I have markers and pens out back. Use what you think best." Yup. Most definitely someone lurking, not window shopping.

Maybe it wasn't smart to hire someone when I knew this might not be the safest place to work. Was I insane to put someone else at risk in my store because I didn't want to be alone?

I ran my eye over her retreating back as I considered just telling her I'd changed my mind. She was halfway through the apothecary gallery when I caught a bit more of the man hanging around the sidewalk. He peeked in the left window, craning his head to see past the fairy lights I had strung around the pane. The large Hecate wheel logo painted on the window obscured most of his face but I caught sight of the scowl sure enough.

My skin did more than crawl at sight of that expression. I felt every invisible rune on my chest and arms ache. My mouth went dry as I took a few more steps toward the window. Maybe he'd run off if I indicated I'd seen him.

"Check the door out back too, will you?" I hollered to Scarlett without taking my eyes off the man. At least if she was near an exit, she could escape should that creepy looking bloke decide to barge in

I made for the window with more than a little anxiety, feeling justifiably paranoid. What the chances might be that in broad daylight another killer had decided to haunt my step had to be astronomical, but not impossible. And if anything, these last weeks proved astronomical odds weren't in my favor.

Even so, the runes didn't lie. I hadn't felt a single burn, ache, or tingle from them since Layne's partner had abducted me and held me prisoner in an abandoned basement. I was still sore and healing from the self-inflicted wounds I'd given myself in order to escape. And while the runes didn't seem the least bit marred by the cuts and scars, they'd gone dormant or quiet or whatever the heck magic did when it wasn't being wielded.

I'd showered, rubbed cream on my chest, loofahed, and all sorts of other activities that involved touching my own skin without incident.

Which led me to believe that the magic I seemed to now possess had to be triggered somehow. It didn't just go off willy nilly although the first few times, it certainly seemed to. I put that down to me just not knowing what was triggering it in the first place.

Approaching the window, seeing that clean-shaven face and blood-shot eyes through the lines of the Hecate's wheel, I was nervous I would set the runes off again and trigger the magic. Because they were on fire by the time I caught the man's eye.

I don't know what I expected from him, but it wasn't for him to lean closer and plant his forehead against the pane. He stared at me for a long moment, holding my eye without blinking with such intensity my heart rate picked up.

I hugged myself as I stood there, frozen by that gaze. My fingers trailed to my chest without thinking. Just before I touched skin to skin beneath the collar of my shirt, he broke the eye contact and stepped away from the window.

The release felt very much like a cold draft sweeping into a sauna. Cold perspiration trickled down the back of my neck. I stood there for longer than I planned, just watching the window, hugging myself as a shiver overcame me.

The street looked the way it always did a few hours before closing on an autumn evening. My shop sat at the crossroads that took traffic on the one side to the piers and boardwalk and the tourist center and restaurants on the other. I had a narrow alley that led to my back door and half a dozen stray cats had taken to stopping by for the bowls of kibble I kept out for them.

The shop across the street had strung white lights around its potted cedar. I knew exactly how it would look in a few hours, warm and yellow and inviting. My sandwich sign sat next to a wooden statue of a gypsy who offered passersby a business card and tea light on a serving tray. The dozens of couples walking by during the summer had dwindled by half in the autumn, and so there were fewer people wandering around.

The scowling stranger had disappeared, probably around the corner. I sidled over to the door and opened it with a ring of the bell strung over the top.

I leaned out against the door frame as I craned to see where he'd gone. It was right about the time I caught sight of a shadow in the alley that I heard Scarlett scream from the back shop.

CHAPTER TWO

I KNEW THE SCREAM of fear when I heard it. I ran for the back of the shop without thinking about the door I left gaping open into the street. My heart pounded hard enough that I thought I could taste the adrenaline.

Scarlett was not in the back shop when I burst through the beaded curtain. The door to the back of my store stood open like a screaming mouth.

I yelled for her, the fear in my throat making the words come out in rasp of tightly curdled syllables. Regret and guilt rode my spine as I sped through the space, my feet pounding the floorboards in a scolding staccato beat. I had no business hiring anyone when I knew damn well no one was safe around me.

I yelled her name again as I pushed past the desk, shoving it hard because I whacked my leg on it. I swore loud enough that I winced at the sound of my own voice. Someone shouted back at me from outside the door.

"Here," she shouted back. "I'm here."

Here, was a few feet into the alley. She was crouched next to a black shadow of fur that I recognized on sight. It had been over a week since I'd seen the black dog that lurked around my shop and appeared, it seemed, to warn me of danger.

The smell of blood cut through the air. When Scarlett looked back at me, I could see she cradled the head of the big black dog, the one Layne was sure was my familiar.

"Fuck," I said and raced to her side. I fell to my knees next to the dog's head.

Someone had hurt it. Wounds, big and round and bloody, peppered its belly, just visible when the beast took large, huffing breaths. When I ran my hands over the poor thing, it moaned and growled low in its throat. Not a threat, just a be careful sort of tone.

"I won't hurt you," I crooned to it. The creature had saved my bacon more times already than I wanted to admit and I would do everything I could to make sure it got looked after.

It moaned and rolled its eyes as though it had its own ideas about what kind of hurt I could administer.

I ran my palm over its snout, stroking lightly with my thumb the way I might a cat.

"It's going to be alright."

I had no idea if that was true. The wounds seemed like burn marks than anything else, but they were too big for cigarette scorches. Whatever instrument had been used made marks as big around as my palm. The dog kicked out with its hind foot as if one of us had touched a sore spot. Its entire body shuddered beneath my hand.

"Who would do such a thing?" Scarlett said. "Is it yours?"

I nodded, not trusting my voice as I rubbed my palms over the dog's jowls. Upon deeper inspection, I found more than just burns. My stomach clenched as I con-sidered the other wounds hidden by thick expanses of fur.

"Bastards," I said.

She stood up and started peeling off her shirt. "You know who they are?"

I looked up at her. "Not really. Just a hunch. What are you doing?"

She squinted down at me as she flapped out her shirt and laid it flat on the pavement. There was just enough light left in the sky that I could see her bra was a pretty purple lace.

"I'm going to roll him onto it and use the shirt as a hammock. You'll need to help. He's a big one."

It took me a second of watching her spread the fabric out next to the dog before I remembered I did indeed have sheets that would work far better. I kept a cot in the shop, a leftover from the days of working day and night to get the store open.

"Hold on," I said. "I have sheets." I tried not to let my gaze drop to the swell of breasts spilling over her demi-cup. "You can put your shirt back on."

She stood with hands on hips as though she didn't believe me, but she nodded and stooped to retrieve her shirt. I left her pulling it back over her shoulders as I sped back into the shop to rummage in the back closet where I kept a bunch of linens along with the roll out cot.

The sheets were white with pretty eyelet lace along the top. I hated to see it get ruined, but I was more concerned that it wouldn't hold the weight of the dog. I dug back into the pile for a wool blanket that was a dark chocolate color. Perfect.

By the time I got back to the alley, she was already sweeping away anything that might impede our progress once we got the dog rolled onto the blanket. I noticed she'd piled up all the cat dishes far to the side so neither of us would inadvertently step into one of them as we hefted the weight through the narrow space.

I snapped open the blanket with a crack that made the dog startle.

"Sorry, old man," I said as I laid it out alongside the heaving muscles and fur. I blew out a long breath as I eyed Scarlett. "You're sure you want to do this?"

"Hello. It's a wounded dog. Of course I'm going to help. We can't just leave it here and let it go into shock."

Right answer, I thought as I bent over to retrieve one end. "I have no idea if he'll let us do this."

She looked at her watch. "Unless your vet makes house calls, we'll need to get him mobile anyway. The worst part will be getting him onto the blanket. He doesn't look like he has enough stuffing in him to fight to get out once he's in."

She was right there. The poor thing was panting hard. We had to at least get it covered up and warm.

"OK," I said. "You take the butt side; I'll take the one close to his head."

I reasoned that if I was close to the biting end, it might not snap at me since it had done its level best to defend me in the past. And if I could talk to it and hold its head steady while we maneuvered him, I might be able to keep him calm.

The concern turned out to be unfounded. The dog worked with us instead of against us, seeming to understand that we wanted to help it. It yipped a couple of times when it moved, but it did find enough steam to get onto a wobbly set of legs as we heaved and hoisted.

It collapsed onto the blanket with a sigh that made its entire body shudder. When its eyes rolled back in its head, I had a moment of panic, thinking it had died, but the hind legs kicked out again in reflex and I let go a sigh of relief.

"On three," I said to Scarlett. She nodded and we started the countdown.

I was glad of her help when we heaved the poor beast a couple of inches off the pavement. She scurried backwards, and I guided her. We got several feet before we had to ease the beast back down onto the ground and catch our breath.

"Fuck, it's made of lead," she said, blowing at her hair and arching backward with hands at her lower back.

"Maybe we should have left him and called someone." I looked down at the dog and it thumped its tail twice.

"I think it thinks so too," she said.

I fanned my face of the heat that washed up from my chest. It was clear we weren't going to make it into the shop with the dog. A half hour more and the vet clinics would be closed for the day. If we were going to call, we had to do it now.

"I'll go make a call," I said. "You stay here with him."

My cell was in the shop and it would take a quick Internet search to find a good clinic anywhere close. As I sped for the counter where I'd left it, I thought I saw movement outside the window again. I sent a harried glance that way but saw nothing but the normal passersby. The restaurant across the street had turned on the lights they kept wrapped around their cedar pots, and the glow was warm and inviting.

I made a quick call to 411 instead of taking the time to search and got a phone number. The answering machine I got listed another number indicating the place to call in case of emergencies. That one was busy.

I sent a quick text to Layne and Parrish both, since I couldn't get through to the vet. It wasn't much, just a note that the coven was peeking out of its dark hole again.

I was dialing the vet emergency line again when Scarlett came into the shop.

"Damn thing," she said. "I could swear the burn marks are healing."

"What?" I brushed past her. There was no way that dog would be healing this fast. Scarlett dogged my steps through the back. My dusk to dawn light in the back had come on and bathed the dog in a wash of light. I knelt at its side.

"You doing OK?" I said to it as I gingerly brushed aside some of its belly fur. The awful rawness I'd seen a few moments before looked decidedly less red. "Do you think it's just the light?" I looked askance at Scarlett to see if she was seeing the same thing as me.

"I'm not sure," she said. "Try the cuts."

I put one hand down on the dog's muzzle, crooning to it as I told it what I was going to do. With tender fingers, I pulled aside the fur around its neck where the worst of the cuts had been. The gash that had been at least two inches long when we'd first looked now had the sugary granulation that indicated it had started to heal.

I whistled softly. "I'll be damned."

We looked at each other, knowing our expressions were reflected in each other's faces.

"What is going on?" she said, leaning closer to inspect the wound. It started to close with both of us watching it.

"Holy Hannah," she said.

"Magic," I said and sat back on my haunches as I gaped at the beast. It caught my eye and didn't blink for a long time. "You incredible bastard," I said. It thumped its tail twice.

A sound from the shop door caught my attention a second before a familiar voice responded to my comment.

"Most folks call me an incredible bitch," Parrish said as she shouldered through the door. "But I appreciate the sentiment."

Scarlett pushed her weight into her thighs to stand next to me when I rose to greet the woman I'd come to call a friend. She crossed her arms over her chest at the presence of a newcomer and I stepped slightly in front of her to give her some space to figure out whether or not she wanted to engage.

"I didn't expect you to come running," I said to Parrish as I eyed the camouflage scrubs. Her hair was uncovered and loose, with kinks in it that indicated she'd pinned it in several clips while her hair had still been wet.

She swept the alleyway with one glance then let it linger on the dog for several seconds before her gaze went to Scarlett who had, admittedly, side-stepped my neat bit of defense. "You think I'd let you face trouble alone after last time?" she said to me without taking her eyes off Scarlett.

"What do you mean, last time?" Scarlett asked and Parrish immediately grinned.

"Our witch here collects strays like nobody's business. Last time, it was a wolf." She shook her head. "Not a pretty sight."

It was near truth, and I admired Parrish her ability to explain the background without saying a single thing.

But Scarlett looked me over in a different way then, her gaze narrowing just a hint as she assessed exactly how I'd managed to wrangle a wolf.

"Which one of you wasn't the pretty sight?" she asked astutely. "You or the wolf."

Parrish chortled. "I like her, Brie. Where did you pick her up?" She stuck her hand out but Scarlett didn't take it. Instead, she curved her arms around her waist and dropped her gaze to the dog.

"It doesn't matter," Scarlett said. "None of my business."

I sent Parrish a look, hoping she'd let her curiosity go for a bit. On a good day, she could be as subtle as an overboard motor. I didn't think Scarlett was ready for the full on Parrish experience. Deflection seemed about the smartest strategy.

"You'd be surprised the things people bring into a psychic shop," I said. "I had a customer come in with a monkey once. Took me two days to find all the places it shit." I waved Parrish over. "Do you think you could help us with this—with *my* dog?" I realized as I asked that I'd never given the thing a name other than stray or black dog and I imagined Scarlett would notice, so I tacked on the first name that came to mind. "Avi met with some trouble."

Parrish closed the distance to stand over 'Avi' and peered down at him with her hands on her hips. She looked at me askance without turning a bit of her body. Just her head, and even in the early dusk I could see the look of dry disbelief on her face.

"You know that's a female dog, right?"

I blinked stupidly. "What are you talking about? It's a male. Just look at how big it is. It would have to be a Newfoundland to be that size and be a female."

"Avi is a female." Parrish nudged the dog's hind foot with the toe of her combat boot, pulling away the leg to reveal a smooth belly. "I know your dog has a lot of fur, and admittedly, I'm not the one to school anyone on male anatomy, but I'm pretty sure a male would have a little bit extra going on down there."

Scarlett snickered into her hand as I glared at Parrish indignantly.

"Well, maybe the next time I'm fleeing for my life, I'll stop to check my guard dog's junk."

Scarlett snickered again and when Parrish glanced at her, she didn't bother to hide the broad smile.

"You haven't always been running for your life, Brie." It was Parrish's turn to downplay the concept of threat that Scarlett seemed to have let sail straight over her head. Either that or she was so accustomed to the notion of running for her life that it didn't register.

I took the cue, though, just in case. "The damn thing comes and goes so much I never get a chance."

Parrish elbowed Scarlett and I felt my face flame. For some reason, I felt the need to keep defending myself.

"I don't go around scouting genitalia on the strays that come around." I crossed my arms defensively. "I have enough to do."

Parrish held up her hands in surrender. "It's alright, Brie," she said. "I might have missed it too if I was dealing with all the shit you've been going through." She squatted next to 'Avi' and ran her hand over her coat. "It does seem sort of rude to be poking around in all the fur she has, so no one is judging you."

The dog stared at Parrish as though it was afraid she'd contact one of the wounds, but she didn't growl or moan. "Good girl," Parrish cooed to her. "I knew an Avi once. He was a dick. Don't let Brie name you after a dick."

"Abbi," Scarlett interjected and Parrish sent her a dazzling smile the likes of which would light an entire concert hall. Scarlett toed the asphalt beneath Parrish's benevolent scrutiny. "I knew an Abbi once. She was a good person. Very brave. Very loyal."

I imagined Scarlett was telling us more with that comment than she'd told most people. "Abbi it is then," I said. "It fits her to a Tee." I jerked my chin at the dog where Parrish was still running her palm gently over the surface of fur. Her hand paused at the shoulders. "She's got lots of muscle beneath all this fur."

"Lots of cuts too," Scarlett said and Parrish looked back at her over her shoulder.

"Not so many," Parrish said. "I'm not sure what had you two in such a tizzy. Here, you can see where an old gash is already closing and the fur already growing back."

"That's not an old wound," Scarlett said with a note of awe in her voice. "That was a huge gash just half an hour ago."

I nodded my agreement. "She's healing really quickly."

"Like magic," Parrish murmured and gave me a knowing look.

"Just like magic."

By the time Parrish pushed herself to a stand again, the dog had rolled onto its belly and was struggling to get up. I rushed to help, but Parrish held me back.

"Let her do it on her own. It's good for her."

I gave her the benefit of the doubt no matter how hard it was to see the stray wobble for a bit and then shake itself as though to rid its fur of the stink of blood. A few minutes later, with us all watching somberly, the dog took a few steps, gave me a long look, and then headed to the back door of the shop.

"I guess she wants in," I said and moved to open the door.

Even as it was yawning open and the dog disappeared inside, someone stepped into the alleyway.

And he was spitting mad.

Chapter Three

Scarlett vaulted for the back door first, and I knew as soon as she did that the man who had barged into the alley was the man she was running from. She let go a little squeak that sounded nothing like the confident woman from moments before.

Parrish must have analyzed the situation quicker than I did, because even as I stepped into his way to keep him from following Scarlett into the shop, she got there first.

"Can we help you with something?" Parrish said in an amicable enough voice, but I heard the threat in the undertones. She no doubt had taken the few seconds to add up the two and two and got the same four I did.

He wore his cap on backwards like a wannabe gangster; his jeans slung low on narrow hips. He had a lush mane of hair beneath the hat that was probably a chestnut brown in full daylight but that looked like bitter chocolate in the dusk. His blue drawers showed a prominent brand name above the waistband of his jeans. Handsome, very handsome man, about twenty-eight or so, give or take.

I understood what had drawn Scarlett to him in the first place just based on his looks. But he was a bully through and through, something he probably eased her into bit by bruised bit until he'd convinced her every blow was a result of something she'd done.

All things considered, it wasn't the tattoos or the clothing he wore that made me think he was a bully. It was the sneer he gave Parrish as he looked her up and down and seemed to conclude that an alley of three women was no match for the likes of him. That kind of ignorant bliss is usually reserved for the young.

"Yeah, you can help me," he said to Parrish. "You can fetch my wife and be quick about it."

"Your wife?" Parrish said with a snort. "I had no idea dudes were marrying dogs now." She gave him an affected shrug. "But who am I to judge?" She called out over her shoulder to some imagined server. "Let the dog out will ya? Her mate is here to pick her up."

"Fucking lesbian," he said. "Tell my wife to get out of here."

Parrish cocked her head at him with a thoughtful, affected confusion. "I just did. Give her a second. She's having a nice bowl of kibble at the moment."

At that, the dude rushed Parrish, who feinted to the side and left him round-house punching the dumpster instead of the jaw he aimed at. The suddenness of both movements took me back several steps in sheer surprise. It wasn't until she launched herself at him that the anxiety prickled my skin and I pin wheeled backwards to get out of the way of the roiling bodies.

The sound of the impact made my stomach lurch. Someone had got struck, and hard. I caught a flash of yellowish white like predator eyes caught in the beam of headlights. I knew then I had to do something or the mess we'd be cleaning wouldn't just be a magical dog's blood.

I took a deep breath and stepped into the fray, expecting at any moment to get hit by a stray punch or kick. Something yanked me back out before I could intervene. A hand on my shirt that made it ride up in front all the way to my throat and dug into my voice box.

I whirled on Scarlett and as she let go my shirt; it loosened enough for me to growl at her. "What the hell?"

She shook her head in warning. Her eyes were huge. Fear. I knew it when I saw it. She didn't want me to get involved, either because she was afraid of what might happen to me if I did, or because she just wanted to let Parrish give him her whacks for her.

Plus, I wasn't entirely sure she wasn't going to use the chance to run through the shop again and disappear into the street on the other side.

I flapped my arms at her in frustration as another wallop sounded on the air and a groan followed it. "We have to do something."

I swung around to the chaos of limbs. Things were going to get too out of hand if we just stood there. I had no idea what triggered a werewolf's change or if they had much control over it, but that flash of yellow was enough to worry me. She was giving in to her wolf and maybe enjoying it a bit too much.

"Stop," I said as an arm—Parrish's, I thought—shot out and made a popping sound as it connected with bone.

Dude was obviously a scrapper. She'd struck him sure enough. The dazed look in his eye lasted far past the grin he sent her as a taunt, pretending it didn't hurt.

Then he went for her throat with his arm, slipping in close so the punch she threw missed him. He hooked her neatly as her fist sailed by him.

"I'm calling the cops," I said.

Parrish laughed out loud.

"You already did," she said in a strangled voice as he put more pressure into his tight embrace.

Footfalls sounded on the air as Scarlett retreated to the shop. Gone, finally, as I'd suspected. I couldn't really blame her. I danced around the two fighters, trying to find a hole in the wrangling mess without getting hit by a stray kick.

Dude wrapped his leg around Parrish's ankle and tried to knock her off balance. She'd planted herself, though, and she wasn't going anywhere.

The door to the shop banged open. My gaze darted to the sound. Scarlett boiled out with a bat in both hands. She waved it wildly at the two. Parrish found a way to use the distraction to wrestle her way out of his hold. She grabbed his arm.

She twisted hard enough that I heard a pop and a groan and then the guy was on his knees with Parrish straddling his back, both feet planted on either side of his waist.

"Seems a lesbian just fucked you over, mate," she said to the back of his head. "Did you enjoy the ride?"

Scarlett prodded his chin with the end of the bat until his eyes trailed to her face.

"Did you follow me here, Kenny?" she demanded. "I told you we were done. It's over. You can't woo me or bully me back."

Her voice wasn't shrill but it was a note higher than she'd used earlier. "Five fucking years you did this shit to me. I'm not taking it anymore." I heard the tears in her voice and wanted badly to gather her into my arms and wrangle her back into the shop out of sight of the bastard who thought he owned her. I even moved to do so, but Parrish caught my eye and shook her head.

Like the dog, it was best Scarlett stand on her own.

I nodded at Parrish and hung back, hard as it was to let Scarlett do her business, it was best for all involved. Parrish held him immobile while Scarlett said her piece.

"So, you're fucking women now?" he snarled at her and then yelped as Parrish applied more pressure to his arm. She lifted her shoulder in a casual, couldn't-help-myself shrug when I sent her a look chiding her for interfering.

Scarlett dragged the bat over his chin and crouched in front of him so she could see his face directly.

"It's none of your business anymore what I do or who I see or who in the hell I fuck," she said. The tears had evaporated from her voice or distilled into something harder, more crystalline. Anger compressed the other emotions from coal to diamonds and I sensed this one moment was one she would use to fuel herself in the months of work she had to face in the future.

"I saw you," he said in a low voice heavy with disgust and something else. Rage, maybe. "I saw you making eyes at her." He jerked his chin in my direction as I stood there, feet shuffling nervously. "I saw you flirting with her."

She barked out a laugh. "Flirting? She was interviewing me. She gave me a job, you fool."

So he had been the one peeking into the window of the shop, watching us, stewing in his own self-righteous juices. He'd made assumptions. He'd hung around to confirm them as true, because if he'd decided it, they had to be correct.

I tried not to be relieved that it was just a plain man, a bully for sure, but a man nonetheless, and not another assassin from the Blackburn cult. Then on the heels of that relief, came the indignation that he'd been hanging around just waiting for a chance to catch her on her own.

He'd been hanging around my shop, lurking with all that anger clutching at his gut.

And the sudden comprehension of what that meant made my blood boil.

"You hurt my dog," I said and stormed toward him. I shoved Scarlett out of the way, grabbing the bat from her. "You cut up Abbi and burned her with something."

Parrish jerked him then, and he howled as his arm wrenched higher up on his back. "You sniveling prick," she said without a hint of mercy or compassion. "What kind of monster does that to a helpless dog?"

"What kind of woman prefers a snatch to a prick?" he said.

One moment, Parrish was twisting his arm up over his back, the next she let it go in favor of grappling for his scrotum. The violence of the movement really made him howl.

"I'd say based on what you have between your legs, your wife should have left you for a woman a long time ago. You'll be lucky if you can find another poor wretch willing to straddle this little needle." She shoved him to the ground and he clutched at his crotch. He sent her a look of pure loathing.

"Bitch," he said. "You're all bitches." He rolled his neck to catch Scarlett's eye. "You know what I do to bitches. I put them down."

Scarlett backed up a step, all bravado gone, but Parrish didn't seem the least bit fazed. She kicked at him with her combat boot and he made a weak grab for her ankle in the hopes he could grab it before it connected. He missed. She grabbed him by the throat, almost as though there was a scruff there that she was holding onto.

I winced as I realized she had him by an inch of hair and not his throat at all.

"I'm giving you one chance to leave here," she said as she hauled him to his feet. He came along with her hand, obviously not wanting to lose a single strand of his pretty locks, at least, not by the handful.

If he was at all surprised by her strength, he was doing his best not to show it. He rose with her but kept his eye on Scarlett and when Parrish angled him toward the mouth of the alley, he swiveled his head so he could keep eye contact with his wife even as his feet aimed themselves for the entry. All I could think was that had to hurt and yet the threat remained fixed over his expression.

"I'll see you soon," he said.

Scarlett hugged herself over her sweater and I tugged at her elbow to distract her.

"Come on," I said. "Let's go inside. Parrish has it handled."

"You heard me, right?" he said again over his shoulder to Scarlett as Parrish force-walked him to the mouth of the alley. "You know what happens to rabid bitches." He drew his finger over his throat.

Parrish gave him one last shove toward a black sedan pulled up to the curb. "I'm guessing that's your ride."

He stumbled but caught himself quickly enough to keep from spilling onto his backside. His saunter to the driver's side of the car was more bravado than anything else. There was too much favoring one side. Parrish had hurt him.

"My ride is back there," he said with a jerk of his chin toward where Scarlett hung at my side, refusing to go into the back shop. "I'll be back for her."

Parrish crossed her arms over her chest.

"They infect their mates," she said to him just loud enough that he knew she'd spoken but low enough he had to ask her what she'd said. Control, that's what it was. Parrish was making him do her bidding whether he liked it or not.

He paused with the door hanging open.

"What's that?" he said.

"You said we should know what happens to rabid bitches," She pointed at him with her fingers shaped like a gun, motioned a cock-back and then pulled the thumb trigger. "I said they infect their mates. You get bit. You get sick. You die."

The way he glared at her would have made me nervous but she merely stood her ground, watching him until he muttered something I couldn't hear and got in to the car. It took the thunk of the door for Scarlett to sag against me. When he revved his engine and drove off, she hung her head and beat a path to the back door. I waited till she was inside and Parrish had approached me before I spoke.

"She's stronger than she looks," I said, thinking of the take charge woman I'd seen inside before her husband showed up.

"She better be," Parrish said. "I've seen women like her plenty in my day. If she isn't strong enough, he'll kill her."

CHAPTER FOUR

I DIDN'T THINK THE bully Scarlett had married was capable of cold-blooded murder. It took a special sort of bully for that, and he didn't strike me as a man who would take any chances that would put him in harm's way. Parrish was speaking metaphorically, I was sure, but even so, I shot her a look before I turned on my heel and followed Scarlett into the shop.

She was crouched next to Abbi, who had spread herself across the floor, barricading anyone from getting into the apothecary galley and beyond to the shop proper. Scarlett looked up at me when I entered.

"I'm sorry," she said. "I didn't mean to bring trouble to your door."

Parrish's laugh from behind me made me jump. I whirled on her and she shrugged.

"You have to admit, it's funny," she said in a voice ramped up by adrenaline. She laid a companionable hand on Scarlett's shoulder. "Trouble finds Brie."

The front door of the shop rattled before I could answer.

"Speaking of rabid," she said. "That would be Layne."

Scarlett bolted to her feet at the sound of the front bell clanging as severe footfalls thudded against the floor as Layne raced towards us. Parrish grabbed my elbow, pulling me with her as she stepped high over Abbi to get to the door.

The dog didn't bother to move. Just lay there panting.

"I'll stay here," Scarlett said and dropped to her knees next to the dog.

Fine with me. I wasn't sure what she'd see if the beating my door was taking was any indication. Parrish outpaced me even though I knew the shop so well that even in the dark, I could navigate without bumping into anything.

My hand ran over the wall where I knew the closest light switch sat, and by the time it flooded the shop with light, Parrish had made it to the other side of the store. She pulled the door open.

Layne barged in like an unwelcome wind.

"Is she alright?" He hadn't caught sight of me yet, but I could see his yellow gaze from paces away. "Where is she?"

When his eye roamed the shop and found me standing there unhurt, a flicker of gold moved behind his gaze. "Brie," he said, and in his voice was a breath of relief.

He brushed past Parrish, who planted her hands on her hips and glared at his back. "Really, Layne," she said. "I had no idea you could get so lathered up over a sick dog."

"Fuck off, Parrish," he said without so much as tossing the words over his shoulder at her. His gaze was on mine as he closed the distance between us.

She tapped her foot four times before dropping into the chair nearby. "Such a drama queen," she muttered and flung her leg over the arm.

He stopped a foot away from me, his eyes piercing, a hair away from that rabid dog look Parrish accused him of. The air between us could have charged my cell phone.

"You said you thought someone was watching you," he said. "A cult member."

"Nah," Parrish answered for me. "Just a mangy little pup."

Layne held my eyes with his. I felt as though somehow he'd put his arms around me with that gaze and I swallowed hard. I didn't need comfort. I felt very different now that the threat was gone. I stepped closer, not consciously, just out of instinct.

"Care to rob Parrish of her witty innuendo and fill me in?" His breath was shallow, as though he'd been running but there was no heaving of his chest. The smallest beads of perspiration clung to his forehead. I found myself reaching out for them.

He stiffened when I touched him, and, feeling foolish, I pulled my hand back close to my chest.

"I thought it was the cult," I confessed. "Maybe I was a little jittery." I smeared my finger against my thumb, feeling how warm the liquid was on my skin. "But it turned out to be my new clerk's husband."

"Dick," Parrish said with a wave. "His name is Dick."

The weakest of grins tugged at Layne's mouth. "I take it he met our Parrish and she didn't like him."

"His name is Kenny," I said. "And yes. Parrish took care of him."

"So no cult?"

I hesitated too long, I knew, when he narrowed his gaze. He hooked me by the elbow and guided me to where Parrish sat. One jerk of his chin and she sighed and vacated it. Once I'd sat, he planted his feet wide apart and crossed his arms, looking down at me with a stern expression that made the nerves ratchet up again.

I didn't exactly feel like a naughty school girl, but the way he watched me put a tremor in my voice, and I hated that I couldn't keep my spine around him. I picked at the threads in the chair arm more to stall out of spite than because I was nervous.

"Well?" he prompted.

"I don't think it was the cult," I said. "It was probably Kenny who hurt Abbi."

His eyebrows climbed an inch. "Did you call 911? Where is she?"

Parrish guffawed from beside him at Layne's mistaking Abbi for my clerk. "Don't you worry your scruffy little head. Abbi's all better," she said. "Just like magic." She jerked her chin toward the apothecary galley where Scarlett stood, hands on both door frames, leaning into the room as though the wood on either side was the only thing holding her up.

"She's gone," Scarlett said. "I got up to get her a bowl of water and when I went back, she was gone."

"See?" Parrish said. "Nothing to worry about." She held Layne's eye for too long and he sighed, understanding we couldn't talk freely with Scarlett in the room.

"Abbi is your dog," he said to me. Not quite a question, just a test to see if he'd put all the pieces together correctly.

I leaned forward between my knees and crossed my arms on my thighs. "Yup. My dog Abbi got into a fight with Kenny, I think." I pushed myself from the chair and crossed to where Scarlett stood. "Kenny is your husband's name, right?"

Her fingers went into the hair behind her neck and she twisted as she spoke. "As a husband, he's not much, but he loves animals." Her eyebrows scuttled together. "No matter how mad he was at me, he wouldn't do that to Abbi."

"Are you sure?" Parrish said and if Scarlett caught the disdain for Kenny in her tone, she didn't react. "Men do all sorts of things when they realize they've lost control of something they think is theirs." Parrish's voice was tight with emotion and I gawked at her, aware she wouldn't meet my eye.

There was cruelty in her past, that was clear. The specter of it sat in the back of her gaze and stooped her shoulders even as her hands clenched at her sides. I noted Layne edged closer to her and she angled her body toward him, like litter mates trying to comfort one another.

I couldn't help wondering how much Layne knew about her past and decided he knew enough to understand she still needed reassurance from his body language. Or, maybe all that was just my own suppositions because I was so used to reading things most people couldn't see.

He reached out for Parrish almost absently and cupped the back of her arm for a long moment. She sagged into his hand and the smallest of sighs escaped her. I had a hard time tearing my eyes from her as Layne decided out loud that if the dog had left, it couldn't be too hurt and that he might as well bring me home since he was there.

I looked down at my watch. It was well past closing time anyway. We'd decided a few days earlier that I'd stay in the guest house in his family manse. I'd slept for two whole days after I'd been abducted by his partner and newly turned werewolf Farrel. Parrish still carried a faint silver scar on her cheek from the fight she'd put up trying to help me.

The police officer was now MIA and the whole department was under the impression he'd been sent undercover or had been struck down by any of the criminals he'd valiantly and one-handedly fought to bring to justice.

No one but Layne, Parrish, and I knew the truth. The new wolf shifter was in league with a pack who worked for the Blackburn Cult, the very killers who had committed several atrocities in the city, including ritualistically murdering several psychics and three others who didn't seem to have any family who cared enough to claim the bodies.

Parrish and the M.E. were still digging through the data she had collected and the bodies were in freezers instead of being cremated because she wasn't sure they were finished giving up their secrets.

Layne had taken to calling her the witch whisperer and she hated it enough to punch him in the stomach the last time he'd done so. Hard enough that he spit out blood afterward. He hadn't called her that again. At least not yet. Watching the two of them was almost like watching a slow motion chess match except the pleasure of witnessing one of the moves had me hanging on every twitch of muscle.

"You take the witch home," Parrish said, "and I'll take the gem." She jerked her thumb toward the door as she bobbed her head at Scarlett. "Come on. I'll drive you."

I was heading for my sweater where I'd left it in the back and caught Scarlett's reaction to Parrish's comment. One of uncertainty, where she sort of leaned sideways toward the door frame again as though she wanted to sneak out but wasn't sure how she could do so with everyone looking at her.

"You don't have a place to go, do you?" I said to her.

She shook her head. "I didn't think much past getting out of there."

Parrish sucked the back of her teeth, a noise that Scarlett seemed to take as disdain for her when I knew it was disgust for her husband. She recoiled, cringing into the door frame.

"You can stay here," I said, putting my hand on her arm. "I have a cot out back and blankets. I stayed here myself when I was getting the store up and running. It's warm and private." I pointed toward the back room. "The door locks as good as any."

She smiled and it felt good to see the movement cross her face again. "I don't know how to thank you."

I waved my hand in a gesture that indicated it was nothing. "Don't bother," I said. "It's more for me than you. I hate mornings. If you stay the night, you'll be right here and can open up for me. There's no shower, but there is a big enough sink and lots of towels and wash cloths. Take any of the soaps you need from the shelf. I might even have a change of clothes in the storage closet."

She inclined her head in gratitude and Parrish made a big show of being relieved she didn't have to go out of her way to deliver her somewhere. I knew better. Didn't matter what was going on, she would have found a way to help this girl but didn't want to let on she would. The woman was complicated. Whatever had happened to her in the past had put a jagged hard shell around her that she didn't want anyone to crack.

"No offense, Scarlett gal," she said. "But I have a date." She winked and Scarlett grinned, catching the light tone. "This chick is not one you want to keep waiting."

"Thanks for the offer," Scarlett said.

"I'd offer more but I think you're into dudes." Parrish stretched, reaching toward the ceiling with her fingers laced together. "Unless seeing Kenny emasculated like that has put you off men." She lifted her eyebrow in query. "It didn't, did it, by chance?"

Scarlett chuckled. "The LGBTQ community is safe from me," she said.

"Too bad," she said. "A threat like that is the kind of thing I live for." She pivoted to face Layne, all business and unaffected self again. "Well, that's that," she said. "I'm out of here." She ran her hand down my arm as she went by and squeezed the elbow reassuringly. She pushed through the shop door and disappeared into the street.

I grabbed my sweater from the coat tree, giving Scarlett an encouraging smile, and then nodded at Layne.

"I'm ready."

"You think you're ready," he said. "Until you see what's waiting for you."

CHAPTER FIVE

WHAT WAITED FOR ME was worse than I could have imagined. Dinner. Formal style. In the main dining room of the manse with several wait staff bustling about as though they were doing their best to distract the alpha's business associates from noticing the simple cotton T-shirt dress I wore. Layne sat next to me, rigid and tense, and I got the feeling that he wanted to be anywhere but where he sat.

To be fair, he'd done his best to warn me. I just had nothing packed and delivered by Parrish to the manse that would fit such an event. She'd brought me over a duffel bag of clothes and basic makeup to accompany the lingerie I'd bought at the shop the day I'd been abducted.

The dress and a pair of black sandals were the best I could manage. I'd rouged my cheeks and spread my favorite lipstick over my lips and while the mirror told me I looked better than passable, the fact that the hired help acted as though I'd come to the table wearing a hat and mittens told me it didn't matter.

I picked at the food on the plate in front of me, a salad course, while the alpha's business associates conversed in louder and louder voices.

The dressing was a spinach and maple syrup conjunction that I could have drank straight from the crystal sauce decanter that sat next to my plate. With a hefty assemblage of fennel and various lettuces and pears all sliced razor thin, I didn't need the dressing, but it certainly helped to drizzle it bit by bit when Layne remained as silent as the dead beside me.

He wasn't much company at the best of times during the course, but as his father kept dragging him into the conversation, whatever I hoped to get out of him seemed impossible. The talk was so far over my head that I pretty much put my head down and attacked the salad with the kind of commitment it took to hold out in a loveless marriage.

And stabbing at the grilled pears that nestled in a bed of arugula was what I was doing when I heard my name spoken amid a bunch of other syllables that were English but might as well have been Latin.

I peered over the silver charger holding my delicate salad plate. The man across from me, a squat man with a thin mustache, looked at me expectantly.

"What's that?" I said.

He blinked, and a haze of yellow clouded his eyes for a second. A werewolf, this one. I'd come to recognize the eyes.

"I asked you if it's spelled like the cheese."

"Cheese?" I said, floundering horribly as I tried and failed to catch Layne's dad's eye.

"Your name," his father said when Layne didn't do more than look miserable. "It is spelled the same as the cheese, is it not?"

I nodded.

"I thought so." Owen flicked his eye toward his son, watching him closely as he spoke. "I love Brie. I could eat it every day."

I felt Layne stiffen even more beside me in a way that made me think I'd completely missed the point of the comment.

"We're not talking about what she does for a living," he said and I swung my gaze sideways to his profile to see a whiteness at the spot where his jaw met his ears. I must have missed more than I thought from the conversation, because he went on without noticing I'd dropped my fork. "I told you earlier. I'm happy to sit here and go over the things I discovered on my research trip, but I don't think it's fair to involve Brie in all this."

Layne reached beneath the table and laid his hand on my thigh.

It made me jump because it was so unexpected. We'd had one date, a desperate offer because he needed someone for a charity occasion, and one that ended with a man dead at the hotel entrance. We'd dabbled and skirted around, not getting much further than that, and then he'd been gone for weeks without caring to let me know he was leaving.

Now, his touch held a familiarity and a possessiveness that confused me.

I did my best to wrestle my heartbeat back into something akin to normal and, as I did so, Layne's grip tightened against the fabric and heated up my leg.

I was pretty sure the elder Garder noticed. His eyes flared with gold as his eyebrow quirked up on the end. I was sure he could either sense my anxiety or the speed up in heart rate. When he swiveled his gaze to his son, I knew for sure he'd reacted to Layne's tense jawline. Reacted the way a shark might to fresh chum spilled into shallow water.

"She is staying in our guest suite, is she not?" He moved the roasted pears over to the side of his plate as he held Layne's gaze. "I would think she wouldn't mind entertaining our guests with a story." He laid his fork down beside his plate and directed a pointed look at the bruise on my cheek, still left over from my skirmish with Farrel. "I'm sure our guests might be thinking you have a jealous lover somewhere."

Layne's hand on my leg spasmed before it clenched into a fist and withdrew to his side. "Her love life is no one's business." He started to push away from the table. It took one second to sight the smug look of satisfaction on Owen's face. "And she's not some bard from bygone days to sing for her supper."

I couldn't let Layne be goaded like that. I gripped his elbow. The muscles tensed but he didn't pull away.

"It's fine," I said smiling my broadest directly across at Owen whose golden eyes had turned a bright yellow. "I'm sure he's just thinking about my day job." I reached for the water glass and traced a line of condensation as I did my best to appear unaffected.

"What kind of story do you think would be entertaining?" I paused, just long enough to see one of the guests drop his gaze to his plate. "Do you fancy tales of lonely widows dying to hear from their late husbands so they can sleep one night without sobbing into their pillows? Or is it the more salacious things you're looking for? The ones where young women come into the shop looking for a love potion to slip into a wealthy man's drink?"

I snaked my forearm over the table between Layne's service and mine to lift the water pitcher and topped off my glass. "Maybe it's the stories about senior gentlemen creeping into my shop with indecent proposals for women far too young for them. I don't do much for my clients then except to suggest they keep a bottle of aspirin next to the Viagra for when the old coot suffers a cardiac infarction."

I smiled blithely into Owen's eyes.

Something cracked next to me and red liquid sloshed over my salad plate. A server rushed between Layne and me with a large white cloth that instantly got stained red as she sopped up the wine he'd spilled before it could collect in too many puddles on the table.

I half expected everyone to make a fuss, it being such a fancy evening, planned it seemed to bully Layne as much as to entertain some business associates. No one moved as the server cleared away the dishes that had caught drops of wine. The electricity in the air as they laid down some equally fancy white linen to cover up the marred cloth tingled on my arms.

Some other server instantly laid down fresh plates of salad, and I eyed mine with some speculation. My stomach was grumbling in anxiety not hunger and a second helping of salad I didn't have the appetite for was about to put me over the edge.

Thankfully, Layne saved me.

"I don't think I have the stomach for more grilled pears with a side of old man's jugular," he said and pushed the plate back into the server's hand. "Brie, are you with me?"

I nodded quickly and lifted my plate from the charger. I held it out to the server. "I'm afraid I ate plenty from the first serving." I tried to smile in encouragement at the still full plate, but my lips caught on my teeth.

The server merely nodded and accepted the plate with the barest of glances at Owen.

"It's fine," the alpha said. "I think we're all ready for the soup anyway." He folded his hands over the table as he leaned toward me. Beneath his gabardine dress shirt, his biceps moved like snakes. "I think," he said as the servers rushed to clear away the course, "that I'd like most to hear about the senior gentleman. Was he handsome at least, if he was making himself available to such a beautiful woman beyond his reach?"

I choked on the mouthful of wine I'd taken to give myself something to do. Sputtering and struggling to breathe, I scraped my chair backwards. My barb had backfired and stuck me right between the I-shouldn't-haves.

It took several seconds for me to extricate myself from the long draping of tablecloth that kept wrapping around my thighs to stand behind my chair.

"I need air," I said with my eyes stinging from the coughing fit. No doubt I looked a sight with the mascara dripping like black rain onto my cheeks as I tried in vain to keep the wheezing from becoming a full on vomit fest. Damn my weak stomach. This was not the time to look weak.

I waved at my face in an effort to send more oxygen into my heaving lungs. The coughing racked my chest and burned my throat. Owen lifted a crystal glass of water and mimed drinking it as I shook my head at him. I didn't care if a swallow might rectify the awkwardness. I just wanted out. A coughing fit was as good an exit excuse as any.

I waved at them to continue and fled the dining room.

The manse had a labyrinthine quality I'd learned during my first few days' stay. As my lungs did their best to settle down and tears blurred my eyes, I struggled to remember which way might take me out of the manse and into the back garden the quickest.

One corridor, lined with oil paintings the way a European castle might in their gallery, I knew would take me to the screening room and one would take me to the back foyer and out into the courtyard.

The pause I took to give it thought left room for someone to enter the hallway from the dining room and I stepped quickly behind a large statue of a Greek god so whoever it was couldn't see me. I bit down on the coughing fit and smothered it with my palm. It tickled my throat, demanding attention.

I was hunched over and choking when I caught sight of the feet beneath my gaze. I'd been found. I just hoped it was one of the servers. I didn't want it to be Layne or Owen. With a sigh that rattled my lungs, I peered up without straightening out of my bent posture.

"Just my luck," I wheezed out as my gaze landed on the handsome but annoyingly cocky face of Layne's dad.

"Indeed," he said as he held his hand out to me. "I would have given a fool's bounty for such luck in my day."

I leaned against the wall behind me and dropped my head against the wall. Thankfully, the coughing had receded and my throat and lungs stopped spasming, but it left me weak and breathless.

I gave his outstretched arm and hand a quick glance. "I don't need help," I said. "I'm perfectly capable of standing on my own without having to lean on you."

His eyebrows climbed half an inch as he flicked his eye to the wall behind me, which made me push off of it reluctantly.

"It's just habit," I said.

"Is it also habit to deface priceless art?"

"I have no idea what you're talking about."

He took my hand gently and laid it on the statue, then guided my fingers over an inch of marble.

"Oh gross," I said as I yanked my hand back to my side. I swiped the palm over the fabric of my dress, cleaning it of the mucus I'd coughed up onto the marble.

"I don't mind bodily fluids so much," he said, edging closer. "You get used to it when you've lived as long as I have as a dual being, especially when one of them enjoys some fluids more than others."

"You mean blood," I said, having a hard time not showing the grimace that wanted to curl my lip. Please let it be blood and not the sexual kind. I couldn't take any more innuendo.

I sobered quickly as I thought about my preference right then for blood instead of anything else. "Were-wolves eat people, so I imagine a certain amount of bodily fluids go with the territory."

He sketched a mock bow but the smile never left his face. "I haven't eaten anyone for many, many years…so long as you don't count the women I've dated."

"Ew," I said, unable to hold back the exclamation of shock.

He cocked his head at me. "You find that repulsive?" He leaned with one hand on the wall beside my head. "I pity your lovers. Or maybe you've just never had a good one."

"I'm not discussing this with you. Not here. Not now."

He inched closer. Something mischievous danced in his eyes. "Did you wear the lingerie?"

I tried to push past him but he planted the other hand down on the wall on the other side of me. I glared up at him to absolutely zero reaction. His placid face remained as before. Smug. Confident. The smell of him, of warmth and heat and something vaguely unnameable wafted around me and for a second my knees softened at the backs.

"Does this really work with women?" I asked, tilting my face up to his. "I mean, do you really and truly score with this kind of macho attitude. It's very misogynistic."

Instead of recoiling as I'd expected, he lowered his head so that his nose buried itself into the fringe of hair at the back of my head. His lips whispered against my ear.

"You tell me, Brie," he murmured with a caress of warm air. "You're the one with a heartbeat like a rabbit and the faintest whiff of pheromone perfuming your throat and skin."

My eyes squeezed closed. He was right, dammit. I knew my heart was racing. "It's the coughing," I said. "Physiological response. I presume as a werewolf, you're aware of that sort of thing."

"And the perfume that tells me you want me?"

"Nothing but alpha energy," said a masculine voice from behind us both.

This time when my knees buckled, it was from the look of anger on Layne's face. I sagged against the wall as Owen straightened up and looked back at Layne over his shoulder the way a man might if he was interrupted from a moment he was loathe to give up.

"Are our guests left alone in there, then?" Owen asked. No remark about the alpha power or the insinuation that he'd been abusing it. No comment about his flat out come on or being caught in the act of it by his son. Not one single indication that he was embarrassed by his behavior or cared that I was.

Layne pulled a stick of gum from his suit jacket pocket. "Our guests came to speak to you, not me." He took his time unwrapping the gum, but I didn't think it was because he felt overly casual about what was going on. Rather, he found the activity necessary to calm down.

Owen leaned into me even as he spun half way around to face his son. "They came to hear your report from your research trip. I'd appreciate it if you'd fulfill your duty."

A shiver went through the air at the words. The alpha power, no doubt, whatever the heck that was. Layne's fists clenched at his sides and the stick of gum he'd rolled up and popped into his mouth went to his cheek.

For a moment, the air sizzled with electricity and it took my breath away. Then as abruptly as it sparked the air, it disappeared.

Layne's shoulders sagged.

"Brie," he said. "If you still need air, it's that way." He pointed toward the other hallway. "It will take you to the courtyard."

I nodded, grateful for the reprieve. Fully expecting Owen to step away and leave me room to escape, I pushed off the wall. His hand snaked around my waist with a smoothness I didn't expect.

"I'll show you," he said.

Layne cleared his throat. "I gave them my report and now they have questions for you, sir," he said, and in his voice was a note of command brushed over with a coat of feigned subservience.

He used the formal title out of respect, it was clear, but also as a means to remind Owen he had responsibilities to his pack.

With a sigh, Owen withdrew his arm with a caress that Layne had to have noticed because his eyes flared yellow. He sucked in a hiss. I couldn't look at either one of them. I gave my shoes far too aggressive a study as Owen withdrew from my side. I did peek up then, and watched him stride past Layne with his hand in his pocket, a casual air that left the hall bleeding with tension.

Layne watched him go and I put my hand to my chest to clutch at the place my heart was hammering.

"I have no idea what that was all about," I said as I blew out a breath of relief.

Layne swung on me as though he'd been storing up a rage for weeks. "I'll tell you what it was about. He smells it on you." His lip curled back in a grimace that made my chest ache.

"Smells what?"

"The lust." He glared at me. "It's all over you, Brie."

CHAPTER SIX

I REELED AT THE accusation and stumbled to find the right words to defend myself.

"He's the one who came on to me." I pushed off the wall, all fit and fury. "I was out here trying to find the door."

"Really?" he asked. "Because I distinctly heard him ask you if you were wearing the lingerie. *The* lingerie. Dammit Brie. After all that's happened, you decide the man with the hefty bank account is your best bet?"

I gawked at him, my mouth working over words that refused to come out.

He stabbed the air between us with a rigid finger, aiming at the floor as though his hand were a pistol. "I might have known," he said with acid in his voice. "You can't deny it, can you? I knew when Parrish took you to that store, it was for him." He ran both hands over his head, scratching at the scalp beneath the hair in a raking motion. "Fuck," he said. "He always does this. I thought you were better than the rest of them." He sent me a scalding look that freed my tongue finally. "But you're the same. Exactly the same."

"You are a prick," I said, storming the distance between us to punch him on the chest. My fist contacted hard muscle that might as well have been a concrete wall, but I refused to yelp in pain. I yanked my hand back with the full intention of cradling it against my chest, even if it did make me look weak.

"You are a *prick*." I yelled the last word.

He grabbed my wrist before I could get away and, with one swift tug, I was up against his chest. That hard concrete wall of muscle flexed beneath me and went rigid again.

"I'll tell you what a prick does," he rasped. "A prick doesn't care if a woman is recovering from shock and trauma. A prick doesn't bother to give a woman space to find herself. A prick doesn't ask. He just takes what he wants."

With that, his free hand tangled in the back of my hair and tugged my head backward. My throat arched for him, offering itself. I had time to see his eyes flicker with gold an instant before his mouth claimed mine.

His lips and tongue violated my mouth in the few seconds it had me. His kiss was full of fury and command and possession, and I barely had time to respond before he tore away from me. He used the thrust of his own movement to push me away.

"I'm a prick. I've always been a prick. And you have always been a con."

With that he swept an acidic look over my face then turned on his heel to head back to the dining room.

I was left staring at the door as it closed behind him. My core hurt so much I had to grasp it with the hand that I'd hurt punching him, and when I did, I realized I was trembling.

He knew I was a con. He'd probably known all along even before I'd confessed it to him in a weak moment during the time we'd worked together. It had been a hard admission, and he'd not made a big deal of it then, but obviously, it had been a major issue for him to throw it up at me now.

In the moment of confusion and anger all I could register was that somehow in the space of moments, I'd lost any chance to redeem myself.

I couldn't go back to the guest suite. I couldn't stay here. Not with Layne hating me and his dad coming on to me so aggressively. I had no idea what this was all about, but I knew I had to leave.

If I remembered correctly, the courtyard had a gate that lead to the street. I didn't have anything in the suite that I needed and I was pretty sure Layne would toss whatever I did have in the trash or send it back to me via Parrish anyway. The lingerie she'd brought that still sat in the bag in the suite could go to the Salvation Army thrift store for all I cared.

My mind's eye roamed the guest suite, searching for things I might need to return for and found nothing. With the lack of things I had to retrieve, my memory quickly settled on the gorgeous bit of fabric Layne's dad had paid for, the perfect gift for Layne, if Parrish was to be believed.

I'd had no intention of wearing that lingerie for Owen at all. Rather, I'd gone along with his request out of curiosity and for the fun outing I so desperately needed to feel half normal again. Parrish, like the intuitive werewolf she was, sensed that and helped me pick out something Layne would like instead.

Just thinking about how hopeful I had been that day sent me fleeing in the direction Layne indicated with such callousness was the exit.

He was right when he'd said I wasn't ready for what waited for me. I just had no idea how bad it might get. I mean, it was businessmen for heaven's sake; what could be so bad about a nice dinner with suited blue collar guys? Like a naive teenager, I'd gone along with the fancy dinner, never thinking the worst hit would come from Layne himself.

I couldn't get out fast enough and it didn't just have to do with my abduction from that shop or the trauma I was still suffering because of it. When I hit the door, I all but fell out onto the step. I slammed the door behind me and stood there for several heartbeats trying to process how it had all gone so badly so quickly.

I didn't even have the chance to ask him how the investigation was going. How Parrish was doing with the tests she'd sent off. How close we were to catching and stopping the damn black coven that had made my life a living hell.

Now, it wasn't just the evening. How it had gone so badly so quickly was a mystery. I felt both confused and humiliated and I wanted nothing more than to curl up in my own bed and sleep for days.

The cool air braised my cheek and raised goose flesh on my arms. I inhaled deeply, doing my best to quell the panic. My head started to clear even if the embarrassment lingered. The sensation of humiliation would probably linger for days.

I took one long look at the cobblestoned courtyard with its wrought iron chairs and benches, the gargantuan pots of foliage and trees with tiny white lights strung through the branches, and I realized I never really belonged anyway. I had no hope of fitting in to such a world as this.

The realization that I'd even considered it surprised me. This wasn't my cup of tea. It wasn't even a plastic cup of chlorinated water. Had I been in my right state of mind, without the threat of danger dogging my steps, I'd have understood much earlier that Layne and I weren't suited for each other, and not bothered sitting down at the table in the first place.

It didn't take a psychic to know Layne and I weren't a good fit. Even his father had inferred Layne wasn't the type to settle with one woman for long. If Owen's inferences were to be believed, Layne used women much the same as his father did, with an eye to soothing his fragile ego.

Plus, he was a cop. I was a fraud. Nothing good could come from that mismatched relationship.

I'd simply been defrauding my own psyche in an attempt to feel safe. Rookie mistake, that. One I would rectify straight away.

I dug into one of the pockets in my dress where I'd stuffed my cell phone before going to dinner, hoping it hadn't fallen out in my escape from the table or that I'd left it on the seat. Relief swam over me when my fingers touched down on the hard case.

I contemplated calling a cab right then but decided the walk might do me good. I'd stroll along the streets for a while until I got tired or my brain finally rebelled at the thought of Layne, and then I'd call a cab and head the rest of the way home.

Decision made, I felt a lot more in control. The thing I missed most about all this hoopla was my self-confidence. It was time to take it back.

So I skipped down the broad cement steps with an energy I faked so I could make it, and strolled across the cobblestones, past the benches and statues and potted trees to the gate. The noise of the traffic beyond swelled on the air, with frequent horn blares and the purring of engines. Layne's manse was halfway across the city from where I lived, in the more affluent part of town, and I'd never make it all the way home on foot.

Not a problem, really. I didn't plan to walk the whole way. It was early enough to take my time. I'd wear myself out so that I'd fall into bed without worrying my brain would keep squeaking along on rusty wheels.

The gate was oiled well enough it made no sound when I went through. That had to be a good omen. I was doing the right thing by leaving. My stay was never supposed to be lengthy anyway. A few days, maybe a week, in the hopes Layne could break the case or at least find Farrel and question him.

The first day, I'd stayed in the guest room and slept. The exhaustion of being abducted and nearly killed, of fighting for my life and powering up a magic I didn't understand had sapped everything from me. No one bothered me. Nobody even knocked on the door, and that included Layne or Parrish.

If they did, I was too comatose to answer.

The second day, I'd hauled myself to work only to discover I still didn't have the juice to do more than toss up a Help Wanted sign in my window. I had every intention of rummaging through my mother's boxes again because I was sure there was more evidence in there about the Cult of Blackburn that might either absolve my mother of involvement or solidify her membership.

That day, I'd poked about the shop but did little else. And the third day, well, that was when Scarlett found me and her husband found her and the rest led directly to the reason I was hoofing it alone in the early dusk of a fall evening.

Three days, it seemed, was the maximum amount of time before a gal wore out her welcome at the Garder manse.

I puzzled over Layne's reaction and Owen's strange behavior toward me and his son. Theirs couldn't be a normal relationship, but who was I to judge? I had a witch for a mother. Whatever was between the Garders, it wasn't my business, and I didn't plan to get any further involved. There was a bit of relief in that. I felt as though someone had taken a hair shirt off my shoulders.

Without the guilt and shame of Owen's attentions, I was left with all kinds of brain power to put on the affairs of a black coven that still held my personal and intimate effects in their storage. My blood. My hair. My nail clippings: all things they could use for countless magic castings.

In truth, it wouldn't matter if I was in the Garder manse or my own apartment. If they decided to use them, I was toast no matter where I was.

I walked virtually alone in the gloom of evening for several blocks and at first, I didn't mind the solitude. The blanket of darkness with sporadic street lamps humming above me and casting a golden glow in puddles of light below was as good a balm to an aching soul as a hot bathtub and a glass of wine.

The thought that I was heading home sped up my step. Layne had dropped the tidbit that he'd placed an unmarked car outside my apartment in case Farrel decided to try again to abduct me, this time from my own home.

Farrel had told me I would find out why they'd abducted me on the waning moon. Time was growing short. I'd wasted the three days I'd been gifted. I planned to change that in the morning.

I was at least ten minutes away from Layne's when the hair prickled on the back of my neck. I paused mid-stride, sure I heard someone behind me. It took all my courage to glance over my shoulder.

The last time I'd felt the presence of someone following me at night, I'd been attacked by a creature who turned out to be the scythe man sent by the coven.

This time, I saw nothing. Not a single shadow marred the sidewalks that shouldn't have been there. I swallowed hard and pulled out my cell phone. A couple of taps and I had the first two digits of 911 entered into the keypad. I gave another cursory glance around me with squinting eyes, and when nothing showed itself, I walked backwards for several more steps to be sure I wasn't being followed.

It took a lot to turn back around. And even as I did, I heard a noise. A shuffling sort of sound, like a dog with its nose to the ground, sniffing for whatever dogs found interesting.

I froze. My heart started to hammer. I could protest all I wanted to myself that I was glad I was out from under the Garders' noses, but right then, I doubted my decision to run.

"Layne?" I said into the growing dark. It was strange there was no one out on the streets, come to think of it. It was a residential neighborhood, bordering on a district with lots of fancy restaurants. There should be more than me on the streets at that time of day. With fear in my throat, I recalled the way my block had gone eerily silent when the scythe man had hunted me.

I clenched my phone with my finger close to the keypad as I started back-walking even faster.

"If you're following me, you should have the decency to step out and show yourself."

Pain lanced my chest and streaked down my arm. My cell phone dropped to the sidewalk with a horrible clatter. When sweat broke out on my brow and made my chest and back clammy, I knew it wasn't the cold grip of magic that had me.

I was having a heart attack.

CHAPTER SEVEN

I FELL TO MY knees, terrified I wouldn't get to the phone in time to call 911. Dread climbed my spine as I worried the glass would be cracked or the technology would be completely dead. Whatever had been following me was second in that moment to the primitive instinct clawing at my throat, the one that forced me to drag in air like it was coming in through a straw.

My phone was my connection to the world, the instrument of my salvation if I needed it. I needed it. I'd not had it with me in the basement when Farrel had abducted me for the black coven's nefarious purposes. Had I that phone in the dark cellar, I might have been able to call for help long before I had to injure myself to bring forth the magic that took so much from me. I might have escaped with Farrel in plastic ties instead of roaming free somewhere.

Maybe he was even in the shadows now, watching me.

Scrabbling on my hands and knees, my hands swept back and forth in search of the phone, but even laying my full palm down on the surface of the glass didn't ease the terror. My body felt drained of warmth, and I was shivering when I brought the phone to my chest.

My fingers were too wet to connect with the heat sensor, or too cold to activate it. I swiped over and over again, trying to get the screen to turn on. It took several tries with me growing more frantic by the second before I remembered I had to press the ON button to get the screen to come to life.

By the time I found the button, my breath was coming in rasps. The cuts and bruises, all bandaged nicely by Layne or Parrish, ached in ways they hadn't since I'd first done the damage to myself in the basement.

With the flash of memory of that moment, my throat tightened even more. There wasn't even enough space to swallow down the fluid collecting in my mouth.

A whimper escaped me, one that reminded me very much of those I'd let go when Farrel was lying on top of me, the threat of violence in his yellow eyes. He'd said if I ran, if I escaped, he'd hunt me down and kill me whether or not the coven wanted me.

By now, I could barely see the screen.

"Sweet fuck," I muttered with a sob. Everything was tunneling down into one pinprick of light, and I did not want to pass out. Not again. Not alone on the sidewalk. Not with something out there following me.

I had fallen onto my side with the phone propped on my chest. I was still angling it to the light, frantically trying to activate the screen, when a noise drew my attention to the bushes beside me.

I craned my head toward the sound, my back arching to allow me to see into the shadows behind me.

Something was there. The something that was following me. It was right there. I couldn't drag my eyes away from the way it moved, rustling on the night air faster now that I was looking at it.

I sucked in a breath to scream just as a cat streaked out of the bushes. My scream died in my throat as the cat yowled loudly and sped across the street, a dog hot on its heels.

My spine sagged against the sidewalk and the air whistled out of my lungs. I watched them go, vaguely aware that the screen had finally blinked on. The keypad was just as I'd left it.

The tightness in my chest had eased at the sight of the pair. My breathing started to ease. The skin that had been prickling just seconds before felt less electric.

I wasn't going to die. At least not right then. I was safe. Cold and coatless, maybe, lying on the ground like a ninny, but not one in danger of dying from anything except embarrassment.

Several long inhales helped. The pain in my chest abated. The icy sweat that collected between my breasts trickled downward as I eased myself up onto my elbows. I clutched the phone to my chest and blew out a long, forgiving exhale.

A panic attack. That's what it had been. I should have recognized it for what it was the moment it struck, but panic attacks are like that. They stole all reason and amped up the dread of certain death no matter what signals got sent from the brain to the muscles.

I hadn't had one in at least a dozen years and it had been so long ago that I'd forgotten what they were like. I almost laughed in relief.

It took the realization for me to really feel the cold of the sidewalk, and I rolled onto my hands and knees. It was bound to happen, I supposed. A gal could only take so much stress. I let my head hang between my shoulders for a moment to let some blood rush back to my brain. I felt logie and stupid and embarrassed.

I was just glad no one was around to witness it.

It was time to call a cab.

I looked around me, looking for a specific location to direct them to but I couldn't see a street sign. The numbers on the buildings around me, lit by LEDs from inside, were useless without a street name.

With the thought that I'd walk until I found a better indication of where I was, I pushed myself to my feet and held the phone against my chest. The smell of roasted meat and spices lingered on the air so I must be near a restaurant. Good. I'd call from a well-lighted area and wait inside somewhere warm.

Shivering, I pressed on, despite the sensation of someone watching me. The panic wanted to rise again, but I stubbornly ignored it. I'd fallen victim to my imagination once tonight and if the dog and cat were lurking nearby, I wasn't in the mood to give them a second helping of idiocy to watch.

I made it to the end of the street without further incident. My breath came easier. I turned in the direction of the smells of food. Several coffee shops lined the strip and I caught sight of a neon sign advertising stone oven pizza. Now that I'd seen the sign, I could make out the light fragrance of wood smoke on the air as well.

My stomach growled at the thought of warm, fragrant pizza. Without thinking, my steps sped up, warming me enough to ease the shivering but not enough to stop the chattering of my teeth from residual adrenaline.

By the time I cozied up to the brick facade and had swiped my phone awake, the radiant heat of the bricks wore down my resolve to head home immediately. The savory fragrance of garlic and lemon reminded me I'd not eaten more than a few forkfuls of salad.

There were people inside. I'd be as safe inside the restaurant as I'd be at home. Safer, even.

And I was really hungry.

I pushed on the door, intending to order a full pie before calling for a cab. A cluster of women hung by the hostess table, talking in lively tones, laughing, their spirited conversation lighting up the hostess's expression as she perused her seating arrangements. I got the impression the place was full up but she was doing her best to accommodate the lively group.

A bushy, bristling head of red hair towered over three companions and I recognized Parrish before she saw me.

I froze. I wasn't sure I wanted her to see me like this. A quick glance down at myself showed I'd ripped my dress and somehow got it smeared with a foul looking bit of black tar. I sniffed. Not tar. Great. I was in a pizza restaurant with cat shit on me.

One back step and I was pulling my phone back up. I spun on my heel and headed for the exit again but before I made it to the door, Parrish called out to me.

Her voice was filled with surprise and I halted with a sigh.

"You're gonna sneak out like a rat, little mouse?" she said. Her companions started making jokes about pussies and cats and my face heated up even as I heard her telltale stomp coming toward me.

I swiveled to face her, arms hugging my waist.

"Oh fuck," she said with a wince as she took me in. "Now I see why you were running."

She closed the distance between us and plucked at my hair, pulling away a dried twig I didn't know was there. "You and Layne decide to roll in the bushes or something?" She sniffed. "And in kitty litter, too, smells like. Bully for you. I usually want Chinese after a good romp. But he does love pizza afterwards."

I blinked at her and my expression must have showed more than I wanted because hers immediately softened from laughter to pity.

"Oh God, Brie," she said. "Don't cry. I'm just guessing he likes post sex pizza. I have no idea." She gestured from her neck to her heels. "Lesbian, remember?"

I swiped at my cheeks, feeling the warmth of tears on my fingers that I couldn't feel on my cold, numb face. "I never thought that. That's not it."

"Of course you didn't," she said. "Because even if I wasn't into chicks, I'd be out of his league." She smiled for me with her whole face and I snorted up a trail of wayward snot.

She put her arm around me, angling me toward the bathroom, but one of her companions caught her eye before we could take a step. "Just going to clean this miserable wretch up," she said to the woman. "Make sure you get a table for four. I'm still coming." She looked down at me. "I'm still having dinner, right? Whatever it is, it's not going to interfere with my pre-sex pizza is it?"

I nodded and clutched my phone closer to my chest again.

"What are you nodding for?" she said. "Are you answering the: 'I'm still having dinner' part or the 'it's going to interfere with my pre-sex pizza?"

"If you didn't ask so many questions all at once, you'd know," I said, feeling more like myself in light of her good humor. I was grateful she didn't make a big deal of how I looked. It gave me a sense of my normal self.

She touched her finger to the tip of my nose. "Much better," she said and guided me toward the restrooms. The doors on both had signs that said, "Whether you're a gal, a guy, or a gruyere, take a pizza paper towel and wash your hands after you tinkle."

I made it through the door before she did and headed directly to the sink. It was a single bathroom much like I had at my shop, but it was expansive, giving the visitor plenty of room to move about. Both of us fit in with space to spare.

She turned on the tap when she noticed I was staring into the mirror. The water ran hot enough to steam the surface and cloud over my features but not before I noticed how blanched my face looked. The mascara had run down my cheeks, standing out like racing stripes on a white face.

"I'm a mess," I said.

She dunked a towel into the water. "You sure are."

I let her run the hot and soppy paper towel over my cheeks. Easing my eyes closed, I pressed her fingers and the towel into the skin and held it there beneath my eyes.

"I'd like to make a sassy remark but you look like too much shit for me to do that," she said.

"Not to mention you already cracked one."

"What can I say? My mouth has a mind of its own."

I felt her shrug and opened my eyes. She was leaning in close enough to kiss me and for a second, I thought she would do just that, then she blew sharply into my eyes.

"What the hell?"

"Checking your vitals," she said. "You reacted just fine so you're not in shock."

I quirked an eyebrow and she released the towel to my grip as she crossed her arms over her chest and regarded me. "These days I'm not ever really sure what I'm going to find when I see you."

"I had a panic attack." There. It sounded bald and bland even to my ears. Nothing like the sensation that made me feel like certain death was coming my way at the speed of a locomotive.

"I guess it was to be expected with everything you've been through."

"I've had them before. When I was younger. I had to see a therapist for them."

"That bad, huh?"

This time it was my turn to shrug. "Didn't help that Layne was being a prick."

She reeled back on her heels with feigned shock. "You mean Mr. Prickly was showing his true colors? I'm gob smacked." She ran another paper towel under the faucet for a moment then turned the tap off. After squeezing it nearly dry, she worked at the gob of cat dung on my dress and tossed it into the toilet, flushed, then put the seat cover down.

"Sit," she said, returning to the soap to clean her hands. "Tell me everything."

It took mere moments to go over the pathetic evening I'd had and she said nothing, not even when I paused to give her space to commiserate. She only spoke when I was done and then it was in a voice filled with caution.

"Layne and his dad have this thing. It's..." she gestured wildly to indicate confusion. "It's tough to explain, but Owen knows Layne could challenge him at any moment. Owen doesn't need to work hard to get tail. It usually comes to him pretty easily. But he has a habit of pursuing women Layne wants."

"By tail you mean women."

She nodded vigorously. "Lots of women."

"And Layne lets him."

"Oh, nothing so uncomplicated as that. Layne hates it. I mean, really hates it. So he usually dates women he has no interest in, just to keep Owen busy." She chuckled darkly. "Then he only sees them once since he's not even remotely interested but his father ends up chasing women he'd never bother with if it wasn't for Layne. It's kind of funny to watch, really. There was this really ugly woman a couple of months ago—"

"So he thinks I'm ugly," I said. "And he isn't interested. I'm just fodder for their dominance contest."

She dropped to a crouch next to me. "Do you think I would have suggested the lingerie Layne would like if I thought he was using you?"

I squirmed on the seat. It was a hard question to answer. She might genuinely believe Layne was interested so the answer might really be moot. "I think you would never be so cruel."

She rose, her knees cracking. "You bet your fat ass. Now, get up and wipe your face. You're having pizza with me and the girls tonight." She narrowed her gaze at me as I stood. "Just so you know. I can't be held accountable for anything you see or hear from me since I'm in woo mode. You might not recognize me."

I laughed and it felt good to do so. I waved a hand between us. "No worries, there. I'm just happy I ran into you."

When we left the restroom, the girls had already been seated. One of them, a curvy brunette kept giving me the side eye and the other two were engaged in animated conversation about a recent news story. Parrish sat down beside the curvy brunette and kissed her on the cheek with an indulgent smile. She murmured something about ordering her favorite wine to go with the pizza and the woman toyed with a bread stick.

Parrish obviously thought the woman was gay, but I wasn't so sure. The way she fidgeted in her chair and avoiding Parrish's direct eye contact told me she was either new at dating women or was incredibly shy. The way she elbowed me when I sat on her other side was a pretty good hint that it wasn't the latter.

"I know you," she said, turning from Parrish's overzealous attentions. She even went so far as to plant her elbow on the table and lean slightly over it, propping her head in her upturned hand to create a wall between her and Parrish. "What's your name?"

"Brie," Parrish said, leaning around the elbow. "She's a friend."

I caught Parrish's eye beyond the brunette's torso. "Maybe you've seen me with Parrish."

The woman shook her head. "I don't think so." She smiled broadly. "I'm Honey."

I shrugged as the server arrived and started taking orders. "Maybe I just have that sort of face."

She canted her head at me and squinted as though she was trying to imagine me in whatever setting she thought she'd remembered me from. "No. It's not that." She mindlessly accepted the basket of focaccia the server passed her. "I have the feeling I've seen you lately."

Parrish grabbed for a piece of bread. "You couldn't have seen her. She's been a bit off the grid." She grinned at me. "Isn't that right, Brie?"

I reached for the bread basket, the smell of olive oil and rosemary making my stomach growl loudly. "Guilty as charged."

At the words, Honey gasped loud enough to make me drop the bread I'd been about to dip into the saucer of balsamic and oil.

"That's it," she exclaimed and bumped her shoulder against Parrish. "She's the psychic."

Parrish froze. I froze. The bread triangle I was holding over the dish of vinaigrette dripped onto the table.

"What do you mean *the* psychic?" I managed to get out without jumping from my chair.

"The psychic from the papers." Honey looked absolutely delighted as she dug into her purse. "The one leading that Satanic cult who strung those women up on the pier."

CHAPTER EIGHT

MY MOUTH WENT DRY as Honey fished around in her purse and finally extracted a cell phone all glitzed up with rhinestones. I thought I could hear my heart rate ratcheting up.

I set the dripping blob of bread onto my napkin. "I'm not sure what you're talking about."

She ignored me, and seemingly unaware of the tension she'd created, swiped open her phone. "It was in the gossip rag today." She ran two fingers across the screen like little legs in a marathon, mumbling about having seen it just that morning.

My stomach started to hurt. I fleeted a glance at Parrish, who glowered at her date.

"It's right here," the woman said and held it up, screen facing me, to see.

The picture was from a few weeks earlier, when the photographer at the first murder scene at the docks had snapped a whole lot of pictures, including, apparently, one of me looking over the crime scene. There was no view of the women who'd been murdered, but in the distance, you could see the markings that had been left on the asphalt when the killer had arranged the viscera and other things into a Hecate symbol. Blurred and indecipherable, they might have looked like Satanic markings to the untrained eye.

What the hell was I thinking? Even the untrained eye would see evil in what had happened there.

In the photo, the photographer had caught me staring off into space as Layne skulked behind me. He looked very official, very angry, and very handsome, while I looked like a mess of guilt and shame. It didn't help that I had been feeling decidedly nauseous at the time the photo was taken or that I'd thought the police were planning to arrest me for drugging a client.

The rest of the detail of the scene was either discreetly cropped out or the photographer had simply aimed his camera my way. I recalled taunting him because he'd given me attitude. Payback was a bitch, I thought.

No one could have accused him of selling crime scene photos based on the picture, but it was clear it was the pier where the murders had happened.

I started to explain, but Parrish took the phone from Honey's hand and laid it on the table.

"That little shit," she said. "I'm going to shove that camera up his—"

"Please," I said, putting my fingers to my forehead. "Don't." I wasn't sure what I didn't want her to do, but it seemed any horrible thing was possible in the moment.

"Why the hell not?" she said. "He obviously sold this for a pretty penny, intentionally misleading everyone." She turned to her date. "Brie is not a Satanist, Honey." This in a haughty tone that should have made the girl quail but didn't. "She's a woman of power. A good one. Someone who helped us close that case."

Honey looked me over with a renewed interest.

"I hear it's not closed at all," she said, pushing Parrish's fingers off her phone and retrieving it from the table. "It says here that although police took a man into custody, he died before he could be charged." She read from the screen in an accusatory tone that managed to sound both intrigued and defensive. "Two more homicides of a similar nature have gone unsolved. The one constant being a woman with a psychic shop located along the piers where she sells, of all things, Zombie Vomit and spells to cast out demons."

So Mr. Photo bug had been into my shop. Bully for him. He knew the aesthetics and no real details.

"The zombie vomit isn't for sale," I muttered and Honey looked at me with an expression of victory, completely ignoring my comment. "It's a joke jar."

"I'm right," she said. "It's you." She turned to Parrish, whose glower had grown very yellow. "It's her, isn't it? You're the coroner. You should have all kinds of inside scoop."

"Honey, I'm the assistant coroner." There was a note of threat in Parrish's voice and I guessed, as she did, that her date wasn't really into her at all, but into the macabre details Parrish might be able to relay.

Even so, a hot flush washed over my chest. "It's me, but it's not what it looks like."

"Damn straight," Parrish said as she pushed back in her chair.

She shoved the bowl of vinaigrette toward Honey hard enough for it to slosh over the bowl, but the fluid missed her and landed on the table cloth in small puddles. "You got it all wrong. You thought I'd want to get in your pants so bad, I'd try to impress you with details of my job? You must be fucking crazy. I had a feeling you were a bit queer. And not in a good way. Fucking prison bride queer." She ran her hand over the bristle of hair that she'd left free for the evening. "God. I hate when this happens."

The other two women, who had already ordered a bottle of wine and were pouring it into glasses, looked distinctly uncomfortable. Neither seemed willing to give up their evening dinner, but they did at least offer Parrish an expression of sympathy. One of them asked Parrish if they should get take-out instead. Good friends, those.

"I'm not hungry anymore," Parrish said then she regarded her date with a grimace that made me wince. "You want dirty details of murder scenes and dead bodies, email Paul Bernardo." She hooked me by the elbow. "Come on, Brie. I'll drive you home."

Her date stood up, wringing her hands, but I had the feeling she was more upset about being found out than losing Parrish. "

"Wait," she blurted out and made a grab for my elbow. "Can I get a picture of you with me for social media?"

I shook her off as Parrish spun on her. If a mere expression could flay a person alive, then poor Honey would look like a skinned rabbit. I said as much when we reached the exit. She inhaled very deeply and slowly before turning heel and guiding me to the door.

We were outside, in the cold air, before I dared speak again, trying for another bit of humor in the hopes of calming the heated tension she was giving off, and partly because the glimpse of yellow I'd seen in her eyes didn't convince me she hadn't seen Honey as a breathing carcass of skinned hare.

I hugged my arms over my chest at the bite of the breeze that had come up. "For a second there, I thought you were going to eat her."

Parrish flung her arm over my shoulder and tugged me close, lending me her warmth. "To be honest, that's why I picked her up in the first place."

We strode up the street, heading for an indoor parking lot. My shivers stopped, but it was tough to walk easily beneath her arm with the height difference.

"You picked her up to eat her?" I said. "I thought werewolves didn't do that anymore."

A gasp of laughter escaped her. "Oh Brie, you're so naïve."

I realized too late what she meant and even though she couldn't see me in the dark, my face flushed with heat.

"I'm sorry, Parrish," I murmured, feeling as though I was to blame for her date gone awry.

"Not your fault I picked a wannabe prison bride. Some chicks are just enamored of death and horror. Funny, she didn't look like a goth. All that pink makeup kind of threw me."

"She wasn't gay," I said softly when we were outside the restaurant. "You know that, right?"

"Hell yeah," she said. "But I thought maybe I could turn her for a couple hours." She chuckled. "One drink away from lesbianism and all that."

I smiled to myself as we entered the parking garage and she guided me left. "You really need to reframe that belief."

"Why?" she asked. "What harm is a couple hours?"

I sighed. "You werewolves," I said. "You really are messed up."

"Maybe it comes from eating people," she said with a hint of humor in her voice.

"Hardy Harr. You're about as funny as Layne is."

We had reached her car and she walked me around to the passenger door and opened it. It creaked so loud, I winced. She shoved me gently into the seat and closed the door. Four taps on the hood and she rounded the front to get into her side.

She turned the ignition and waited till it was purring evenly before she looked askance at me.

"You know, the last person I ate moaned and begged for more."

I clutched at the dash as she hit the gas and sped out of her parking space. "Please spare me," I said.

"It's a fact, Brie. Werewolves like me eat all sorts of people," she went on as though I'd asked. "There's the little Latina who liked to cosplay as Red Riding Hood, the chubby Korean girl who liked to roller skate, the very hard to understand Scottish chick who introduced me to haggis, the--"

"Stop. Please. Just stop."

"Oh come on, Brie. You worried I might be interested in eating a little cheese?"

"OK, now you've gone too far," I said with a laugh. "I know what you're doing."

She turned a corner a bit too sharply and the car tilted. "Is it working?"

I gripped the dash and rolled with the car as it leaned to the right. "I can't say I'm pleased about being in the papers, but at least I'm not about to have a panic attack. Thanks."

"Just doing my duty."

I shifted in my seat as she slowed to a regular pace, but weaved in and out of traffic like she had a death wish. It took several moments before I realized I recognized the direction we were heading in. The neighborhood looked too distinctly elitist to be my part of town, and I knew she was taking me to Layne's.

"You're heading in the wrong direction," I said.

Her sigh filled the car. "You know I can't take you to your house. Layne would kill me. Literally. And I can't take you to my place." She didn't offer up a reason, but I didn't care anyway. I wanted to go home and said so.

She shook her head. "Impossible. You're going back to the alpha's. We'll break in. They won't even know you're back."

"I doubt they even know I left." I sunk down into the seat, knowing I wouldn't be able to dissuade her and trying to work out how I could slip out of her sight and call a cab and still make her think I'd gone in. Because if she thought I wasn't obeying, she'd come right to my house to get me.

"Oh, they know you've left," she said.

That made me bolt up. "Oh my God," I said. "He called you."

"Messaged me, actually. It was a happy happenstance that you walked into that pizza joint." She chuckled. "I'd just told him he'd have to go looking for you because I was about to eat." She paused to chuckle at her joke then went on. "I told him I'd bring you back when we were finished."

I was about to comment something nasty about being finished myself when my phone chirped. Then it chirped again, and then in rapid succession, went all haywire with so many noises, it left me frantically trying to shut down the sound so I could think long enough to start reading the notices popping up.

"What in the hell?" Parrish said. "You got some demon in there or something?"

I stared at the screen in my hand, dumbfounded. "I have a new friend, it seems." My back went clammy as I brought up the notice that my business had been tagged on my favorite social media platform. "She got a picture," I said, my voice flat. "She snapped a picture when I was at the table. Fucking bitch."

The car swerved past two vehicles and darted to the right. Parrish pulled it to a stop, double parking. "Let me see that." She shoved the car into park and grabbed my phone. "Sweet Jesus," she said. "There are at least fifty comments."

In the few seconds I'd seen it, the post had managed to burn itself into the back of my eyelids. Me at the table looking cold and wet and pathetic juxtaposed against the article Honey had shown me at the restaurant. There were cute little stickers with knives and stabbed hearts and captions that said: met a witch tonight.

"She's dead," Parrish said. "I mean literally dead."

"If that's got you upset, don't look at the comments that say I need to be drawn and quartered or burned at the stake." I squeezed my eyes closed. The panic I'd beat back earlier was nothing to the dread that climbed my spine.

"This isn't going to go over well," she said.

"Captain Obvious over here," I said with a weak laugh.

"There's at least twenty texts," she said. "And a hundred emails."

"Delete them," I said. "I don't even want to look."

"Already doing that," she said. "But I don't think I'll be able to keep up."

"Then just keep the phone." I opened the car door, the sudden need for air overcoming me. The blast of cold took my breath. Or maybe it was the sob that stole its way from my lungs.

I slammed the door and walked briskly back in the direction we'd come. There was no way I was going to Layne's now. There was no way I was sitting in the car with Parrish, listening to the damn phone blip and burp and steal more of my life with every second. The adrenaline was already kicking in and I had to fight the urge not to run.

Parrish's car door thunked open and closed. I stepped up my pace. She wouldn't force me back to Layne's. I'd hail a cab. There were plenty enough this time of night.

She called out to me twice before I turned around to see her standing by the car, my cell phone in the air.

"I think we should go to your store."

Something about the way she stood there made the hackles raise on the back of my neck. I swallowed hard, trying to remove the fist that seemed to have me by the throat. When she noticed me heading back to the car, she lowered the phone to her side. She'd turned it off, I guessed, because it wasn't making noises anymore.

"What's wrong?" I said when I reached her.

She jerked her chin at the passenger door. "It's Scarlett," she said.

The dread I'd felt, the hair-raising claws dragging a line down my spine rested on the small of my back and dug in so hard I nearly lost my balance.

"What happened?"

She jerked her chin again at the door on my side. "Maybe nothing."

Maybe nothing. I clung to that hope as I climbed in. Parrish tapped the wheel four times before putting the car back into drive. I noticed she had set the phone between us in the cup holder. She kept her eyes on the road, driving more sedately but at a quicker pace than before.

"I messaged Layne just in case," she said. "And 911."

"911?" My hands went to my chest instinctively. "What's happened."

"Maybe nothing," she said again. "But there was a message from her along with all those emails and pings. She said for you not to come in tomorrow. Just send the police."

CHAPTER NINE

WE FOUND SCARLETT LYING just beyond the open doorway that led to the back alley. The dog lay at her side, its legs tangled in hers. It lifted its head for a moment when it heard us. The red glow in its eyes died to regular brown by the time my mind let me process everything and sort it into one cohesive image.

Scarlett was in the same shirt she'd worn when I left her, except it was torn and blood stained. Her jeans were missing and she wore a pair of mauve lace panties that peeked out from beneath the hem of her shirt. My gaze froze on the single bloody palm print on her thigh and I hitched it forcefully back up to the purple smudge of her panties, unmarred and pretty still despite the horror of blood everywhere else.

I halted midway through the door, gaping at the scene as I tried to process it all, and tried to get past the explosion of guilt. She didn't deserve to get hurt. It was all my fault. I never should have hired her when I knew, just knew, my shop wasn't safe anymore.

"Fuck," I said. "Oh sweet Jesus, they found me. They fucking found me and now she's dead because of me."

I was aware I was weaving on my feet as Parrish shoved past me with her phone to her ear. She shouted an address into it. Told them to hurry. Then she dropped to her knees beside the girl.

All while I just stood there, half in and half out of my shop like a deer in the headlights.

Everything swam around me like weeds in a pond. Colors morphed and changed. Parrish's voice as she shouted something at me was distorted.

Watching Parrish as she pumped Scarlett's chest, paused, pumped again, was like being stuck in a time loop that didn't end. Ever.

Several long moments passed like that before sounds caught up with images and even then, I couldn't move. The paralysis held me in its grip with claws sunk deep into my psyche. It took Parrish yelling at me in a voice so shrill it hurt my ears to release me.

"What?" I said. "What do I do?"

"Get a fucking blanket or something. A first aid kit. Bandages. Dear God, we have to stop this bleeding or all this CPR isn't going to amount to an ant's fart in the wind."

She kept pumping but altered the cant of her voice, readjusting so the syllables bobbed along with her torso as she adjusted back to a rhythmic pace and yelled at me at the same time. "Ah ah ah ah staying alive staying alive," she sang out as she pumped. "Get a fucking med kit staying alive. Staying alive. Didn't you fucking hear me, Brie, staying alive. Staying alive."

I staggered backward, holding onto the door frame and used it as leverage to thrust myself deeper into the shop. I didn't have a med kit. I didn't even think I had roll of bandages. But I did have a change of clothes in the back room. Sheets. Yes. Sheets. I had sheets for the cot. Scarlett would have taken them out already to make up the bed for herself.

As I flew through the back room, I tried not to look at all the things that had been toppled over or smashed. I tried really hard not to envision the scene that must have unfolded as Scarlett fought against any number of coven members who had come, finally, to take me back to that God-forsaken basement or somewhere worse.

The sheets and blankets were lying on the cot unused. She must have just dropped them onto the mattress when they came. I scooped up the sheets, thanking the gods that they were white cotton and not polyester or fleece. I ran back for Parrish, halting only for a second to grab the shears from my desk on the way by. Drawers had been pulled out and flung across the floor and everything but the basket had been swiped clean off the surface, but the scissors still sat in the basket.

Thank God for small miracles.

I was panting when I made it back to Parrish, the adrenaline making my breath shallow. My lungs felt like someone had banked a smoldering fire in there, expecting a long cold night.

I thrust the sheet at her and held up the shears. "I can cut whatever size we need."

She didn't bother to look up, so I had no idea how she saw what I was holding. "Don't bother with the scissors staying alive. Just drop the whole thing on her leg staying alive. Lean on it for pressure alive staying alive. And for the love of God do NOT fucking' puke. Ah ah ah ah."

I looked down at the legs that were sprawled out on the ground pointing toward the street. There was a lot of blood on one of them. The entire reason I'd been so happy to focus on those pretty panties.

"She's bleeding."

Parrish did look up then, but she didn't stop pumping down on Scarlett's chest. In that one second I knew what she couldn't say to me. What her whole face was telling me. The girl was dead. We'd put the sheets down and we'd lean on them with all the pressure we could manage to try to stem the flow of blood and we'd deliver CPR perfectly and it still wouldn't matter.

"Do it," she said, breaking the rhythm for an instant before returning to it.

I dropped the cloth onto the unmoving leg and leaned on it. My stomach came up into my throat. Sirens split the air and I wondered how I hadn't heard them coming till just now when they seemed to be right out front. I think I sobbed. I might have gagged. There was an odor that shouldn't be coming off a living person unless they were homeless.

"It's all my fault," I murmured. "I killed her."

Paramedics rushed into the alley, accompanied by the metallic sound of equipment being unloaded from the back of a vehicle. Red lights flashed all around me, making the dizziness worse.

Someone shouldered me out of the way, a husky fellow with kind eyes. A wiry man removed Parrish and put an oxygen mask over Scarlett's face.

I stumbled backward and fell against a trash can. Parrish moved toward me like a zombie. Her eyes were wide and black-lined. She'd worn mascara for her date and the sweat had ran into her eyes and watered the makeup right off her lashes. When she blinked it was long and slow.

I looked past her to the paramedics who were already loading Scarlett into the back of the ambulance. She was covered with a sheet. I was reassured to see they hadn't pulled it over her face. They were working on her even as they hoisted her into the back. So. Not dead. Not yet.

I let go a shuddering sound that drew Parrish's attention.

"The police will be here soon," she said.

I nodded, not sure what to say and not trusting my voice anyway.

She ran both hands over her head and clasped them at the back of her neck, a very masculine gesture that somehow just made her look vulnerable. "It's not your fault."

I wrapped my arms around my midriff and realized I was shivering. It wasn't until she pulled me into an embrace that the tears finally came and she shushed me like a mother might. I cried into her chest and clung to her as she rested her chin on my head.

"I think we got to her in time," she murmured into my hair. "We weren't too late. One more minute and—"

She clamped her mouth shut with a noise that made her jaw click audibly above me. She wasn't soft and yielding as she held me but it didn't matter. I clung to her just the same, just happy to feel her heartbeat against my cheek, sense the way her chest rose and fell with each inhalation. I was still trying to gather the sobs into some sort of control when she stiffened even more against me. She pushed me gently away.

She was looking at something behind me. I spun on my heel to see Layne standing at the mouth of the alley. He looked shell shocked, his arms held stiffly against his sides, his spine rigid. When he swallowed, it looked like the Adam's apple struggled to plunge down his throat. The gaze that flicked from Parrish to me blazed through the darkness like a predator in the darkest shadows.

He said nothing, just turned on his heel to retrieve two blankets held out to him by one of the uniformed policemen gathering behind him. When he faced us again, Parrish swiped her face with the back of her wrist and side-stepped, giving me room to wipe my eyes and gather my control. Maybe so she could gather her own.

Her voice was low and throaty. "This has to stop, Layne. You have to do something."

"I'm doing everything I can," he said, his expression carefully masked but his eyes flashed. He shuffled the blankets each to one arm. They looked to be made of wool with a Sherpa lining. I shivered just thinking how divinely warm they would be.

Three uniformed cops flanked him, busily setting up a perimeter. My shop was now a crime scene. Again. Someone was putting up yellow tape at the mouth of the alley, blocking the entrance.

Layne acted like they weren't there, and maybe to him they were as invisible as he headed for Parrish. He ignored the blood all over her shirt and hands, blood that I knew coated me as well. Scarlett's blood.

Parrish stood there, rigid under his gaze, her fists clenched at her sides in a perverse echo of his own posture upon entering the alley.

He took one long look at her and draped one blanket over his left arm, leaving his right free to shake out the other. With great care and what seemed like wary caution, he then wrapped the other around her shoulders.

She trembled visibly beneath his touch, making the blanket ripple like a pond disturbed by a pebble. For the first time, I realized she was working really hard to keep it together.

Only once she was cocooned in the warmth of the blanket, did Layne reach for her, and when he did, it was with one hand that went round the back of her neck. He cupped the back of her head with his hand and used the motion to pull her roughly against his chest.

His other arm circled her shoulders as he inched forward at the same time, giving her no space to fight him if she wanted. And she did fight him. I could see it in the way the blanket moved as though it was being pummeled from the inside. She tried to wrench herself from his embrace with a ferocity that reminded me of a cat in a bag.

But he was immovable, and so then was she. There was determination in the way he gathered her in, and compassion, even gentleness in the way he held her despite her struggles. He was her safe harbor in a torrential storm.

That was when she broke down. She shuddered violently beneath the weight of the blanket and he let her sob into his chest. The murmuring sounds he made were for her ears only and she nodded many times as he held her.

I watched with a mixture of fascination and envy, my own body trembling with the after effects of adrenaline, the longing to be held and cared for an ache that burrowed in my bones.

But I was an interloper. I shouldn't have been there in that moment. I felt like a voyeur, but I couldn't turn away. The intimacy of the act they shared was a balm even for my spirit.

The activity behind them, the scent of blood in the air, the traffic on the street beyond resided somewhere outside the bubble of energy they created and it took long moments before he released her. He held her at arm's length and looked down at her as she hung her head.

"You will be alright now," he said. It wasn't a question but she nodded as though it was.

I wrung my hands in front of me. I was freezing now. My teeth were chattering. I'd not thought to close the door to my shop so no doubt it was just as cold inside since the furnace couldn't possibly heat the entirety of the outdoors.

I made a move for the shop and that was when his gaze shifted to me as though he'd been waiting for me to make a move. He hadn't forgotten me, that was clear by the way his shoulders squared when my eyes met his.

"Would you like a blanket, Brie?"

It was so polite, so carefully enunciated that he might have been talking to a stranger instead of the woman he'd kissed not a few hours before. A woman he'd kissed and insulted in between one breath and the next.

"Of course she wants a blanket," Parrish said in a faint imitation of her usual tone. Even with just the light from the street lamps, I could make out the faintest echoes of sorrow that she hadn't yet been able to erase. "Can't you see her shivering for fuck sake?"

He sent her an indulgent look before he inhaled and headed toward me as though were braving steps to the gallows. I wasn't sure what to do so I just stood there like a ninny until he was close enough that I could smell his aftershave and mint gum. The air between us pulsed like it wanted to explode. My throat ached all the way to my chest.

At first, I thought he was just going to hold the blanket out to me, giving himself distance and to avoid having to touch me. But a heartbeat later, he swooped in and wrapped me so quickly I wasn't ready for the warmth of him. I gasped at how good it felt. I all but sagged against him.

His sharp intake of breath was the only thing way I knew he was as afraid of this moment as I was, but that what had happened between us didn't matter right then. My forehead leaned against his chest of its own accord and if I thought I'd wrung myself of tears before, I was naive.

His arms tightened on me. I yielded completely with a sigh of longing and relief, and he dropped his chin down on my hair. When he spoke, his voice was strangled by emotion.

"I thought it was you," he said in a voice strangled by emotion. "My God, Brie. They told me the emergency was at this shop and I almost lost it."

"It wasn't me," I said stupidly. "It was Scarlett."

Scarlett. The coven had attacked Scarlett. Maybe they'd sent an assassin and they'd thought she was me. I had a hard time caring it could have been me lying half dead in the alley way when I was pretty sure she'd fought like a banshee against them. She had spirit. She deserved to live dammit.

"I thought I'd lost you, Brie," he said. "I couldn't--" His voice broke and I looked up at him. He struggled with the words. He was looking down at me and each word was a battle. "I couldn't lose you. I just can't."

"You won't lose me," I whispered. "Not ever. I promise."

I wasn't sure what to expect. His wasn't a declaration of love or an apology for earlier, but in light of the evening, it didn't matter. My words felt right. Whatever had happened before was swallowed by the depth of emotion in his voice. I didn't want him to ache like I was aching. "It's alright. I won't leave. I promise."

He buried his face in my neck then and I felt the wetness of his tears. I reached for him from beneath the weight of the blanket and wrapped my arms around his waist. I thought I felt a wave of heat come off him, warming my bones, my marrow, my spirit. I felt like everything would be alright so long as he was there with me.

Someone cleared their throat behind him and I eased away from his embrace, too shy now to look him in the face. Instead, I peered around him at the officer who was holding out a knife inside a baggie.

"We found this," he said to Layne, who nodded sedately. "Probably the weapon the suspect used to inflict the wounds on the victim."

Layne turned to retrieve the bag and as he did, something sparked my memory. It wasn't just Scarlett who had been hurt. She'd been the ones with the wounds, yes, but there was another casualty of the coven.

I scanned the alley way with a frantic eye. "The dog," I said, noting an alley filled with dark brackish puddles of fluid I knew was blood, several discarded items from inside my shop she'd no doubt used to throw at her attacker.

"Dog." The officer said. "What dog?"

I sent a harried glance to Parrish who had to have seen the same thing I did when we found Scarlett. The black dog, Abbi. She'd been lying beside Scarlett just as unmoving as the woman had been. I'd forgotten it in the chaos. But I remembered now. She should have been lying in the alley.

"My dog," I said. "She's disappeared."

Chapter Ten

I HAD TO ACCEPT the fact that the coven had killed my dog. Or spelled her out of existence because she was nowhere to be found, no matter how hard we looked. We checked the store as much as we could without disturbing things. We scanned the alley, even canvassed the streets around my shop by asking late night passersby if they'd seen it.

Parrish, by then, was cranky and completely out of sorts. I didn't want to ask her how she was feeling. She kept casting stolen looks at Layne as though she was afraid he'd catch her doing something she shouldn't. Even when she threw her hands up in the air as we stood in the middle of my storefront, saying she was done, simply done, she sent a furtive glance his way.

If he saw it, he paid no mind to it. That just seemed to make things worse, and the fidgeting was enough to drive me around the bend.

"It's clear the dog is gone," I said. "You might as well go home." I ran my hand over the back of my neck and stretched to ease the kinks. It was nearly midnight and all of us had to get up for work. "I'll just sleep here."

Parrish whirled on me like she would bite my head off. The bark in her voice lifted me an inch off the floor. "Like hell you will."

Layne's hand descended on Parrish's shoulder, and she jumped. I guessed she was too busy growling at me that she didn't hear him approach her.

"You said you were alright," he murmured.

She swallowed and canted her head to look at him. Her finger pointed in my direction. "You can't let her stay here after that."

I saw his fingers tighten on her shoulder, but she didn't wince. "I don't intend to."

"Good," she said and dropped her gaze from his, unable to hold it any longer. She stepped away, out from under his touch, but it didn't escape me that he watched her every move as she strolled across the shop.

I guessed some sort of dominance contest had gone on in those microseconds and Layne had exerted his will. I knew she wasn't submissive, but was willing to bet there was some pecking order I didn't understand. I vowed to ask him about it all now that we'd what? Patched things up? Made up? I had no idea what we'd done. It just made me feel better to think there would be an 'after'.

She picked up one of the candles Scarlett had been looking at earlier. "Maybe the dog just got called back to wherever it comes from." She peered at the wax undercarriage. "Here doggy doggy doggy."

Layne narrowed his gaze at her as though he were uncertain of her mental state. The ghost of her smile disappeared beneath his solemn scrutiny and she put the candle back down on the shelf with a soft thump. "Sorry. No touchie." She held her hands up in surrender, but her expression was anything but. "Well, you tell me where an invisible dog could be."

"It's not invisible," I said. I thumped my chest to show just how solid I thought it was. "At least, not anymore. You saw it, right?"

She shrugged. "I saw it earlier in the day, but not here tonight. Are you sure you saw it lying next to Scarlett?" she winced as she said the woman's name and I guessed it had come out of her without her thinking much about saying the name until she heard it again.

I hugged my waist. "I'm as sure of it as I am of all the mess those bastards made of my shop." I skirted around another mention of Scarlett, and not just for Parrish's sake. "Parrish probably just didn't notice it because she ran to help Scarlett straight away."

Nope. There was no way to talk about this without mentioning that poor girl. The guilt was overpowering.

Layne stooped to pick up a few books that had been tossed either in defense or attack at some point during the evening. He caught himself before touching them and rubbed his hands together absently as he straightened back up. As though afraid he'd give into some compulsive desire to clean, he shoved his hands into his pockets as he addressed me.

"Tell me more about the dog."

I closed my eyes, willing myself to see the scene again despite the horror of it. "It was lying next to her," I said, again avoiding mention of Scarlett by name. "It wasn't hurt in any way I could see, but it wasn't moving."

"And when did you notice it was gone?"

"When you came. But it must have been gone before then because I don't remember seeing it when I came out with the sheet."

"So other than the dog not moving, and Parrish not seeing it, nothing out of the ordinary?"

It was said with sarcasm, but he wasn't being unkind. I got the sense the entire situation was bothering him more than he showed. Like he thought there should be something more that he should be seeing but wasn't.

I dropped my head back, thinking. "It looked kind of gray maybe?" I paused to consider what I'd said. It was true. It had looked sort of gray. "Like it was less dense. Like the black was fading."

Parrish halted mid-step and bit down on her thumbnail, a screaming violet color that was chipping from her thoughtful chewing on it. "Like it's being erased, maybe?" she said. "Maybe it was mid-disappearance when you saw it. Going back to wherever the hell it lurks in between these horrible harbingers of death visitations. Good riddance."

"Well, wherever it is," Layne said. "It's not here." He let go a heavy sigh. "The team will want to sweep through and finish come morning. We best not mess with too much more." He gave Parrish a meaningful look that had her throwing up an insult with her middle finger. "Parrish, you go on home. I'll take bring Brie back to the manse with me."

Parrish sent a worried look in my direction. "You alright with that, Brie?"

I sank into one of the chairs and flung my leg over the arm of it. "I don't care where I stay, to be honest. I might just fall asleep right here."

A uniformed officer coming into the main shop from the back drew my attention right about the time Layne's phone chirped again. Both of them had the same expression on their faces.

I sat up, pulling my leg off the armrest and planting my foot on the floor.

"What is it?" I said.

The officer crossed to Layne and took him aside by the elbow. As they whispered together, Parrish sidled over to the chair.

"Doesn't bode well," she said.

I was clutching the arm rests by the time Layne broke away from the officer with a nod. He revealed nothing by his expression, but the slight tremor in his fingers when he pulled a stick of gum from his pocket and unwrapped it with such acute attention that Parrish sucked in a breath, made it abundantly clear something was wrong.

When he finally swung his gaze our way, it was to capture Parrish's eye. Some communication traveled the air between them because she swore beneath her breath. The officer who had approached Layne made his way over to us.

"Get up," Parrish said to me. "If you have something you need from this store that might be useful later, grab it now as though you came in with it."

My legs were like rubber at her words, but I stood just the same, my eye roaming the shop as my brain tried to tackle her meaning and fizzled back out again.

The officer had pulled out his notebook and pencil. Not a good sign. I'd seen Layne do the same thing. Notes. They were going to take notes. That was all. And yet, I couldn't control the tingling at the base of my spine that said this wasn't just going to be an inventory of things I thought might be missing.

"Ladies," the officer said and Parrish snorted. He looked her way with a quirk of his eyebrow. "Lady," he corrected himself.

"Officer Wright," she said with a mock bow. "You're looking judgmental this evening."

"We'll be closing off the store for the day," he said to me. "Do you have anything you need that we should catalog before it leaves the shop?"

"Here it comes," Parrish said, nudging me. "You best make sure you got all your drawers on, Brie. Officer

Wright might confiscate anything he finds in the spare dresser."

He glared at her. "You know the procedure."

She shrugged. "I've never known procedure to include stealing panties from crime scenes."

His lips tightened into a line that could open a soda bottle and Parrish stared him down, daring him to argue with her even though it was obviously untrue. In the end, he turned to me, deciding, evidently, to ignore Parrish.

"You won't be able to open tomorrow," he explained. "So please take only those things you need to work from home."

I spread my arms out. "This is a psychic store, Officer. I sell things. I can't sell all this from my home."

He waggled his head side to side as though he agreed, but had his hands tied. Layne, I noticed from over his shoulder, had started wandering the shop, studying things without touching them.

"Take what you need," Wright said. "You want the person who did this to get caught, right?" he didn't wait for me to nod because of course I did. "Then let us do our job."

I scoured the shop with my gaze, letting it slide over the books and candles and ephemera that had fallen or got thrown during Scarlett's attack. I really couldn't think of anything I should take until my eye landed on the appointment book on the counter.

"That," I said, drawing Layne's attention as well as Officer Wright. "I need my agenda."

Wright jerked his thumb at the photographer, who had slipped into the store unnoticed. The spindly young man headed for the counter at the same time Layne did. I crossed the room to gather the book and waited while the officer snapped photos of it where it sat and then, with gloves, lifted it to snap several more. He then bagged it.

"I thought you were letting me take it," I said.

Layne put his hand down on my shoulder. "They'll wait to clear it first, Brie," he said.

"But he said I should take something." I pointed at Wright.

Layne guided me away from the counter. "You'll have it early in the morning," he said. "Someone will be working tonight to clear it for your use."

"But, he said—"

"Brie, this is a crime scene. You can't just take things from it."

I gestured toward my back room. "The crime scene is at the back of my shop. The crime scene is the alley where those bastards hurt her." My voice sounded thick and uneven and even hearing it, I knew he'd not relent.

He ran his hand over his head and sent a look toward Parrish. She started and her face fell. I looked from her to him to the officer and then the photographer.

"Oh my God," I said. "You think I did something to her?"

"No," Layne said. "It's not that."

Parrish shouldered her way past the photographer, her posture rigid and tension so tight in her jaws that her lips were blanched.

"What's going on?" I asked.

Layne's arm slipped around my waist and he tugged me close. The smell of him, intoxicating as it was, did nothing to ease my anxiety.

"This is now a homicide investigation," he said. "Your friend is dead."

CHAPTER ELEVEN

Hearing about a death should make you cry, express shock, want to offer comfort. I felt none of those things in the moment Layne told me Scarlett was dead. No. I didn't feel grief. I was past that the moment I watched her being loaded into the back of an ambulance.

What I did feel was fury.

That I was going to be kept out of my shop like a criminal, like someone who had done something wrong when I'd done nothing but try to help a poor girl off the street. This was my payment. This was what that poor woman got for trying to get out from beneath the thumb of a bastard.

Now I couldn't even ply my trade and both Layne and Parrish knew it well. They knew exactly what was going to happen, and they were going to let it.

My legs felt like wooden stilts as I took several deliberate steps toward Layne. I poked him in the chest, not even feeling the contact as my finger dug into his chest.

"We know who did this," I said, fully aware my voice was shaking. "They are out there getting away with it. They are going to keep getting away with it unless we do something."

He held still under my furious gaze. I thought the officer and photographer might have backed away. I didn't care how I sounded.

"They killed her," I said in a low voice. "They came right into my shop and they chased her and did God knows what else until she fought back. You see the mess." I gestured wildly without pulling my eyes from his. "She tried to defend herself, Layne. Like I did. But she didn't have any magic to help her. The coven killed her right here."

The photographer cleared his throat, and I swung my gaze on him, glaring at him. "What?" I asked. "You think I'm crazy, bringing up a coven of witches?" I laughed without humor, a dark sound that made the photographer look hastily down at his camera.

For some reason, that infuriated me more. "You're all ignorant. You have no idea what these people can do."

"Do you?" The voice was Officer Wright's. He'd somehow sidled up to the counter without me noticing, and his voice was filled with suspicion.

I slammed my palm down on the counter in front of him. "I know they've killed half a dozen people in the most horrible ways and you all are doing nothing but closing down a little side shop. You've still got my amulet in evidence and are refusing to simply return my property when you know, you KNOW, I had nothing to do with any of this. A girl is dead for fuck's sake and you're here telling me I can't even have my damn agenda?"

My stomach felt like it was in knots, but I wasn't anywhere near done. I thought I felt Parrish tugging on Layne's arm and I spun to face her, just as angry at her for not coming to my defense in this.

"You know," I said. "You were there." I tossed a gesture in the direction of the back room. "You saw her. You told Layne it was the coven. Do something. Make them do something."

"Brie," she said. "Just because you've been through hell doesn't mean it's the coven. Maybe it was that bastard, Kenny."

"Kenny?" Layne said and Parrish nodded.

"Her husband. He was here earlier. Threatened her." She made a slashing motion across her throat. "Real piece of shitty work."

I snorted. "Too easy."

Layne's expression softened as he regarded me. "Sometimes easy is the right answer. I can't tell you how many domestic violence cases end up the same way."

For some reason, that just infuriated me more. I was shaking with the adrenaline of fury. "You're barking up the wrong tree. They're trying to make it look like that's what it is, but I know in my heart it's not. It wasn't Kenny."

The officers stood nearby, waiting for things to re-solve, no doubt marking it all down in their little note-books. I figured I'd be brought in for questioning the next day. Because that's what they did, this police de-partment. They ignored the obvious and blamed every-thing on the poor psychic.

"It's the coven," I said. "Why else would the dog have been there? Explain that."

Parrish exchanged a look with Layne, who ran his hand over his head. "Brie, this crime scene looks noth-ing like any of the others. No one saw the dog but you. Maybe you just wanted to see it."

"I didn't want to see it. It was just there. Right beside her. It's the coven, I'm telling you. I know it."

I had to turn away from the sympathy in his gaze, but when I did, I caught sight of the worry in Parrish's face and that did something to me that I didn't expect. I screamed. Loud. The way the clichéd tribal screamers are taught to loosen their inner angst. Just dropped my head back and aimed my face at the ceiling and let fly a guttural scream that clenched my fists into tight balls.

And then Layne was herding me out of the shop, pushing me to the front door and I was fighting him because how dare he do that to me? It was my shop. My door. My damn anger.

"It's my damn shop," I yelled as he grabbed my hands and held them behind my back. "You can't make me leave." I tried to yank my hands from his grip but it was like trying to pull cold taffy through a pinhole. "Let me go, you prick. I have a right to be here."

"Not when the police are performing an investigation, you don't," he said with an infuriatingly rational tone. "You can come back tomorrow when they're done, Brie. And you'll have your things back when they are finished with them."

"Fuck you," I said, giving one more last wrench of my arm and ended up hurting my shoulder for the trouble. I was aware he had changed tack and was herding me toward my back room, out of sight of the roaming officers and Parrish as they combed my store proper.

"You're angry and you're grieving and you're scared," he soothed. "That's all. It's a lot to process, and no one expects you to be calm and cool when everything around you is falling apart. But if you want to help find the killer, you need to let the police do what they need to do."

"But you heard them," I argued. "They won't be looking for the coven. Just like Farrel—" I froze right then.

Whatever I was going to say clumped up in my throat, choking me. The thought of the detective who had abducted me and nearly killed me came so hard and so fast, that I saw him again in a flash. Not in my mind's eye, but in front of me, sneering at me. He was real in that instant, not a memory or a trick of the light.

I sobbed at sight of him. And I sagged in Layne's grip as my knees buckled. Some sort of flame licked through my chest and down my left arm. My fingers tingled, and the room started to tunnel down into a pinprick of light. The beaded curtain that separated the apothecary galley and the private rooms of my office and back shop brushed against my hand as I pushed through to find a place to lay my hand down for support.

I might have cursed.

If not for Layne's hold on my arms, I'd have sunk to the floor. It took him no more than a second to realize something was wrong. He scooped me right off my feet and held me cradled in his arms. Pulling me against the warmth of his chest.

He laid his back against the door as he hitched me higher.

"You're OK," he murmured into my hair. "I've got you. Nothing will hurt you with me here. I won't let it."

"Fucking damsel," I said in a voice filled with self-loathing and grief.

He shushed me by lifting me high enough to lay his lips against my cheek. "You're anything but a damsel," he murmured against my skin. "No damsel could have survived that basement. Only a warrior could come out of that alive."

I snaked my arms around his neck to burrow in closer and thought I heard his breath catch. If he was insulted or revolted, I didn't care right then. I was greedy for each inch of warmth I found. The heat that radiated off him burned out the cold and the fear. The words, the tone, all of it was a salve. Maybe the only salve I needed for the heartache I felt. The panic started to subside.

I wasn't sure if it was being on the other side of the curtain, in the inner sanctum of my office, or if it was the feel of Layne's steady heartbeat against my ribs, but I could breathe again. My mind cleared. And with it all came the realization that I had burrowed down into his embrace as though it was a plush blanket warm from the dryer.

Farrel had gone the way of all bogey men in the light. Not magic. Not black spells. Just my own vivid imagination partnering with the post-traumatic stress. And Layne was there holding the pieces. I felt like a weakling.

"I can walk now," I said.

He tightened his grip. "I know you can, but I'm not letting you go."

"Because I'm a mess," I said with the tightness of embarrassment putting a hard edge to my voice. "Because you think I can't manage."

He looked down at me, his gaze yellow and the corners of his eyes tight.

"No," he murmured. "Because *I'm* a mess. Because I can't manage without you. I need you, Brie. I need you whole and hale and safe and right now, the only thing keeping my wolf from tearing to shreds anything that moves is the feel of you in my arms."

The threat in his gaze wasn't for me, it was for the maniacs who dared come on my territory and threaten me. It was for the man who would lay an unkind hand on me.

The need behind the gaze, the intensity, was riveting. I couldn't pull my eyes from his.

"You do have magic in you," he whispered in a voice equally tight as my own. "But it's not the kind of magic you think. It's the magic the darkest sides of my wolf needs to lay down like a docile lamb by the fire while the man clings to his humanity. You're the thing keeping my wolf at bay. I need you, Brie."

I felt the baldness of his confession echoed deep in my marrow. He was already filling me up. He had to know that. He had to know what he was doing to me. Every breath he took in time with mine pushed one more inch of darkness aside.

"I need you too," I said.

His forehead touched down against mine. When he captured my eyes with his, I was sure something sparked in there. I felt a rumbling in his chest that vibrated against my ribs. I felt safe then. I reached up to touch his chin with my thumb and something broke in him. I sensed it in the way he shuddered beneath my finger.

He let go a ragged sound and then he was crossing the room with a determination I felt in the sudden, desperate tightening of his arms around me. By the time we reached the tiny room where the cot was stored, I knew what he was going to do. I knew, and I clung to him with the same desperate abandon.

The storage closet had at one time been a pantry with a broad counter and several wooden shelves. It was roomy enough to hold three people and have space to spare. I'd left the shelving on one wall and torn out everything except the counter and framework of the bottom cupboards. The old smell of sugar and spices still lingered in the air, mixing with that of fabric softener from the sheets and clothes I stored there now.

In one fluid gesture, he released my legs so my feet dropped to the floor. Then he back-walked me against the counter, pinning me between his hands as they gripped the lip. The edge of the counter dug into the backs of my thighs. His head lowered like a dog's, hooded eyelids drowsy with lust and possession.

"You need me," he said in a low voice. "But do you want me, Brie? Because it can't just be out of need. I have to have more than that."

I'd never wanted anyone more than I wanted him in that moment, but I was afraid to say so. I was afraid to admit it. Even with the smell of his arousal in the air, I was terrified he'd reject me. That he'd leave me the way everyone did. Casting me off as though I was a ragged sweater with no use.

"Brie," he prompted. "Say it, love. Say you want me."

He flicked the light switch on without taking his eyes from mine. The yellow had melted to a golden honey color and if I stared just right into them, I could see the wolf looking back out at me. It felt like I was in the arms of two men: one, a civilized man and the other, a very sentient but primal creature with a need that surpassed speech.

I couldn't bear for him to see the nakedness of my fears. I reached over his shoulder to fumble for the light switch. Darkness was all I'd ever had, and darkness was what I expected.

He caught my hand and gathered the fingers together.

"Don't," he said. "I want to see your face. I want to watch you."

I swallowed nervously, but nodded.

"You want me?" he said. "You have to say it, Brie. You have to consent because I'm not sure how gentle I can be. I am on the verge of control. My wolf is rattling my cage. He wants you too, and he's not so civilized as I am."

My throat was too thick to speak no matter how badly I wanted to say yes, yes I wanted him.

Instead, I lifted his hand to my mouth and kissed the knuckles, peeling my fingers from his grip and instead wrapping his hand with my own. When I guided his hand to my mouth and sucked his thumb inside, the sharp intake of breath that escaped him cracked something in my core.

A moan escaped me, one that released the pent up consent.

"Sweet Jesus, Brie," he said at the sound, his voice hoarse and ragged.

I pulled on his thumb, tasting the mint gum he always chewed when nervous. He let me swirl my tongue around the pad before he withdrew it slowly, his eyes on my mouth. His fingers splayed across my cheek, finding the tender spot behind my ear. I felt my pulse against his ring finger, pounding hard, a rapid fire that I saw echoed in his own throat.

I had the feeling we were both suspended in the moment, not sure if we could survive all the way through it. Then, testing, he slid his thumb inside again and I opened to accommodate it as he stroked my tongue and found the back of my throat with the pad of his finger, then danced away with it before I could gag.

"My God," he said in response. His forehead dipped down to mine again, his breath a rasp as he held my gaze with his. "My God you're going to kill me."

My hands were already working at his buttons. It was degenerate of me, to want him so badly when I knew a woman had been murdered just hours before, just yards away. That her killer had sought her out here and taken her life so brutally, but I couldn't help myself. I wanted him. I wanted the balm he had, to forget the horror of the things that had happened in my shop. For him to erase all that.

I wanted to feel alive.

"They do call it the little death," I said.

"Then kill me, Brie," he murmured. "I'm not afraid to die. Not with you."

I spread the panels of his shirt apart and let my palms whisper over the brush of light hair between his nipples. A wash of aromas mingled with the old scent of cinnamon and fabric softener, a mix of mint and pheromone and lust.

He roamed my throat with the tips of his teeth, dragging them across my skin, raising goosebumps until I hooked my ankles around his waist and yanked him closer.

"They're going to hear," I said.

His hand slid down to the small of my back. "I want them to hear. I want them to know I'm taking you. That you're mine. That you're giving yourself to me and I'm losing my very soul in the taking."

He took me hard and fast. I clung to his neck with my leg hitched over his waist. The act wasn't loving so much as it was desperate, two souls rampaging through a devastated landscape burnt of its foliage and devoured of its fauna.

We raced to the end as though we feared we wouldn't have the time to get there, and when it was over, I sagged over his shoulder and buried my nose in his neck. We both breathed like it was a labor. At some point I didn't remember, he had torn open my shirt dress, and it hung to the sides. My bra was hitched up over my breasts and the under wire dug into my skin.

A soft rap sounded on the door and Parrish's voice filtered through.

"Take her home, Layne," she said. "Damn you take her somewhere dignified, you fucking' degenerate."

Chapter Twelve

He peeled away from me, the mingling of our sweat making his chest stick to my bare stomach. He lifted his gaze to mine, his face flushed with shame and guilt.

She continued to curse on her side of the door as he caught his breath, the sound of her voice growing more distant.

"She's right," he whispered when she'd got far enough away that we could only barely hear her swearing. "I'm sorry, Brie."

I tugged at the panels of his shirt, pulling them together. "Don't be sorry. I wanted it too. Maybe more."

A soft, bitter laugh escaped him. "I doubt that."

"She's going to give you hell, isn't she?" I said.

His head dropped back, and he clasped his hands behind his neck. "She's going to rip me a new one is what she's going to do." He scratched at the base of his skull before dropping his hands to his sides where the fingers tapped his legs.

"But I needed to feel alive, to feel your pulse on my skin. There was no option for me. The wolf was too close. Too agitated. I took advantage of you. I should be ashamed."

His shirt was still open and I could see the sweat on his skin. It glistened in the light. I fought to keep my fingers from touching it. It was only when he raked his hand over his hair that I realized he was struggling too.

The shirt dress was still wide open, my thighs bare and white in the harsh light of the overhead fixture.

He looked down at me with a face filled with remorse and still, there was bald need there. Whatever he needed, it hadn't been sated. "I should have taken my time, taken you somewhere beautiful, not taken advantage of you in a closet."

He took a step backward and his eyes trailed to my bare shoulder. He tugged my bra back into place, the backs of his fingers brushing my nipples. I might have moaned beneath my breath, hussy that I was.

"Take me home," I said. "And stay with me." I almost added a please at the end, but I didn't need to. A low rumble moved its way through his chest and wafted over me in a growl that indicated he'd been waiting to hear exactly that.

He led me from the shop through the back and tucked me into his car. We drove to the manse without another word. The air in the cabin could have sparked a fire. I wondered briefly if it was appropriate, the lust I felt, in light of the grief and passing of a girl I'd hired to help me in the shop. Then I didn't care. I needed him. I needed to feel alive and forget for a few hours that the cult was out there doing unforgiveable things.

I needed to drown in something other than fear.

He didn't carry me from the car to the guest suite. He let me go on my own steam, maybe offering me one last chance to change my mind. I wouldn't, though. I took his hand and led him through the door and down the hall to the suite.

This time when the tingling took my body, I knew it wasn't fear or dread. When my heart started to pound, I knew it was anticipation. I was going to kiss him. I was going to pull him close and breathe in his smell and let it intoxicate me. There would be no worry or self-reflection. He was going to wipe away every horrible thing I'd ever suffered.

It had been so long since I'd been with anyone, I felt at once shy and excited. My throat ached so much I couldn't trust my voice, so I said nothing. I just dropped his hand long enough to wrap my arms around his neck and pull him closer.

He held my gaze with his. The yellow had become molten gold. I let my fingers trail up into his hair and he shivered, the tension in his neck releasing under my touch. If he was at first stiff and unyielding against my body, I knew it had nothing to do with his own desire. He wanted me too. I could feel that much.

"Again?" he said. He sounded so uncertain. Was he worried I wanted his father more? Was he afraid his declaration was made out of gratitude, or did he think I was just so glad to be safe? Whatever it was, it didn't matter. I somehow found the way to speak past the clump of lust in my throat.

"The lingerie," I said. "It was for you. Not your father. Didn't Parrish tell you that?"

He shook his head. "She wouldn't. It's not how she works."

"And you?" I asked. "How do you work?"

"Slowly," he murmured. "Slowly and tortuously deliberate."

When his lips claimed mine, he showed me exactly what he meant, and it took me several long moments before I could breathe again with any regularity. My heart raced. I returned his kiss with the same deliberation, even when he took control and pressed me ever backwards toward the wall.

He kissed me still, when he unlatched my arms from his neck and lifted them above my head, pinning them to the wall with one hand. The movement lifted my ribs, thrusting my chest upward to meet his touch. He roamed beneath my dress, tasting my skin with his fingers, making me moan until he smothered the sound with another deep kiss.

What happened after that was a blur of delirious pleasure. I returned each kiss, each caress, each thrust. I lost myself in him, and when I emerged from the darkness, my skin felt electric. Like someone had turned on a light that had been off far too long.

After, he held me close, his fingers trailing down my arm, making lazy circles as both of us remained silent. There was a reverence in the air, as though we'd done something sacred, the ritual one of magic created by touch and respect. Something wholly different from the rituals we'd been witnessing played out on other, unfortunate souls.

When he finally lay sleeping next to me, spent and snoring lightly, I took stock and realized I felt alive like I hadn't felt in years. I felt powerful and invigorated.

I felt like anything was possible.

I dropped a bare foot to the floor and slid from the bed. Pausing to look down at him, I drank in his physique with my eyes when just moments before, I'd touched every inch of it with my fingers, my tongue. His taste was still in my mouth, of mint and salt and something wild that might have been a mossy forest.

I didn't bother to dress. Somehow, what I planned to do seemed more fitting to be done naked and vulnerable. I thought of the coven in that dingy basement. I thought of the way they'd bared their flesh to the ravages of magic and I thought that if they could do those things with the evil intent they'd possessed, then I could do better with the pure heart I had in that moment.

I didn't have my mother's grimoire. Her amulet had yet to be returned. But I had her picture. Layne had returned it to me, and I kept it crumpled in my cell phone wallet. My mother's blood ran in my veins. I had her magic in my marrow.

And I had Scarlett's blood as well. She'd baptized me with her dying fluid. I could use that to call to her. I could use all those things that ritual required to help find her killer.

I didn't know the ritual I needed, but I'd seen my mother perform before. She'd used language and blood and sacrifice to amplify her magic.

I'd use what I had. Ritual was a funny thing. Borne of intention and energy and the prescribed actions of a thousand times before, they had a seed in the now. The genesis of ritual needed a seed, an act, an intention that could be carried on later. But what of the now? What about the start of the ritual?

I lifted my dress, bloodied and cold now, from where I'd dropped it when Layne peeled it off me. I inhaled the scent of Scarlett's blood and I took it with me to the fireplace.

Quietly, so I wouldn't wake Layne, I turned on the propane. It squeaked a bit from lack of use, but it flared with a whoosh of fuel. I sat cross-legged in front of it.

Then I prepared to call to the dead.

CHAPTER THIRTEEN

THE MAGIC CAME WITH a whisper, but it landed like a shout. The sound of ocean waves crashing on rocks roared in my ears. The flames as they consumed the bloody fabric, crackled and spit and screamed as though they were consuming kindling. My skin crackled and bubbled along with the fabric. The blood cried out to me, piercing something inside that was deeper than hearing. It lanced me. I tried to scream the pain away, but my mouth dropped open, wordless, soundless.

I'd not burned sulfur for protection, I realized in that moment. I'd not cut into my runes to call to the magic. In my arrogance, I'd simply held my mother's photo against my chest, asked for her guidance. That ritual seemed enough. Maybe it was too much.

The viselike squeeze of power was unlike anything I'd felt before. The pain from the basement, the dizziness, the sensation of falling through blackness had launched themselves into a void and left me with the aftershocks.

For a moment, I hung suspended on that power with my entire body, all my cells and viscera tangled in it as though I were merging with the magic. Suffocating fear came along for the ride and no matter how hard I tried to scream for help, all of it went into that void.

All that existed was that power. I had no choice but to surrender to it and even in letting go, I thought I was dying.

I fought the magic. I thought of Layne and the moments we'd shared and I wanted to return to it. I wanted to be safe in his arms again. But the magic was a greedy beast. Once it had finished chewing me over, rolling me around in its mouth and scraping my psyche with its teeth, it swallowed me whole.

And then the darkness enveloped me completely.

I landed in the void with a thud that jarred my teeth. The photo I'd clutched was gone: the first hint that the magic had taken me somewhere. The second hint came when I bit down on my tongue and tasted blood. Something moved in the shadows, restless and urgent. A chattering sort of sound rose and multiplied around me, like the sound of bones being knocked together or of teeth clacking. The hairs rose on my arms.

I wasn't alone here.

"Scarlett," I said, calling out the way I would in a séance. "Scarlett, I am here beyond the veil with you. You are safe to show yourself to me."

I listened, but I didn't close my eyes the way I would in a regular session. The tingling at the base of my neck and spine warned me it wasn't safe to leave myself that vulnerable.

"Scarlett, I ask you to show yourself to me. Let me know you can hear me by rapping three times on the floor."

I waited and as I did, my skin began to crawl. At first, it was tolerable, but then pinpricks, as though fire ants were roaming my body and biting at will, stung my skin. My breath came in gasps as my chest burned. I coughed, smoke clawing its way down my throat.

The magic wasn't going to hold me here for long and I didn't want to stay. But there was a presence, something black and hulking in the shadows. From the side of my eye, I could see it shuddering now and then as though it were trying to shake off something and move into sight.

"Scarlett," I said again. "Show yourself to me." I thought of Layne's words, the ones that helped push back my own panic. "You're safe here. I won't let anything harm you."

At first, the darkness shivered. I cocked my head, sure I'd heard something, a soft whisper or a rapping against the wall.

"I'm here to help you. You're safe."

There was a strange sound, like a mass of fluid being disgorged from a resistant pucker. Then that darkness grew lighter, not much, just enough for me to notice. I held my breath, both in wonder and fear that I had managed to affect a change, that the veil was real, that I might ruin everything with a single breath.

When she came forth, a dull pain struck my stomach. I sucked in a breath and bit down on the pain.

She looked at me.

"He punched me in the stomach first," she said, now she was more visible. Light streamed through her from an unseen source. Her voice sounded thready.

I gripped my belly, the pain still radiating outward. "He who?" I asked, gasping the question through the pain. It wasn't just a force moving from my stomach now. It was stinging slices of agony peppering my body. I flinched with every strike but forced myself not to let go the thread holding me with her. "Was it a warlock? A man with eyes that would see through you? Was he tall?"

It was the best way I had to describe the shade man, and I hoped she'd be able to remember him.

She canted her spectral head at me. "Kenny," she said. "Kenny killed me."

The words gutted me. Not the cult. It was exactly as Parrish and Layne had said. The disappointment was so acute, I curled into myself.

"You came to help me?" she asked. "Make sure he's caught."

A blow across my back dropped me to my hands and knees. My chest heaved with the exertion of breath, so easy before, now an agony with every inhalation. Somehow, though I couldn't lift my head, I could see her still. She hugged herself. The frailty of hopelessness pinned to her by years of abuse sat on her features the way they had in life. But there was something else there. An echo of her strength as well. A knowing.

"Don't let him do this to another woman," she said.

"Don't worry. They'll catch him," I ground out, meaning the police. Domestic violence. Easy for them, apparently. So many cases so similar to hers. It wouldn't be long before they found his prints, evidence to bring him to justice. It had been me who doubted he was the killer. Me who believed something far more nefarious was afoot. If not for the dog, I might have gone along with them too.

"He won't stop," she said and a jolt went through me, unlike the echoes of her own pain delivered by a man she loved. This jolt had more force and yet it came from nowhere and everywhere. My own nerve endings sizzling on a cast-iron stove.

"If someone doesn't make him stop," she said, "he'll hurt someone else."

I could barely breathe now, so all I could do was nod my promise to her. Yes. I would do what I could to stop him. Colorless fireworks played over my vision as I lifted my head. She stood in the same place, her arms extended. Her mouth was still moving, but I couldn't hear what she was saying.

There was a peculiar shift, like a hitch in a video, and suddenly she was kneeling in front of me. She was bloody and bruised and wounded. Her cheekbone pulsed. I flinched at the nearness of her. The smile she gave me was one of sad comfort.

"Thank you," she said. "For trying."

Another sharp pain cut through me, forcing a moan from my lips.

"It's alright," she said. "I'll be fine. But you need to be careful. I want to help you."

She ran fingers over my cheek and laid her hand on the back of my neck, and the whisper of contact tore a sharp inhale from me. Where her fingers touched down, my skin burned, then the skin went immediately cold, so cold it hurt more than the burn.

I rolled back onto my haunches, swaying beneath the pressure building inside that seemed to come from the spot our skin met. My hands flew to my head, trying to contain it all. It took everything in me to withstand the pressure.

Just when I thought the pressure had mounted to a point beyond what I could stand, it shrank down to nothing, sucking everything back in with such a ferocious speed that a whirlwind swept over me. Where my skin was cold before, now it felt raw and chaffed by a wind that clawed at each inch it found exposed.

"Hold on," she said, dropping her head back. "It's coming."

An instant later, I saw it all. From the moment she opened the door for Kenny and stood back to let him enter, to the opportunity he took to exert his dominance. I watched as she fought him. Things I had placed throughout the shop so carefully got flung in panicked defense as she ran for the back.

He caught her. His grin was so clear and so visceral it was all I could see for a full heartbeat. Then the nausea rose and roiled through my stomach as I knew her terror, her certainty that this time she wouldn't escape.

The rest I saw with a blessed detachment, as though whatever spirit that connected me to the moment had been delivered to the veil and had no energy left to fuel my fear. I watched as the dog leaped from the shadows, emerging whole and solid, with its teeth bared.

She didn't see it in her terror. One moment she was running, the next she tripped over the dog's rump and landed solidly on its back. The dog dropped like a stone beneath her. She wriggled and squirmed as she fought for purchase, only to find a furry body beneath her that tangled its legs with hers. She was afraid in the moment that she had killed it. In he last moments, she balked. One split second of indecision that Kenny used against her.

I let her last moments soak into my psyche, storing her rage and fear and betrayal for her because she had let it go. When she rose again, it was to see us working over her. The dog rose as well. She watched it approach her and wag its tail. Some sort of communication went on then, between a beast of magic and an immortal soul.

"You see it," she said to me. "You understand now."

"Yes," I murmured. "I see."

"Don't forget," she said. "She gave me the message to give to you. Don't forget."

I shook my head. "I won't forget."

She smiled wanly, the bruises and wounds gone. She was Scarlett again, the girl I'd seen come into the shop with the tentative grin and heart of a lion.

"I bit him," she said. "At the end. I bit him hard enough to break his skin. I held his blood in my mouth as long as I could. He burned his shirt in the trashcan but it didn't burn all the way. You'll find it in the dumpster behind our apartment."

She pushed herself from her haunches onto her feet and stood back, watching me struggle with the pain and overwhelming emotions that seemed worse than a bit of agony I knew would dissipate when the session was over and I was back to myself. The tear in my soul from carrying her story would not heal quickly or well.

She took a deep breath, although I was sure she didn't have to breathe anymore. I took it to mean she was bracing herself for what was coming next. Her shoulders sagged, and she shook out her hands.

"Don't forget," she said again and then she backed into the shadows once more.

With her disappearance, the horrible pulsating sense of *someone* in the darkness returned. It seemed she'd been holding back the sensation, creating a bubble of time and space where I would see, feel, and hear only the things she wanted me to. Protecting me from the things outside it.

But while I wasn't stuck in the void of her soul, I was lost in the chasm of magic with no protective spells or crystals to guide me home or keep me safe. I'd leaped with arrogance and now I comprehended the fullness of my mistake.

The darkness came alive again with the chattering of teeth and the pulsing sensation of a fire growing and sending out waves of heat. My skin prickled and then crawled, and I knew whatever was in the darkness with me didn't possess the same sentience or corporeality as I did. It took shape or shapes at whim and they were exploring my flesh.

I imagined a beast with hundreds of tentacles and thousands of pinprick sized suction cups whipping at me with stinging poison. Welts rose on my skin. Each point felt like a hot poker had branded me.

I screamed, hoping Layne would hear me. As I spun in a circle, looking for a way out, the tentacles became bolder. They encircled me. One went around my mouth, silencing me mid-shriek while another slid underneath to invade my mouth. I choked. Then I gagged.

When I clawed at the arms, trying desperately to free myself, even just enough to gasp in a breath of air, two more came round to pull my hands away and pin them against my sides.

This was what awaited me in the darkness as I landed without the correct ritual, without the protection of spell and language. I would suffocate right there in the guest room of the manse a few feet away from the man I loved while he slept, completely unaware of the danger I was in.

I would die right in sight of him.

Frantic, I struggled in earnest, kicking and flailing and managing to do no more than move my arms a mere inch.

Just when I thought it was all over, a great whoosh of air swept across the expanse. The tentacles pulled at me as they retreated, as though something was pulling at them, yanking me free. I caught sight of Scarlett braced, hands deep in the eye sockets of a monster, yanking like a donkey, bucking and hauling.

And then I could breathe. My throat had been scoured and abraded and each inhalation was like sucking in ground glass, but I could breathe.

I staggered backwards from the force I was exerting as the thing released me. With nothing to catch me, I fell on my back, chest heaving.

The darkness began to recede. I blinked the rest of it away only to see Layne looking down at me. I sobbed at sight of him.

"Jesus, Brie," he said. "What have you done?"

CHAPTER FOURTEEN

I WOKE NEXT TO darkness with my arms pinned down against my sides. Something burned in my veins. I tried to sit upright and found I couldn't move. The scream I let go hurt my ears.

A soft touch moved across my hair. Calloused fingers lay against my forehead. I twisted my head, trying to bite whatever was holding me immobile. Images flashed across my mind's eye before I could open my eyes. Witches and magic and dead women and a werewolf leered at me.

Terror took my limbs, but my limbs refused to obey me.

"It's alright," said a familiar voice. Layne. Layne was here. "You're safe, Brie."

Everything in me relaxed at the sound of his voice. I inhaled slowly as I blinked him into focus. My night vision was still adjusting. The light over my bed bathed him in yellow light as he leaned over me.

The room smelled of antiseptic.

"I'm in the hospital," I whispered and winced at the rawness of my throat. So it hadn't been just my imagination. My voice sounded charred.

"Yes," he murmured, but he didn't say more.

I tried to get up and discovered I couldn't move.

"Don't try to move," he said. "You've hurt yourself." His voice sounded choked.

I swept the room with my gaze, trying to take every-thing in. When I settled on his face again, his brow was creased with worry.

"How did I hurt myself?" I asked.

"Damned if I know, but it was—" He cleared his throat. "We thought it best to restrain you to keep you from doing more harm."

To keep me from doing more harm. That sounded odd and weirdly specific.

"Tell me what happened," I said.

His palm whispered over my cheek before he ran his thumb across my temple. "I can only tell you what I know. The rest they're trying to figure out."

I leaned my face into his palm. As long as he was there I could take anything. Any truth. No matter how difficult. "Tell me."

He sighed heavily and his hand moved down to my shoulder as though he wasn't sure whatever restraints they had bound me with would hold me. Maybe he was worried I'd fight them again.

"I found you out cold just like before," he said. "But this time, your mouth was wide open as though you were screaming, but no sound was coming out." He dropped his gaze to his own hand, and I felt him squeeze me reassuringly. "My wolf almost came out then," he said in a soft, rasping whisper. "He didn't like seeing you like that, naked and in pain."

I squirreled my eyebrows together, and he seemed to understand without me asking what my question was. "I knew you had to be in pain," he said, "because there was blood everywhere."

He leaned closer, letting me see the wolf in his eyes that blinked out at me as he told the story. When I tried to speak, he laid his finger against my mouth. "I don't know how you did it. There was nothing there to cut yourself with. No knife, no letter opener, nothing remotely sharp."

When I didn't say anything, he reached down to lace his fingers with mine. His gentle touch was reassuring until he spoke again. "I called 911 and they're the ones who realized you'd dug into your own skin. There were peelings of skin beneath your nails." He swallowed audibly and his features tightened. "You were there for hours, Brie, with me sleeping." He squeezed his eyes shut, but not before I caught the flash of bright yellow in his eyes. "My wolf and I both. Drunk on pleasure and passed out like a glutton after a big meal."

"It's not your fault," I said. "You couldn't know what I was doing."

He shook his head. "I'm not that sound a sleeper, but I guess I was so damned comfortable after..." his voiced trailed away and his hand spasmed in mine. "It wasn't worth it, Brie. I'd forgo ever touching you at all if it would mean this never happened, to have been awake to save you."

"I'm not dead," I said with an attempted smile. "And I'm not a damsel, remember?"

"It wasn't just the scratches, Brie," he said. "It was the burns." He shuddered. "Like little sparks from a fire had spit out at you and peppered your chest. The propane was going, but I've never known it to throw off sparks."

He laid his forehead against mine, and the smell of mint washed over me. His aftershave smelled warm and comforting. "I had a devil of a time letting them work over you. My wolf wanted to tear them to pieces when they moved you and you moaned in pain. God, Brie. You were a mess. It's cleared up some now, but at first—"

"Couldn't have been too bad if it's healing already," I said.

He pulled back. "Already? You've been here for three days. They've given you plasma and fluids. For a while, we didn't think you were going to pull through. You lost a lot of blood, Brie. And your body was in such a state, they'd never seen such a state of shock. Usually people die from that sort of stress."

Three days. I'd been unconscious for three days. I'd almost died.

Something in my chest flip-flopped as I considered it all.

"Not unconscious for all of it," he said, as though he read my thoughts. "Once they got you stable and pumped fluids into you, you responded well even if you were in and out. They restrained you to keep you from scratching at the burns. They're already looking much better. You don't even need the I.V. anymore. They took that out this morning."

He leaned close enough that his lips touched my ear. "We have a pack member on staff here. I called him from the ambulance."

I couldn't find the words to respond. I knew what had happened even if I'd never be able to explain it to the good doctors and nurses. I wasn't even sure I was ready to explain it to Layne. The answer was simple. The power was too strong for me. I'd accessed the magic within without a single bit of protection or real ritual, and I'd miscalculated just how potent the magic was.

The thought that I'd been mucking about with such an incredibly powerful unknown put a knot in my stomach. The waking up in the flophouse, the zoning out as I'd held the grimoire for Layne to test out the connections. Forcing the magic back in the basement, thinking it would save me, when all that time any of those actions could have snuffed out my life just like that.

I started to tremble beneath the stark white sheets. Layne scooted even closer, and he was already so near he could have crawled into bed with me, either oblivious to the trembling or noticing it and trying to warm me.

From somewhere out of range of eyesight, he pulled a heavy blanket over me and tucked it beneath my shoulders. So. He noticed. I tried to feel grateful but couldn't get past the fear that had lodged itself in my gullet. I could have died. I almost died.

"You're fine, now, Brie," he said. "Much better than you were when I found you. Our doctor has done a whole raft of tests. I demanded they check you for epilepsy if you can imagine that." A nervous laugh escaped him and he dropped his elbows onto the bed beside me. Clasping his hands together, he said, "Ultrasounds, MRIs, EKGs, the lot. I had them checking for everything. It's going to be a hell of a bill but worth every penny."

I lifted my eyebrows.

"All clear," he said. "There are some blood tests still out, but they're confident they'll come back fine, too. Our good doctor understands magic the way we all do. He's ready to accept that you're a witch and that some sort of magic had you."

He blew out a long breath, the kind that leaks out after an extended period of stress is finally relieved. "I'm paying him overtime to be here. And he's sure he'll find nothing in the tests, but we had to check. I'll go get him so he can take off the restraints."

He kissed me lightly on the mouth, lingering a little too long as though he was testing me. I yielded, enjoying the feel of his lips on mine, and I watched him go with my mind whirling.

I'd been out for three days. I'd slept through tests. I'd nearly killed myself.

That one was the most terrifying. I'd not respected the magic, and taken its existence as a sort of entitlement, a gift for having endured a traumatic childhood and should therefore have received compensation.

Whether it was ignorance or arrogance, I had tapped into the power without ritual or anything more than sheer desire, expecting it to come to me. I'd not protected myself. I'd not given it the proper respect or fear.

Somehow, however, I didn't think any of that would have mattered. The things I'd experienced in front of that propane fireplace were stranger, more confounding, and far more powerful than anything I'd accidentally accessed before.

I'd not brought forth a magic that I could have shielded myself from or feared enough to give proper ritual to the things I did. I simply expected it, like the grimoire, the amulet, and the dog, to keep me safe.

The truth was frightening to consider. It seemed, I did possess power, and whatever inherent magic sat in my tissues or my blood or my cell membranes, it was too much for a mortal body.

I had no doubt that if I tried to access that power again, it would kill me.

I closed my eyes, thanking whatever gods there were that I was still alive.

I felt weak and slightly dizzy, but underneath all that, a thready whisper spoke of something greater. The magic was mine. That magic allowed me to connect to a real ghost, and more than that, it allowed me to speak to her. I felt her death and her struggle, and I'd known her despair when she realized it was over.

Scarlett. The grief of the trauma was only outweighed by the guilt that I was culpable for her death.

Had she not been in my shop, had Parrish and I not taunted Kenny, maybe he wouldn't have returned to hurt her.

The greater, more terrifying worry that the cult hadn't been involved was a small consolation.

My eyes flew open at the thought of the cult. There was something else in the memory as I gave consideration to the culprits being members of the black coven. That something slipped away like a silk thread being tugged free of a garment. I tried to grasp the end, to keep it from unraveling even as it escaped my grasp.

Scarlett had given me the means to nail Kenny to the wall, and I would tell Layne about it as soon as he got back, but she'd given me more during the visitation.

Don't forget, she'd said.

I'd assured her I wouldn't. I assured her I'd remember. It was important, so important, that I'd never be able to lose it to the fog of ninety percentile synapses blinking back to sleep.

I was still struggling to bring the experience back to mind, to replay it so I could hear those words again that she'd whispered in my ear, when a noise at the door drew my attention and whatever fabric of truth I'd managed to clutch at was gone.

Parrish. Shoving her way through the doorway with an armful of balloons too big for the width of the door. The entire wadding of them caught on the frame and squeaked against each other as they shifted and elongated, trying their best to fit. One of them popped as it hit the corner of the latch.

Both of us startled and I let go a shriek that made her let go the clutch of balloons. They scattered across the floor in a slow-moving tsunami of latex.

"Fuck, Brie, you scared the risen bejesus out of me." She had her hand on her heart and the violet thumbnail flashed at me, reminding me of blood. I cringed without meaning to.

My eyes welled up at the sound of her voice.

"I'm scared too," I said. I hadn't been afraid at all until I'd begun to imagine the consequences of my actions. Now that I had, I was terrified.

She stooped to pluck balloons from the floor by their plastic stems one by one and, once she had the whole bouquet of them again, she broke them into two waddings and took the time to plant them all over the room. Some she stuffed into the sink, some she pinned to the corkboard, and some she jammed into water pitchers and bedpans alike. That last I hoped was clean and empty. By the time she was done, my room looked like a clown's boudoir.

I loved it.

"Thanks," I said as she spun around to face me from poking a plastic stem with a bright yellow balloon into the curtain rod.

"Don't mention it." She hitched one leg up so she could sit at the foot of my bed. "Where's our lovelorn hero?"

I felt my face flush and as she trailed her gaze over my cheekbones, and then dropped it to the sheets, it seemed she noticed for the first time that I was restrained. She swore loudly and with gusto, then without asking, dove for the buckles and started tugging at them. "Who in the bright yellow fuck decided this was a good idea?" she growled.

"Actually," Layne said from the door before she got through the first restraint. "Our good doctor decided she needed them."

When he stepped into the room, giving space to the towering giant behind him to enter, Parrish dropped her feet to the floor and circled around the bed to the other side. If she'd have been a cat, her back would have been arched and her hackles up. As it was, she all but hissed at him.

"You let this quack deal with her?"

"Nice to see you again, Parrish," the good doctor drawled. "I see you're no less feral than the last time we saw each other."

"Fuck you," she said.

"No thanks. We tried that, remember? I'd rather not relive the experience."

As I pondered the suggestion that the doctor and Parrish had been involved at one time, the doctor overtook Layne and approached the bed, keeping his eye on me even as he directed his words to Parrish. "I've been paid very well to look after our mortal patient here. I wouldn't dream of losing her with so much money riding on her recovery." He grinned down at me.

"You always were a completely selfish prick," Parrish said, pressing her back into the wall and crossing her arms.

"Parrish," Layne said in a warning voice and the doctor raised his hand as though it didn't matter to him. In fact, just the way he leaned just slightly toward Parrish told me he was rather enjoying her discomfort.

"It's true," she said to Layne. "And you know it." Her bottom lip pooched out just enough that it made her look like a pouty child.

Layne pinched the bridge of his nose. "It's been a century, Parrish," he said. "Let it go."

A century. That was a new one. I stored that tidbit away, knowing Layne hadn't intended to let the bit of information slip and figured I'd broach the fact later when he wasn't so stressed and she and the good doctor weren't finding ways to juice the air with tension.

The doctor propped one elbow on his forearm as he regarded me, stroking his chin the whole while. "I'm Doctor Zachariah Goode," he said and Parrish muttered something derogatory that had to do with the oxymoron of his moniker. A comment that made the ghost of a smile tug at the good doctor's mouth. "Call me Zach," he said.

Zach had a scar down the side of his throat that ran from the back of his crew cut to the hollow of his throat. He also had the most massive hands I'd ever seen. Clean, trimmed nails spoke of manicures while the hardness of his jaw indicated he probably had to take a few verbal jabs over his metrosexual tendencies.

Still, he didn't look genteel by any stretch.

"You're very lucky," Zach said. "Or you have a werewolf's stamina." He chuckled. "But since you are mere mortal, we'll chalk it up to Dame Fortune."

"She best have good luck to survive your quackery," Parrish grumbled.

"My quackery might be the best thing that could have happened to her. If some other doctor had got hold of her, I'm not sure she wouldn't be someone's lab experiment right now."

All this said without looking at Parrish for one second. Instead, he held my eyes with his so intently I started to squirm.

"What do you mean, lab experiment?" I asked him, keenly aware he hadn't moved to undo my restraints. I looked at Layne, whose face was so tightly closed off the only thing that indicated something was bothering him was the movement of yellow in his eyes.

Zach sighed heavily as his index finger stroked beneath his chin. "Your blood work is a bit disconcerting."

Parrish came off the wall, then. She flicked her gaze to Layne, and again, some sort of communication whirred through the air.

"What?" I asked. "What's wrong?"

"Do you know your blood type?" he asked instead of answering my question.

"Of course I do. I'm A negative."

"Wrong."

I pulled at the restraints. "I'm A negative. I know because I wanted to donate blood when I was ten and she said I couldn't because no one would want my blood."

"Well, whoever 'she' was, she was right there," Zach said. "But not for any reasons she might have given you. Have you had any surgeries, any transfusions, any blood work done in the past that seemed odd?"

I shook my head. "Healthy as a horse. At least physically. At least till now." My lips pressed together as I thought of all the ills my body had taken these last weeks.

He made a thoughtful sound deep in his throat and Parrish finally came out from behind the bed to confront him.

"Your bedside manner sucks," she said. "Tell the woman what she needs to hear."

He looked at her for the first time and though she bristled with irritation, his expression softened when he regarded her. "I'm going to ask you once, Beatrice, to back off so I can attend to my patient. After that, I'll just have you removed."

It wasn't the words, but the tone, that did it. The seriousness of it, the deadpan, but not unkind way they were delivered made her blink once before she whirled on her heel and went to Layne's side. I thought she was so thrown off, she didn't even realize he'd called her by the wrong name.

She and Layne both watched as the doctor sat on the edge of my bed, an uncharacteristic thing for an unsympathetic medical professional to do, and I knew right then he was someone to be trusted. Whatever it was he was going to tell me, it was bad, and he knew it.

"Tell me," I said.

He rolled his shoulders, easing out some kinks that had settled in during long hours. "I'm not sure I can tell you," he said. "If I didn't know better, I'd swear someone had turned you."

Chapter Fifteen

Turned me. The term Layne used when a person was intentionally infected by a werewolf shifter. I thought back to the time Layne had been out of town on business and he'd asked me if I'd been turned while he'd been gone. The thought of it scared me.

"You think I'm a werewolf?" I said in a trembling voice.

Layne pulled himself up straighter. "Impossible," he said and directed a long, studious glance my way.

Parrish stepped back, the look of panic on her face as clear a message as if she'd spoken out loud. It was the last thing she wanted for me.

Zach rolled his eyes to indicate what he thought of our concern. "I said, If I didn't know better. But I do know better. You are not a werewolf, and yet you have been changed. Somehow. Your blood doesn't react the way it should. In fact, I'm not even sure we tested your blood. If you say you're A negative, then that's not what we tested. We tested AB. And as it sat in the tubes, it somehow changed to O negative."

He shook his head. "I've only seen similar behavior in new shifters, as their blood shifts from human blood types and antigens to a mix of animal and human. But this," he paused there and ran his hand over the top of his head, making the crew cut bristle. "This is stranger. A person just doesn't exhibit multiple blood types."

"Impossible," I said, echoing Layne's sentiment, and Zach shrugged helplessly.

"If it was impossible, it wouldn't be happening." His eyes fell on the restraints and he reached for them with a quirked eyebrow. I nodded, and he started unbuckling the ones on the left closest to him. "I'd like to run more tests if it's OK with you. What was your mother's blood type?"

"Not sure." I lifted my freed hand and rotated it at the wrist as he went for the other restraint.

"Your father's?"

"Wish I could help you. Surely it's in the records somewhere?" I rubbed my hands together over my chest, enjoying the sensation of liberation. I caught Layne's eye, and he looked as worried as I felt. "Are you sure the lab work isn't a fluke or a mistake, or something?"

"I did it myself," the doctor said. "I do all the pack."

I didn't miss the inference that he thought I belonged to the pack. It made me feel warm despite the growing concern that something was terribly wrong with me.

"There's an old saying in the pack world," he said. "Gods and dogs are a jumble of letters apart. Meaning there isn't much separating the two, but it's still a world of difference." He took out a notebook from his pocket, as well as a pen, and jotted something down. "I'll run a few more tests while you're here. Maybe at some point we can look at your parents. See what that shakes out."

"While I'm here?" I said. "I want out."

He chuckled. "Oh, Ms. McAllister, you'll be here for a few more days yet. Do I need to put the restraints back on?"

"I fucking dare you," Parrish said, stepping up and shouldering him aside.

He gave her a long look. "As much as I might like to take up the gauntlet, Bea," he said. "You would lose. I'm her doctor. I say when she leaves."

"Shows what you know," she said. "She might be Layne's mate, but she's my friend. I have some rights here."

Mate. She'd said mate. I flicked my gaze at Layne, who avoided my eye as studiously as Parrish's attentions on the sheets. I started to say something, but a thought struck me that had nothing to do with mates or packs. It had to do with dogs. And gods.

Gods. Something Scarlett had said while I'd been under.

"A god's blood is too strong for a mortal body," I murmured, staring fixedly at the footboard as I tried to pull the moment back from the ether.

"What's that?" Layne said.

I lifted my gaze to his. "God's blood," I said again. "Or rather demigod. That was it." I squinted at him because his handsome features were interfering with my recollection. When he blurred, I concentrated, doing my best to slip back into that space where Scarlett's words would come back to me without actually having to travel.

"God's blood," Parrish said. "What the hell—"

I cut her off with an upraised hand. I almost had it. "Scarlett told me something when I saw her."

I felt Layne's movement rather than heard it. His sharp intake of breath accompanied a quick step toward the bed and the next I knew he was lurking over me, his eyes pinned to mine. They'd gone yellow again.

"Scarlett?" His hands splayed out on either side of my hips. "Scarlett is dead, Brie."

"I know. It's what I was doing in the suite." I scrabbled backwards on the bed, pressing into the pillows. I wasn't afraid, exactly, but his gaze, his expression, were too intense. I wasn't ready for it. "I called to her. With the magic. I used the dress I was wearing. The one with her blood on it. And I called to her."

Parrish laid her hand on my head. "So you used your juju to call up the dead, huh? Did she come?"

I nodded. "She gave me everything you need to nail that bastard," I said, and Parrish made a small sound, like fear but mixed with a satisfied grunt. "She also told me not to forget."

"I'm sure it was all a pretty horrific nightmare," Layne said and sent a pointed look at the doctor. "One the good doctor has no interest in."

"I have rounds to do," Zack said, taking the hint. "I'll be back later.." He pointed at me with his notebook before slipping it back into his pocket. "You aren't discharged." He turned to face Layne. "She isn't discharged. You need to understand that. No stealing her out of here in the dead of night. Absolutely zero abductions on my watch."

Layne went tense. "That only happened once."

Parrish jutted her chin out even as she cocked her hip. "And that abduction as you call it was a rescue."

The good doctor sighed at both their reactions and spun on his heel. I had the feeling he'd come up against the two of them more than once and knew better than to argue. He opted to send me instructions to rest, then headed for the exit.

After he'd left, Layne asked for the entire story and I gave it to him, including the information Scarlett had given me that would help nail Kenny as well as the strange feeling of tentacles invading my throat. I left the message from Scarlett till last because I was still trying to grab the edge of the fleeting memory.

"I can't remember all of it," I said. "But it had something to do with blood and gods and..." I hesitated as I tried to bring the rest of it back. "Don't forget," she said. "Don't forget because 'she' wanted me to get the message."

"She?" Parrish asked. "You mean Scarlett?"

"No. I think she meant my mother."

Parrish hopped onto the foot of my bed and leaned on her palm as she faced me. "Scarlett gave you a message from your dead mom." She sounded breathlessly excited over the notion. "So? What is it?"

"I wish to hell I could remember," I said. "It's pretty fuzzy. Kind of like a dream where you're waiting for a trigger to yank the memory back into your mind." I noticed Layne was typing into his phone. "Who are you calling?"

He finished typing but spoke over the equipment as he answered. "Not calling. Giving directions. My new partner will go check out the details you gave me. If it checks out, we'll pull the bastard in for questioning."

"Guys like that don't answer questions," Parrish said. "They respond to pressure." Her voice held a threat directed at Layne and he nodded.

"I am more than capable of exerting a little pressure."

"But is your partner?" She leaned over the bed to rub my shoulder before hopping back off and poking Layne in the chest. "You need to get off your ass and do your job. Never mind tending to your woman here. She looks pretty much OK right now." She looked back at me over her shoulder. "Am I right, Brie? Tell this lovesick moron you need your rest so he can go fuck over that little bastard."

"Hell yeah," I said. "You guys get out of here and get to it. I'm more than capable of lying here and sleeping."

Parrish narrowed her gaze at me. "You're in an awful hurry to get rid of us. You aren't planning to call to the dead again while we're gone, are you? I mean, now that you know you can pull a ghost from the ether, you might be thinking you'll just dial up your mother?"

I placed my fingers on my chest in mock indignation. "I barely lived through the last phone call. I have no intention of trying again."

I said it in jest, but I meant it. I wasn't ready to start mucking with the magic again. I wasn't sure if the reactions were because of a buildup of use or if I hadn't been doing it right in the first place, but there was no way I was going to attempt another trial until I knew more about how it all worked. "I'm tired. And I'm safe here." I said this directly to Layne. "Plus, I'm sure you're going to place some ridiculous guard on my door the moment you leave the room."

His shoulders sagged, and something in the back of his spine relaxed enough for his jaw to unclench. He approached the bed and leaned over to kiss me full on the mouth. His lips lingered on mine in a way that made my belly tingle.

"Do not summon your mother's ghost," he whispered against my mouth and I tasted mint and chocolate on his breath. "Because if you do and you survive it, I will come back and bite you."

"That's not much of a deterrent," I whispered back.

He snagged my bottom lip with his teeth to suggest it wasn't much of a threat either. With a lingering stroke of his palm on my hair, he pulled away and turned to Parrish.

"She has been sufficiently warned," he said.

"You and I have different ideas of threat," she said to him. When she leaned down, I thought she was going to kiss me too, she was so close, but instead she snagged my wrist in a viselike grip as she growled low in her throat. "Do not cast any spells while we're gone," she said. "Or I will kick your scrawny witch ass."

"No worries," I said. "I'm too tired to raise the dead."

She let go my wrist with a nod. "See you stay too tired to raise the dead."

"Parrish," Layne said. "Let's go. Brie needs her rest and I have to convince Zach to keep watch on her room for me. I have a feeling he'd opt for that over me stationing a surly-looking pack member in a chair next to the door."

"Please make it Zach," I said. "I'd rather him too." The thought of a strange werewolf lurking nearby gave me the shivers. Farrel's shadow was a long one, reaching into the darkest parts of my psyche.

I watched them head to the door with a longing that made me feel both warm and fuzzy and sad. Both of them cared about me. I hadn't had that in a long time. That sense of belonging was so acute it ached inside. When Parrish paused at the doorway, I was delighted.

She halted at the door at the last moment, then came back to the bed, robbing me of that delight when she indicated what she wanted. "The dress," she said. "The one you used to summon Scarlett. Do you still have it?"

"It's at Layne's," I said, feeling my face flush as I remembered him peeling it off me.

She chewed her bottom lip as she considered that. "I'd like to test it," she said. "Do you mind if I pick it up?"

"What sorts of tests?" I asked.

She shrugged. "DNA, blood typing, stuff like that. I don't really trust the idiot doctor and his obviously botched results."

"That's a good idea, actually," I said. "Layne will get it to you."

She nodded mutely, then spun on her heel and left with Layne. A veil of quiet fell over the room. I stared out the window, watching the darkness thicken like oatmeal. The sounds of the hospital around me came to life once I was alone.

All the droning noises lulled me into a sort of trance that felt very restorative. I'd never been great at meditation, but I could see how it helped to clear the mind to just be for a while. The white noise of the ward outside, the nurses walking back and forth to check on patients, the snoring from a man across the hall, all vibrated through some deeper sensory organs than ears and eyes.

Without intending to, my mind turned to the session with Scarlett. I recalled the way she'd looked so solid and corporeal, the way she'd been able to fight with that thing that held me in its throes. I'd not thought it odd then, I supposed, because I wasn't really thinking of anything except finding her killer and surviving the session.

But it was strange. The ghosts I'd seen these last weeks were very spectral, the sort you expected to see via special effects in movies or recordings.

And in the moment of her death, she'd connected with the stray dog. I'd forgotten that. The dog had tripped her, I realized. That one moment, I'd not been sure when I'd witnessed her fall, but I was sure now. The dog had tripped her and Kenny had taken her life. And in the afterlife I called her from, she'd given me a message from my mother.

The lingerie clerk had said that the dog belonged to my mother. The coincidence was too strong. Was my mother trying to contact me from beyond? She'd disappeared, the clerk said. One day, my mother had just disappeared while all along I'd believed her dead.

The small hope I'd harbored in that one moment that she might actually be alive was dashed now. If Scarlett had a message for me from my mother, then she was dead. Just like Scarlett.

The tangled mess of it all wore my brain out. The white noise of the ward soothed me. Soon enough, I knew I was falling asleep. I could feel myself dropping into slumber.

I wasn't sure if it was knowing I was falling asleep that jerked me back awake or if I'd heard a noise, but my entire body spasmed with the jolt of coming awake.

And the scream I let go died behind a meaty palm that covered my mouth before I could shout the name of the man holding me down.

Farrel. Come finally to finish the job.

Chapter Sixteen

Farrel's hand tasted of onions and blood and I sucked in all the disgusting taste of it as I tried to inhale enough air to scream past his skin. His other hand planted itself on my chest, pinning me to the mattress. I fought him, grateful the doctor had untied me from the restraints before he left. Had he left me tied, I'd have no way of defending myself.

Since I was unrestrained, I didn't hesitate to fight. I dug at his face. My legs kicked to give me thrust as I bucked off the bed. The panic sent my heel straight into the iron footboard and I arched back in mute pain, doing my best to scream under his palm but getting nothing out but a muffled grunt.

"Lie still," he hissed. "Lie still or I swear I will tear your throat out right here."

Eyes wide with fear, I took in all of his features that I could see in the dim light. He was still human for the moment. A mask hung around his neck, tied at the nape and hanging down his chest. The top ties dangling over me as he bore down. The surgeon's scrubs he wore were stained with a dark fluid that I suspected was blood.

Could he tear my throat out with human teeth? I didn't dare find out. I went still, even as my mind frantically rattled along a train track to nowhere.

"Good," he said as he untied the mask from around his neck with the other hand. "Good. Now, I'm going to take my hand off your mouth. You need to keep your mouth shut."

I nodded and the taste of blood intensified as my lips shifted just enough for my tongue to contact more of this palm. I grimaced but stayed silent. At least for now. The doctor had lain the buzzer somewhere handy, hadn't he? I could press that and someone would come running. I mean, they had to. That was the point of the damn buzzer in the first place.

I reasoned I could nod at Farrel in tacit agreement because pressing the buzzer would not break my promise not to scream. I hoped that meant I'd keep my throat wonderfully intact.

He jerked his head toward the window. "The wane is coming. They need to prepare."

I didn't like the sound of that and I must have indicated how I felt with some movement in my body because his hand bore down heavier on my chest.

"Easy," he said. "I don't want to have to hurt you."

I knew my eyes were wild with fear. It took everything I had not to struggle and do as he bid. I wanted that hand off my mouth and I'd have done anything to get rid of it in that moment, even disobeying every instinct that told me to scream bloody murder the moment he peeled it away.

I held his nasty gaze even as I scrabbled my fingers toward my pillow. I wasn't sure what luck was with me that he'd not noticed I was looking for the buzzer. Maybe he was just too busy acting threatening or struggling to hold onto his humanity. Because he was struggling. The glimmer of neon yellow behind his gaze was a sign I'd come to understand well.

Bring it, I thought. A few more seconds and I'd have the buzzer in my fingers.

He leaned heavily on me as he leveraged himself to pull off his mask. It was only when he started to shove it into my mouth beneath his hand that I realized I wouldn't have a single second to scream anyway. I gave up trying to be clandestine. My fingers scrambled for the wire.

The side of my hand brushed against the buzzer right about the time he realized what I was doing. With the mask stuffed in my mouth and his hand down on top of that, he raked the mattress with his free hand, grabbing for my arm.

I fought him then with the arm he'd left unmolested. I bucked and kicked on the bed. If I made enough noise, maybe someone would hear and come running anyway.

One of his fingers slipped inside my mouth as he fought to stuff the mask in. I bit down as hard as I could.

"Bitch," he growled and planted his entire torso on my chest, then. The mask wadded into my cheeks as he worked it in up to the strings.

With his weight on me and the fabric pillowing into my cheeks, any minuscule amount of air I managed to pull in through my nose wasn't nearly enough to keep my lungs happy.

Blind panic struck then, and I thrashed on the bed. My head collided with something solid. Bright stars exploded behind my eyelids.

I only knew I'd cracked his head with my own when he growled low and threatening, much like a wolf about to tear into a rogue trying to steal its dinner.

"Fuck the coven," he said through gritted teeth. "I think I'll just kill you right now."

Fuck you, I wanted to say, but the mask had shoved my tongue to the back of my throat. Dizziness swept over me. The lack of oxygen and the full-on bloom of panic taking the last of the air that kept me conscious.

I wanted to sob. He was going to kill me. He'd wanted to ever since I'd run from him in the basement. Now, he would finish the job and I'd end up bleeding out here in a hospital bed.

One small thought fluttered in the recesses of my mind like a red flag, taunting a bull. Hadn't Parrish said they ate people?

I would not pass out and let that happen.

I found one last bit of energy to buck beneath his weight. My foot hit something solid and I sobbed with pain into the mask.

"Fucking bitch," he said. "You're dead. I'm going to kill you."

"You will do no such thing," said a female voice from the doorway.

He froze for a moment. His growl indicated just how he felt about being ordered not to kill me. Then, his hand curled around my throat and he squeezed, just enough for my voice box to beg to release a cough.

I knew the voice. The recognition was enough to paralyze me. Parrish's date. The one so enamored of the coven. What was her name again? Honey. That was it.

The door clicked closed. The sounds of clothes rustling and footsteps whispering against the tiles indicated there was more than one person in the room with Farrel and I. Not just Honey, then. She'd brought friends, apparently.

The buzzer and its wire fell against the railing, clunking loudly enough for me to know it was still there but out of reach with my arms pinned beneath the werewolf's weight. He swung his head in her direction and I followed suit. I'd always been the type to want to see what was coming for me. I seriously doubted she was there as the cavalry.

"Our famous black-magic psychic," Honey drawled in a voice that sounded nothing like the simpering woman I'd met at the restaurant.

She came into view, finally, as a shadowy, bulkier figure stood off to the side.

"You can let her go," she said to the werewolf. "I've cast a cloaking spell. No one will hear."

Farrel released me with a grunt of disappointment, and I screamed the moment his hand left my mouth, forgetting for the moment that it was fabric and skin that had smothered the sounds before, not just his hand.

The mask soaked up all the noise, leveling me to whimper helplessly and in frustration. He still held me down, but not with all his weight. Just a heavy hand on one wrist. I yanked out of his grip and he let me go, not seeming to care now that Honey was there.

I tried to shove the fabric from my mouth with my tongue long before my fingers reached for the ties. I was pulling it away like a clown yanks out scarves. The retching was automatic. Spasms racked my stomach and I longed to hang over the bed and heave up every nasty taste his skin had left on my palate.

"You were hard to locate," Honey said as she approached the bed. One short look at Farrel and she shouldered him aside as though he were no more than a gnat.

He barely glanced at her, instead, craning to see over his shoulder. Whoever stood in the shadows was far more interesting to him than the witch.

I looked past her as well. If Farrel was afraid of the man at the door, then it stood to reason he was the one I needed to be worried about too. No matter how bad ass she thought she was.

As Farrel shifted to accommodate her, she laid her hand down on my arm. At her touch, I felt cold. In protest, I tried to pull away from her touch, only to discover my arm had turned to a leaden weight. I couldn't raise it to save my soul.

I blinked at her as I tried to form the words I wanted to throw her way.

She smiled down at me, those white teeth flashing in the light over my bed.

"You'll find it quite impossible to move," she said conversationally. "Or even scream, for that matter. I have an affinity for energy."

I glared up at her, feeling the words trying to erupt despite her declaration. She watched me struggling to speak with a haughty smile. "You're stubborn, it seems," she said. "But you'll figure it out, eventually." Her fingers trailed up my arm to my shoulder and while I couldn't move away, I found I could grimace just fine.

I grimaced like mad. I grimaced like a badass. I grimaced like looks could kill her.

She just snorted and pinched my shoulder.

"We've been looking for you for ages. We were beginning to think we'd never find you. Your mother had you cloaked really well." She sat on the edge of the bed, further shoving Farrel to the side. He sighed heavily and moved to the other side of the curtain, out of sight but for that hulking shadow that darkened it like a pool of tar.

"You won't be so hard to find when I get out of here," I said in a threatening tone that had whoever was standing in the shadows by the door chuckling beneath his breath.

Honey bounced on the bed once as though testing its weight. If she heard my threat, she didn't respond to it.

"The others don't think we've found you yet, to be honest. They don't think I'm right. They don't trust the wolves' noses for magic." She tossed a look over her shoulder at Farrel. "And they aren't pleased that a fledgling let you go before they could test you themselves, but I'm sure. They think I'm too young, too inexperienced, that a little gossip here and there is a useless tool. I fooled them. I have knowledge they don't." This time, she cast a quick glance over her other shoulder at the shadow near the door before pinning those zealous eyes back on me. "I know you have power in your veins. It took a lot to pin down your location, Brie. It is Brie, right? That's what Parrish called you. I'm so glad she took the bait."

I tried to shift on the bed but found that everything seemed very leaden. It put sourness in my tone that I probably should have held back.

"Maybe you should get your lady bits checked if you think of yourself as bait."

At that, she leaned down to look into my face. She cocked her head sideways, first one way and the other. "I almost hate to do this to you," she said. "I think in other circumstances we could have had fun together, casting spells, raising the dead."

"Is that what you are doing?" I asked. "Raising the dead? Exactly who is worth all this?"

She tittered and I realized she wasn't really fully sane. She let go a soft sigh and reached into the purse she had dangling from one elbow.

The sharp snapping sound of the clasp rang out in the room for a second before she lifted what she'd extracted to dangle it between us.

My amulet. It caught the LED light over my head.

She let it sway back and forth like a pendulum. "This thing," she whispered in an awed voice. "This was quite a piece of magic. I wasn't sure at first you were the one until Farrel tested it on you."

"Is that what he was doing when he stole it from evidence and threw it at me." I sucked my teeth. "Clumsy maneuver, but then what can you expect from an idiot?"

Farrel growled and moved into the light. Honey swatted him with the back of her hand and shoved him away. There was a long, hard stare from her in his direction before she turned back to me and leaned closer. I could smell old wine on her breath. Her lips were red with waxy lipstick. I thought of Scarlett and my heart hurt.

"Do you know how many women of power had to die to find you?" she asked in a voice that tightened her timber to something akin to a child's.

"I'm thinking one witch too few," I said, trying not to show my grief for the poor souls. They deserved better remembrance than to kowtow to their killer and I wouldn't dignify her question with anything other than disgust.

She tutted as she pulled the strap of her purse higher onto her shoulder. "Their deaths are on your head. Yours and your mother's.

A moment of irritation in the shadows indicated she was wasting too much time. Farrel touched her on the shoulder. "He wants you to get it over with. He has other things to do."

Honey looked at Farrel over her shoulder, pulling the amulet close to her chest. "He doesn't command us. We command him." She cast a look toward the shadows at the door. "You have no power here, dog. Mind your place."

The wolf in the corner growled. A glimmer of yellow pierced the shadows for a long moment, reminding me of a cornered predator, but she just chuckled as though it meant nothing. I knew what it meant. Whoever stood in the shadows was the alpha we'd been looking for. Farrel's alpha. Our guess had been correct. Someone had turned the detective for the explicit purpose of being a nameless, expendable soldier. I almost felt sorry for him.

"Get on with it," Farrel said with a growl. "We don't have much time."

The air shivered with energy, but I knew it was coming from the corner and not the witch sitting on my bed. The alpha was testing the witch, trying to exert his power. I wondered if she knew how close she was to losing the battle.

"I know the shape and scent of my spell, wolf," she said to the alpha as though she expected him to kowtow to her. "We are fine for a few moments more. Do as you are bid and guard the door like a good pup."

She looked at me again and touched her lip with her knuckle. The amulet swayed beneath her fist. "I almost hate to begin," she said. "So many years of searching and here you are just lying in a hospital bed. No fight in you. No spine to you. It's almost a letdown. Maybe my sisters and brothers are right and it isn't you, after all. I would have expected it to be more difficult than this."

I didn't want to say that this wasn't easy by a long shot. All she'd had to do was waltz into my hospital room with a couple of werewolves at her beck and call.

I had to suffer the horror and terror of her coven's evil machinations. I was the one who almost died.

But she wouldn't care about that. It was what she and her coven were after, in the end. They wouldn't appreciate the work that had gone into evading their evil.

"I guess we'll find out in a moment or two, won't we?" She gave me one last long lingering glance before she laid the amulet on my chest. I sucked in a sharp breath. Just like the first time Farrel had tossed the amulet at me in the precinct, where it contacted my skin now, it burned. Beneath the hospital gown and sheet, my runes stung like they were branding me again.

But this time, unlike the first time, I knew the power would be too much. I wasn't fully recovered. I could die beneath the power it drained from me, the pain it seared into my tissues. Because I couldn't help it, I writhed on the bed while she held the amulet against my skin, my arms unable to move, my legs pinned to the mattress. I felt like a serpent held down by a stick.

"Yes," Honey said, sucking in a hissing breath. "Yes, I was right."

She tittered again, the sound of a young girl who has found herself in the position of being right in the face of all odds being too high to bet against. "I was right. It's you. It's really you. You are her daughter." A soft laugh of victory escaped her.

"Blood of blood and bone of bone," she said in a breathless, almost shrill voice, "Daughter of Hecate. I have found you."

CHAPTER SEVENTEEN

A TERRIFYING IMAGE FLASHED through my mind as I writhed on the hospital bed, pinned by my own mother's amulet and another witch's power. In one second, I saw each and every one of the horrifying scenes from my childhood that had terrified me into running away as a kid and sent me seeking solace in an entirely different country as an adult.

One second shouldn't have been enough to blast those memories through, but they came anyway. They came, and they gutted me.

I stood at the bottom of the cellar steps, my bare feet digging into the cold concrete. The floor wasn't smooth as new buildings possessed. Rather, it was rocky, the way old-fashioned mortar had been cobbled together with derelict pebbles of various sizes and poured out over a ground hand dug by shovels and man power.

At first, I saw only her back as she knelt before a small pile of stone and flat river rocks built up nice and high. It wasn't until I heard the crackling of burning fat that I filtered out the smell of it. The flames on her altar cascaded over the top of her hair, making a halo of her red tresses. The adult Brie knew she was looking at an altar, that the circle of white that lay before her feet was a casting circle, that the sleeping dogs that lay on the stones were sacrifices.

Adult Brie recognized the stink of charred feces. She knew the sound of chanting. She understood the chills that ran over her body were from the power of the spell being cast.

But the child did not know the woman kneeling in all the blood was a witch of considerable power. She only knew it was her mother. A woman she should trust. A woman she loved. A woman who had done terrible things to innocent animals, and she couldn't separate her fear from the sense of betrayal long enough to let the love win out over both.

But neither the adult nor the child would have been foolish enough to believe her mother was a god. Honey thought I was a witch, a woman of power, and I almost laughed at the irony of it all. I wanted to tell her it was her coven's bullying that brought out any magic at all and I'd gladly have ignored it the way I had all my life had they not decided to sacrifice a trio of women.

Daughter of Hecate. Every witch might have called herself that. Every witch was, in essence, the daughter of the mother of witchcraft.

Honey called out to Hecate once again, and this time she lifted her voice the way a singer in a choir might. She wasn't just gleeful. She was rapt.

"Such power," she said, dropping her head back. "Ripe for the taking. Almost too much for one mortal body."

Her words had the faintest whiff of the familiar, but I didn't have time to ponder them. The amulet surged with heat. My back arched with the transference to my skin. I didn't bother to bite down on the scream that erupted from my throat.

The witch began chanting beneath her breath, and as she chanted, the words came faster and faster. Her movements became more caressive, like a voodoo priestess in a trance, she swayed to and fro as she held the stone against my solar plexus.

The air I managed to pull in grew more and more the closer she got to me. She was stealing all my air with the frenzy of her movements. I got the feeling from the frantic timbre that she wasn't in control of the amulet, not by a long shot.

Fear sizzled through me at the thought that she wasn't in control, and someone needed to be in control. Someone had to manage the power or it was going to kill me. She was going to kill me. And for what?

She'd come to prepare me, according to Farrel. He still stood off to the side like a well-trained Labrador retriever and didn't seem the least bit worried that the amulet was more than she could manage. That whatever preparations she was using the amulet for, the stone had no intention in cooperating.

It was fighting back.

So I fought my own body's inclination to fight the pain the power was inflicting on me. The only one who had a chance of controlling this rogue power was me. The only one who cared if I lived was me. Just like when I'd been a kid, I had to pull on my reserves. I had to do something. Save myself.

I squeezed my eyes shut, bit down on the agony, and willed myself to lie still. Even if the burning in my chest was too much, even if I thought for sure my organs were going to catch fire. I. Held. Still.

The tone of her voice shifted, as though she was grateful for my submission. Maybe she thought my compliance would help her. Stupid witch. I might die from what I was about to do, but I wasn't about to let her prime me like a pump. Not without a fight.

I concentrated. Really hard. I thought I heard her mutter something about gods and mortals again. Again, she called out to Hecate. I bit down on my tongue with the back of my teeth. Hard. It was the only way I could get any amount of blood, and I knew blood was the key to the power. It had always been the key. I'd just never truly known it.

Something shifted in the air as I tasted the coppery tang of blood in my cheeks. An electrical current or a buzzing charged the space between us.

The pressure on the amulet eased. Not much. Just enough for me to breathe again. Enough for me to slip my hand over hers. I didn't wait for her to notice my hand on hers. I grabbed for the stone the way Grasshopper did in those old Kung Fu movies.

At once, the chanting stopped. Her eyes bugged out as she looked at me. Those full lips Parrish had so wanted to kiss, worked silently, chewing over words that no longer exited her mouth.

She was strangling, I realized as her hands flew to her throat. The amulet dislodged from her hands as though a suction had pulled it free. In my grip, it burned no less, but it also began to glow.

She staggered backwards at the same moment something burst from the stone. A loud crack sounded. The wolf in the corner let go a howl. Farrel fell to his knees.

I scrabbled backwards on the bed, climbing the incline of the mattress and headboard as though I could scale it like a fence.

Too late, Honey realized the same thing we all did. That we weren't alone anymore.

The shade man stood at the foot of my bed, as did the big black dog. She made a sound in the back of her throat at sight of the dog. It might have been a genuflection, but that couldn't make sense.

In that moment, I knew the two were connected to the stone somehow, connected to each other. The many times the dog had warned me of danger, had rescued me from threat, I'd never considered it a part of whatever the shade man was. But seeing him and the dog together, I knew they'd both ridden the magic of the stone.

Honey knew it too. So did Farrel. The new werewolf howled as though something had driven itself into his stomach, no doubt remembering the wound inflicted on him in the basement by the shade man when he'd bid me escape. Farrel clutched his stomach and arched his back the way a man might if he was feeling the injury for the first time. I thought he was going to collapse.

The alpha rushed to catch him before he fell, and as badly as I wanted to catch a glimpse of him, Honey recovered and staggered to her feet. She spun to face the shade man, blocking my view of Farrel and the alpha.

"You," she said. "You should be dead, old man. We used you up. And that awful creature, too."

He looked much the same as he had the day he'd entered my shop and tried to yank the amulet from my neck. That day, I'd thought he was there to harm me. But there, in the basement of my imprisonment, he'd been the instrument of my salvation.

Now, I knew him for what he was. An enemy to the cult. And an enemy of my enemy or something like that. I scooted over to the side of the bed, intending to drop my feet onto the floor and get the hell out of there.

"Don't move, daughter," he said.

I hesitated. He'd called me daughter back in the basement. I stood next to the bed, holding onto the rail, feeling the cold tiles against my bare feet, and mulled over whether I should completely ignore him and save my skin before things got much worse.

I tugged at the hospital gown as the draft at the back reminded me I'd been naked when I'd called to Scarlett. Didn't matter. I only needed to get out of the room.

"This woman is not your daughter, old man," Honey said in a voice filled with scorn. "You're delusional in your death."

The shade man cocked his head at her. "You're delusional in your living, witch. It's not an old man you called forth. You called to me. I am here." The grin that stretched the shade man's lips looked strangely feminine and out of place on the man's face.

The dog snarled at Honey and he looked down at the stray. "*We* are here," he said, as though correcting himself.

Honey backed up at the words, her features widening along with her eyes. "It can't be," she said. "You're dead. We have your bones."

"You have bones, yes," he said. "But you don't have our essence." He smiled. "It's that essence which you call to and that essence, free of its shell, which will be your death."

He crouched down next to the big black stray that had so many times come to my rescue, and as he did, Honey took a step backward. Everything in her demeanor screamed she was about to bolt. All of them were, I knew. Even Farrel had gained his feet. The alpha was tugging him toward the door. Maybe I should be running too. I measured the distance from where I was and knew I couldn't get out before the shit hit the fan.

The shade man whispered a single word to the dog, but it was clear even where I stood, clutching the bed rail and considering diving beneath the bed.

"Go," he said.

One snarl and the dog launched itself from the shade man's grip toward Honey.

She called out to the alpha at the same moment, demanding his protection.

With a curse, the alpha shoved Farrel at the witch.

He knocked her onto the bed just as the stray collided with his side. Jaws clamped down on the werewolf's stomach. Farrel attempted a transformation. His spine cracked beneath his clothes and tore along his back. He moaned in pain and the dog released his belly and went for his throat. The man didn't have the time to affect a full change. He went down beneath the weight of the dog.

The sound of a door opening and closing told me the alpha had escaped. I hoped the spell had broken with his exit.

I collapsed on my side of the bed. The sound of Farrel's death a sickening reality just out of sight but not out of every other sense. His dying made me retch. My head hung between my shoulders as wave after wave of nausea brought up every bit of bile in my stomach. My nostrils burned from its release. My ribs spasmed.

I was still laboring over another ounce of bile when someone grabbed me by the hair. Honey. She pulled hard, sending my scalp into its own spasms.

I howled in pain and rose to ease the tension in her grip. I sagged against the edge of the mattress. She was on the bed, kneeling forward to hold on to my hair. The shade man stood alone next to the dog, which looked wet and slick with fluid. Blood, I knew. I caught sight of Farrel's foot in the shadows, twitching for a moment, then going still.

The dog's eyes glowed red as they landed on Honey. The shade man chuckled.

"We are fortified by your dog's magic," he said. "We thank you. It was just what we needed."

"Stop," she shouted back over her shoulder at the shade man. "Call off your dog or I'll kill her."

The shade man's chuckle at her declaration was dark and throaty. It sounded all wrong. As though a bull frog was being strangled. Honey paused, so distracted by the creepiness of the sound, that she slackened her grip on my hair.

"You won't kill her," he said as he advanced with a slippery movement that put me in mind of an eel. "Blood of a god, bones of a mortal. Your coven has been searching for her too long to take her life now."

A grin crept across his face that made me shiver. Honey responded to the smile the same way I did. I saw her shoulders tremble, though she did a good job of gathering her control over them faster than I did.

I crept along the mattress, hoping to knock the bitch over. She clenched her fingers again, sending renewed waves of pain across my scalp. I twisted onto my side, trying to relieve the pain. She yanked once, then tangled my hair deeper into her grip. I howled in pain.

The dog whined and the shade man made a move to approach, but Honey held the amulet up, letting it dangle over my chest.

"Let me go," she said. "And no harm will come to her."

The shade man paused. It took several seconds before he looked from her to me, but in those seconds, something in the room shivered. I had the same feeling as I'd had back in the basement when he'd stabbed Farrel. "Run, daughter," he said, the same faint echo of those words made my skin crawl. "Her spell is broken."

At that, he rushed Honey, the dog, a split second ahead of him. In her haste to protect herself, she ignored me to cast a second protective spell against

Smith. That moment gave me time to fall onto the floor and roll under the bed.

I was scrambling beneath to the other side when a blue light erupted in the room. I didn't stop to see what caused it. My toes dug into the tiles and I clawed my way out from beneath the bed. The dinner tray knocked over, crashing its contents onto the floor behind me as I gained a sprinter's stance and ran for the door.

I had time to hear Honey casting the last of her spell before I ran from the room into the hall. But I was sure I heard her call out to Hecate with a loud scream that was like a cascade of icy water over my back.

"I am here, you fool," the shade man responded. "And the blood you've spilled from my daughter's holy body means your death."

Chapter Eighteen

I reached the hallway on my hands and knees. My breath in my ears was the loudest thing to register and I was still dragging in a draft of it so I could scream bloody murder when Honey bolted past me. The amulet clutched in her grasp, still sparked with energy. It spit out long, cracking trails of magic and seemed to be thrusting her from the room. Whatever had gone on inside in those moments I'd fled for the door, she wanted out like she wanted to breathe.

Her foot came down on my fingers. Pain lanced up my hand as her stacked heel stomped on my tender flesh. It was enough to drop me flat onto my stomach, pulling the sore hand against my chest and rolling over to my side, cradling it against me as I moaned.

All I saw in the dark was Honey's retreating feet as she streaked down the hall and slipped through the door to the stairwell.

Weakness kept me company as I strained to survey my environment. Each time a dizzying round of blackness tried to steal across my vision, I blinked hard until it retreated.

I might have passed out for a moment because one second I was lying on my stomach with my face aimed up the hall, and the next my face was smashed against the tiles with drool pooling around my mouth.

Apparently, I was either invisible to everyone on the ward or I just hadn't been passed out long enough to draw attention. I shouted for help, but all that coughed out was a weak, gargled sound.

My ward room, I discovered, was at the end of a long hall, with the nurse's station several darkened yards away. No one sat at their post. The entire wing seemed empty and silent. A film of some sort seemed to discolor my vision and I blinked several times before realizing it wasn't on my eyes but on the very air around me.

Honey had reset her spell, apparently, leaving me to wonder if I was seeing actual reality or just a version of it she wanted me to believe I saw. Another reason to think I'd not been unconscious long. No matter. I was moaning and yelling in pain loud enough that whether the nurses were at their posts or down the hall, they'd have to hear me, eventually.

I expected someone to hear my anguished moans, to come running, to find out why a patient was out of bed in the middle of the night and lying on the floor in obvious pain.

No one came.

A cold draft fingered its way up my spine where the hospital gown had come untied. I rolled to my shoulder and craned my neck to see behind me and up the hallway. Empty. A noise from behind me reminded me that the shade man and his dog—my mother's dog—were still in my room.

And so was Farrel. At least, his body was. I shivered at the thought of seeing him again. I decided I'd much rather lie on the cold floor than crawl back into that room again and risk planting any part of my body accidentally into any part of his.

But the reality of him still lying dead in my room gave me greater pause. I had a dead man in my hospital room. A man who had been mauled to death. That sort of thing would require a hell of a lot of explanation. And it wouldn't be easy convincing anyone that a wild beast had run loose into my room.

Maybe it was a good thing no one heard me and came running.

I found the energy to flop onto my back, letting my head fall against the cold tiles. It took an extreme amount of effort and I realized the only thing that had kept me going had been adrenaline, pure and strong. Fear-soaked muscles had kept me conscious and given me the strength to flee. But I'd run out, and I knew it.

But I also knew it wasn't over. I had to find the strength to go back in to that room because the only person who would believe the impossibility that a werewolf had been attacked and brutally killed by a ghost dog was Layne, Parrish, or the pack doctor.

And none of them were right handy. Not to mention the fact that I had nowhere near the energy I needed to flee the building and leave a man to decay quietly in my room until morning rounds. Bad enough, I was already suspected of being some savage Satanic practitioner. Another picture of me in the media came to mind, and I saw myself with a quaint little caption that said, "I didn't kill him, honest."

I squeezed my eyes shut at the impossibility and futility of it all. I could only hope the doctor would find his way to the room before a nurse did.

As hard as it was to go back into that room, I had to do it. It made far more sense to get the pack to take care of pack business than it did to try to exit the hospital wearing an untied hospital gown with no purse or phone in hand to call a cab.

I swallowed down the residual panic and revulsion and braced myself to crawl right back into that hospital room. The door would need to be blocked to keep anyone except Layne's pack from getting in. Then I'd dig around to find where Layne had put my cell phone. Because surely he'd brought it along to my room. He was too organized and prepared not to. So I'd call him and make sure he got hold of Doctor Goode.

The good doctor would know what to do with the body, and if he wasn't still on site, Layne would make sure it was taken care of. Because I was pack business now.

Just moving through rational thought eased my mind somewhat. I started to breathe better. I could do this. Hadn't Layne said I was a warrior? Warriors did not balk from sitting in a room calmly with a dead body and perhaps a ghost and a supernatural dog. After all, both dog and ghost had done what they could to protect me in the past. They weren't about to harm me now.

I exhaled my fears and sucked in a bracing breath, then laid my hands down on the cold tiles and worked to push myself onto my knees, then I pushed off onto my feet. I swayed a bit at first as I locked my knees, but when I steadied myself with a palm against the wall, I was able to hold my ground.

Going into the room after all that took the last remnants of courage I had, but I did it. I closed the door behind me and laid my back against it until it clicked and I could survey the room.

Both dog and ghost were gone, but Farrel remained. My gorge rose as my gaze landed on the pool of blood around his head. I refused to look any farther than the immediate floor around him. That way lay madness.

Instead, I focused on the priority task of muscling the chair beneath the doorknob. That done, I started the visual scan for my phone.

I found it on the rolling tray beside the bed. Eyeing it meant I had to step over Farrel to get to it. I hesitated long enough to hear voices outside my room, then I bolted for the tray. Each time my feet slapped noisily against the floor as I made a run for it, I muttered a quiet prayer of thanks. It meant I didn't step in anything fluid on the way to the phone.

I kept my back to the body on the floor as I swiped and tapped in Layne's number. The other end didn't ring more than once before he answered.

"What's wrong?"

"Farrel's dead on my floor." I didn't think how it might sound to a man roused from sleep or how he might feel at the bald confession. The whole thing needed brevity, not mincing admissions. I gave him a moment to let it sink in before I went on. "He and his alpha came by with a witch. I didn't kill him."

"That's something I suppose." The rustling of material on his end indicated he was getting dressed. At least, I hoped so. The hollow echo of a door closing and footsteps came along with his voice. "I'm on my way. Bar the door."

"Already done."

"Smart girl. I'll call Doc. You call Parrish. He'll need her."

Seemed I didn't need to explain how awful it would be to have a nurse find a dead man in my room. I wondered how often this sort of thing happened in the pack that he had a head start on the problem solving. I tapped on Parrish's number and waited a long time for it to ring. When it did, it rang much longer than it had for Layne. I counted seven rings and when she answered it was with a curt growl.

"What?"

I took a breath. "It's Brie. Layne told me to call."

"I know who it is. Layne better have a good reason for sicking his paramour on me. He knows this is my dominoes night."

"Farrel died in my room." That sounded like a good reason didn't it?

"Fuck me with a soft boiled egg."

OK. I would ignore that one. "He said the doc would need your help."

"I would fucking say so. Fuck." She swore again under her breath but at least there were the telltale sounds of fabric rustling. "Fuck, I hate that man."

"Well, he's dead," I said. "So it shouldn't matter."

"Doctor Goode is dead too?" she said and unlike with Layne, the rustling of fabric partnered with the sound of multiple zippers and snaps. "Hell, what a night. How hard are you on men, anyway? Please don't switch teams. We have few enough good lesbians as it is."

I wasn't sure what constituted a good lesbian, but at least I understood she didn't mean Farrel when she indicated her hate of the man. "Doc Goode is just fine, at least I think he is. Layne is calling him. Please just get here ASAP."

A car door slammed and I was impressed with how quickly she'd managed to get on the move. "Gimme ten," she said, and the phone went dead in my hand.

With nothing left to do constructive, I crawled onto the bed and squirreled my way to the top of the mattress, pulling my knees up to block any view of the floor. I sat there with my arms wrapped around them for what seemed an eternity before a soft knock sounded on the door.

"Ms. McAllister? I'm here to help. Layne tells me you might need to come to the door."

Coy, that doctor. I guessed someone was outside with him that he didn't want to hear I'd barred the door.

"I'll wait till you're dressed."

I climbed down from the bed by the same route I'd crawled on. Namely, by navigating to the topmost edge and dropping down one foot at time and feeling around to make sure the floor was clear. I didn't have the least inclination to step in Farrel.

Carefully, making sure I followed the same path to the door that I'd made getting to the bed, I advanced on the door and pulled away the chair. As far as blockades went, it wasn't high tech, but it did the trick. When I swung open the door, he pushed in so fast I stumbled and had to grab for the wall.

I hit the light switch, and the room flooded with a bright glow so harsh it made me squeeze my eyes shut and shield them automatically.

"Holy Hannah," he said with a whistle.

"I don't want to know," I said, but I did know. I knew all too well. Pretending I'd not seen the mess the ghost dog had made of the fledgling werewolf was the only way I could cope without completely losing my shit.

He sighed heavily. "I'm going to need Parrish," he said, and then he swore at the prospect.

"You have the same effect on her," I said.

"I'm sure I don't have the same effect at all." He spun me around so that he could guide me to the en suite bathroom without having to encounter Farrel's remains. I wished I'd thought of it. It occurred to me that I might have found close proximity to the toilet handy and then realized I'd not thrown up. Score. Small victories right?

I aimed myself for the toilet, but he steered me to the sink.

"How are you feeling?" he said. "You've been through the mill. Probably the soaking of adrenaline is the only thing keeping you on your feet." He ran a practiced eye over me, measuring, analyzing, all with one quick assessment. "Doesn't matter, anyway. We can't waste a single second. Not a single helping hand. Shit." He started running water in the sink and muttered to himself about letting Layne bully him into guarding my door.

"But you didn't," I said, weaving on my feet now. "If you had been there, maybe I'd still be sleeping."

He raked me with a look that said more about how guilty he felt about that truth than my comment. I collapsed on the toilet seat, the adrenaline he'd mentioned starting to leak out my knees. I was pretty sure I was going to faint.

"Take this," he said, pressing a cold cloth into my hands and raising it to the back of my neck. "Lean over. You can't pass out. Not yet. I need you. Without Parrish here, I need your help."

I waved a weak hand over my head.

"I'm sorry, Brie. I know this is hard. I know you don't feel well, but if we don't get started, you'll feel worse the moment a nurse comes in on rounds."

He was basically telling me to suck it up, every last bit of illness and weakness, and lend a hand. Because if I didn't, things were going to get much worse.

"Parrish and I will take the body. Can you wash up some of the blood? Can you manage that? If not the floor, then...other things?"

He didn't need to indicate which things. Arterial spray seemed to go a long, long way. Farrel had bled all over everything.

My stomach started to roil.

He gave me a hard look. "You aren't going to puke, are you?"

"Are all you shifters that queasy about a bit of vomit?" I complained. "Or are you just worried you'll be drawn to it like a dog?"

I expected him to growl at the insult, but he broke into a grin, lighting up a flare of amber in his gaze. "That's good," he said. "A bit more finesse and I can use it on Parrish."

I decided he would regret my snappy mouth more than I would by the time he turned that quip on Parrish.

"I'm sorry," I said and planted myself on the toilet seat cover. "I'm beyond terrified and angry and a whole hell of a lot of other things I never knew I could feel all at once."

"Just think of it as Jell-O that wouldn't set."

I peered up at him. "I don't think that will work.

"Then I'm guessing this isn't the best time to tell you he might still be alive."

Chapter Nineteen

Do you really think he could be alive after all that?"

He shrugged. "Our kind heals well. And quickly. Especially when we're newly turned. It's a sort of survival mechanism, I guess, to ensure we make it through the first transition."

"I think I'm going to be sick," I said and flipped the toilet seat up.

He rubbed the spot behind my shoulder blades. "Just make sure it all gets in the bowl. We'll have enough to deal with cleaning up Farrel."

My stomach twisted. I fell to my knees and hung over the bowl. At least the hospital kept things neat and tidy and there was no smell washing up from the water. I stared at the rim line and willed my belly to calm down.

"What you're saying is that if he isn't well and truly dead, you are going to make sure he's well and truly dead."

"Do you really want to know?"

I clutched the rim of the bowl and leaned closer. My toes had started to curl. "No," I gasped out. "I don't think I do."

I hung there for several moments with him lurking nearby and to be honest, I think the distraction of knowing he was about to witness a mighty hurling managed to quell the nervous reaction. I stopped thinking about Farrel out there maybe being still alive in the state the dog had left him in and I started thinking about how I'd look heaving my guts out with a pretty damned handsome doctor watching me, the gaping hole in the back of the gown, baring every horrible spasm.

Was it self-centered? Sure, but the nausea went away, and for that I was grateful.

I leaned back onto my haunches, breathless from the residual anxiety, and put the lid down with a thwack.

"Lovely," he said in appreciation.

I sniffed up a trail of snot that had started to leak from my sinuses and swiped my arm across my nose. Lovely, maybe not, but not puking, so at least not gruesome. Small victories where they could be found, I always said.

A door opened and closed on the other side of the bathroom, and I bolted to my feet. He leaned out of the bathroom.

"Oh goodie. Our jolly lesbian is here," he declared, and Parrish made a hawking sound like she was pulling a lot of fluid from her nasal cavities.

"Fuck," she said from outside the bathroom, as she no doubt caught sight of Farrel's remains. "I was hoping you were the body I had to clean up."

The doctor stepped out into the room, leaving me sitting alone in the bathroom. "If it makes you feel better, I haven't showered in two days. I wouldn't mind a sponge bath."

"And I thought that stink was coming from the ca-daver."

I might have found the two of them entertaining if I wasn't so freaked out about said cadaver. It seemed I was going to have to remind them there were more important things than bickering.

Parrish popped her head around the door frame. She tossed me an oversized sweatshirt that smelled faintly of roasted pineapples, a pair of sneakers and track pants. The pile struck me in the chest, spilling the armful of wash clothes onto the floor. I made a clumsy catch and caught the sleeve while the sneakers fell to the floor with a splat.

I was never so grateful for a bit of jersey material and filthy runners. When I pulled the shirt on over my head and smoothed it down, it came to mid-thigh, and that was plenty to make me feel less like a flasher. The pants helped too.

She waited till I had shoved my feet into the sneakers before she leaned in past Zach help me to my feet. With one hard yank, she managed to pull me all the way to the doorway.

"You are really an evil magnet, aren't you?" she said.

"Is there a way to demagnetize me?" I asked. "It's sort of becoming a bummer."

Her grin wasn't an encouraging one, and I only felt better when the two of them left me to stand over Farrel's body. Their mutterings were a welcome distraction as I considered the best way to clean up the mess they were going to leave for me.

"Can't we just get a mop?" I said as I blinked rapidly to chase away the dizziness. "I mean, I'm just out of my sick bed. You of all people should know that."

Zach touched my forehead as though testing for fever. "I declare you well enough to get off your ass and help us with this mess you made. I'll pump you full of fluids and vitamins later. Right now, shit needs doing."

"Spoken like the compassionate doctor he is," Parrish said and he glared at her.

"Listen, I was having a nice chat with a pretty nurse when all hell broke loose here. I could just walk away and let you and Layne take care of it."

"Except Layne pays you well," Parrish said, leaning against the door frame. "So let's not pretend, alright?"

I ran my hand across the back of my neck. It felt too clammy. I wasn't sure how much more energy I had in me. "OK," I said. "Hospitals must have to deal with blood all the time. They have to have cleaning protocols. Buckets. Laundry. Cleaning staff."

"With this much spray, they'll need to see the patient," Doc said.

I thought about that. "But you're the one who sees the patients. What do you do when you want someone to clean up? Do your janitorial staff always ask to where the blood came from?"

"In the operating room, no, but here in a patient's room—"

"You're a doctor. You think too much like a doctor. Most people just do their jobs, wait for their breaks and live to go home at the end of their shift. You really think they'll care?"

Doctor looked at Parrish, who shrugged. "She has a point. Let's get this bag of shit on a trolley and call for maintenance." She didn't bother looking at me as she started barking orders at him and surprisingly, he did everything she said, which seemed to include stripping Farrel of what bits of clothing remained on his body.

I didn't want to know why. Instead, I turned to leave and Parrish called out over her shoulder without breaking the efficiency of directing the doctor with a few strategic orders.

"Don't think you're going home, Brie," she said. She waved her hand in the air in a gesture that indicated she didn't believe me. "Take a step out that door and you'll end up wearing nothing but your Brazilian."

My face heated. "That would be nothing at all," I said.

She tilted her face my way and grinned. "The image of you in that lingerie shop still haunts my dreams. I hope Layne appreciates the effort."

The doctor, who had grabbed Farrel by the ankles and was trying to roll him out of his pants by tearing what wasn't torn all the way up the man's thighs, snorted.

Parrish held her hand up to me to tell me to remain where I was as she addressed him. "Don't," she said. "Don't even go there."

He looked at her as she hooked Farrel's ankle onto his hip. His silence only seemed to make her angrier.

She lifted a finger at him. "I should wipe the blood off the fucking floor with your smirking face, Zachariah."

"I think I'd like that, Beatrice."

"Don't call me that."

"Then don't call me Zachariah." His voice was so matter of fact that I knew he'd used her dead name as a way to instigate her response. I couldn't imagine why but I was sure he'd done it on purpose.

He then did the unthinkable. He looked away from her, not in a way that showed her as more powerful but in a dismissive gesture and in that one second, she closed the distance between them and muscled him against the wall with a loud thud. Farrel's legs fell to the floor with a sickening splat.

I wasn't sure if the heavy breathing coming from their direction was him or her, but it had me backing up so fast, I butted into a solid form behind me with such surprise I let go a squeak.

"Let him go, Parrish," Layne said.

Parrish swung her gaze to Layne, who had gently pulled me aside and tucked me beneath his arm. She didn't look very much like herself in the glimpse I caught of her face. Her eyes were a dangerous shade of molten yellow. She had her hand around the doctor's throat and I noticed his feet were off the floor about an inch.

Even hanging suspended by her grip, his expression hadn't changed from the calm demeanor, nor had his eyes changed color. He'd been in control the whole time of his own emotions. I was sure he'd baited her, but I had no idea why.

"Parrish," Layne said with exaggerated calm. The room pulsed with energy much like I'd felt earlier when the alpha had tried to exert his power over the witch. "You need to let him down without hurting him. We need the doctor. I don't care how much he hurt you. You do not have permission to do Zach harm."

Her lips peeled back from her teeth, but she lowered Zach to the floor just the same. I heard his scrubs rustle against the plaster.

"Now let him go."

Her fingers slipped away from the doctor's throat. Even in the dim light of the room I could tell it was red and swollen from her grip, but he didn't rub it.

A lesser man might have smirked at her. The good doctor didn't. What he did was swing his gaze to Layne.

"She wouldn't have hurt me."

Parrish's grating laugh came out in bark and I was inclined to agree with the sentiment behind it. One second more and I was pretty sure I'd have ended up stripping the good doctor of his pants.

"She wouldn't," he insisted.

"I would have eaten your voice box."

His lingering look that took in her face, her hair, her throat and then finally her heaving chest was so full of compassion and empathy that my heart hurt just witnessing it. I don't know what it did to Parrish, but I had to turn away from it just to keep from tearing up.

"I can't stay here," I said to Layne.

"You don't have to." He pulled off his jacket and wrapped it over my shoulders. "I'm taking you home."

The words lit a fire under Zach in a way Parrish's reaction hadn't. He stormed Layne.

"You can't take her. I haven't signed her out."

"She's not a book in a library," Layne said. "And try to stop me."

Parrish's chin lifted at Layne's tone. Defiant. Angry. And something else. Were there tears glistening in her eyes?

"She doesn't need rescuing, Layne," Zach said. "She needs rest and fluids. Look at her. She can barely stand."

"That's exactly why she needs rescuing." Layne scooped me beneath my knees and hoisted me against his chest. "I left her here, and she got attacked and a man died." He flicked his gaze to the floor where Farrel lay. "I don't know what kind of care you think that is, but in my book, it's negligence. Send me the bill for her care. I'll take it from here."

Layne was backing toward the door and I had a great view of Parrish's duck-clapping behind him.

Zachary crossed his arms over his chest as he glared at Layne. "Sure thing," he said. "I'll do that right after we dismember and burn this poor sod. And I'll be sure to add it to the bill."

I snuggled in, happy to be going somewhere I would feel safe, but I knew that the sight of that hospital room was going to be one I'd never be able to forget.

CHAPTER TWENTY

THE STREETS WEREN'T DESERTED by a long shot, even though it had to be way past midnight, but Layne drove as though he had the road to himself. The nausea started to rise again, even as everything started to go dim in my vision.

"Layne," I said. "I'm not well."

His quick glance at me made him slow his pace. "I'm sorry, Brie."

I sighed. "It's ok. I'm guessing you're upset."

He shifted gears smoothly. "I'm glad you're OK, but I need to know what happened."

Of course. Things had been so hectic, I'd not had time to explain about Honey. No wonder he was so sullen and silent. So I told him. Every horrible detail of it and he let me speak without interrupting.

And when I was finished, he simply laid his palm on my thigh and drove silently, thoughtfully, until he turned into his driveway. I both ached to know what he thought and was grateful I didn't have to say more.

He helped me out of the car, but when he made to carry me into the mansion, I swatted his hand away.

"I can walk."

He snorted. "Zach seems to think you're an invalid."

"Zach can kiss my ass. Do you know he almost made me clean up that...Well, I refused."

"Sounds about right," Layne said and offered me his arm instead to lean on. "You're feeling stronger, then?"

"I think the IV drip helped my body. Not sure what's going to help with the mind."

We walked slowly, Layne letting me set the pace, and I found that with his strong arm to bear down on, I did indeed feel better. The soft yellow glow of the veranda and the foyer fully lit looked welcoming.

"And Scarlett?" I said. "What have you done to find her killer?"

He sighed heavily, and I felt his body tense under my hand.

"We're still gathering evidence. I don't want to arrest the bastard until I can nail him to the fucking wall with his own teeth."

We had reached the steps and when I tried to lift my foot onto the first tread, I realized I was shaking all over. The exertion and exhaustion was getting the best of me. Maybe Zach had been right. Maybe I wasn't ready to be released.

"Brie," he murmured. "You don't have to be a warrior the whole time. I'm a big strong wolf."

I sagged against him then. I was too tapped to argue. Instead, I nodded, and he scooped me into his arms again and climbed the five stairs in less than three seconds.

"See?" he said. "Big strong wolf."

I chuckled and melted against him, feeling the weight of my eyelids so acutely I could barely keep them open. He opened the door without so much as jostling me and I realized exactly how light I must be to him. Not a burden. That felt nice in more ways than just physical.

A sigh of contentment escaped me. There was just such a feeling of safety in his arms. I felt cocooned. I wasn't sure what I expected of him after all that had gone down, but I didn't care what happened so long as I was with him. He strode to his room and set me down on the bed.

"Take off your clothes," he said.

I tugged at the jacket he'd thrown over the hospital gown when he'd rescued me from Zach, knowing what he'd see beneath it. "I'm flattered," I said, "but I'm also really, really tired."

"Sweet Jesus, Brie," he said. "What kind of monster do you think I am? I just meant you need to put on something a bit more comfortable than that soiled hospital gown. And to be honest, I don't think I can sleep with you wearing Parrish's workout clothes." He feigned a shiver.

I peered down at my chest, moving aside the jacket and lifting up the sweatshirt. The fabric was indeed soiled. Not just with dirt. There were spatters of blood all over it and something that made me think it was skin. Farrel's skin. I shuddered and pulled off the jacket and laid it next to me on the bed. Parrish's clothes went the way of the jacket, but suddenly, irrationally shy, I stopped short of the gown.

It wasn't the image I wanted him to think of when he thought of sleeping with me. When he finally saw me that way, I wanted to be wearing something lovely.

I twirled my fingers at him. "You'll need to turn around."

He smirked but spun on his heel to face the wall while I peeled off the filthy hospital wear. After tossing it on the floor, I hugged my chest, shivering in the coolness of the room.

"You know I'm going to have to turn around to pass you something to sleep in," he said. "Unless you're planning to go to bed nude, and in that case, I have to warn you I'm pretty tired, too."

"Just get me a shirt," I said. "And toss it over your shoulder. I'll get it."

He rummaged through his drawers and pulled out a heavy cotton t-shirt with his department logo on the front. When he tossed it over his shoulder, I was pretty sure he intended it to fall just short of my reach. It did, and I climbed down from the massive King sized bed to fetch it from the floor. I pulled it over my head and smoothed it down across my stomach. It smelled like him, and I laid my nose down on the shoulder to inhale deeply.

"Can I turn around now?" Layne said.

I didn't answer, just padded close to him and wrapped my arms around the back of his waist. I hugged him as though I needed him to stay on my feet. Maybe I did. His soft, thoughtful sound vibrated his ribcage and transferred to my solar plexus.

"You are tempting my resolve," he said and turned in my arms. "But a promise is a promise. I won't let anything hurt you. And that includes me."

"Come to bed then," I said.

He lifted me off my feet, and I found the energy to wrap my legs around his waist. When he laid me down, it was on the softest micro fleece. The warmth as he pulled the blankets up around my chin surprised me.

"Did you have someone come in and warm the bed?"

He grinned. "Heated mattress. Turns on with the lights and goes off after an hour. You like it?"

I tried to say yes, but all that came out was a mumble of syllables that didn't sound coherent. I felt him climb into bed next to me and as he pulled me close, I was already drifting off.

"Brie," he said, dragging me unwillingly back to the surface.

I slept the sleep of the dead and woke long before Layne. His soft, whistling breathing made me feel safe, and I lingered in bed just so I could listen to him breathe. The soft glow of morning bled in through the cracks in the curtain, lining the window with a pink hue that looked almost garnish against the charcoal fabric.

I snuggled into Layne's side, and he reflexively pulled me even closer. The crook of his shoulder gave off so much heat, I wondered if he'd leave scorch marks on my skin.

I lay there for a long time, mulling over the events of the night before, trying to decide how I would explain it all and how I would tell him that it had been one of Parrish's dates that came to my room. I had no doubt she'd feel horrible, even if it wasn't her fault.

Eventually, though, the wakefulness made me aware of how full my bladder felt. I slid my feet to the floor and eased the blankets back. By the time I was standing next to the bed, I knew I wouldn't be climbing back in again. I wasn't the kind of chick to lay in bed long after I woke, and a quick grope for my cell phone told me it was already seven A.M.

There would be no way I'd get back to sleep now.

I dug in his closet for a warm sweater and pulled it over the shirt. A pair of ratty sweatpants lay slung over a chair in the otherwise immaculate room. I stepped into them and drew the string tight.

I knew I looked like a homeless chick, but I wasn't about to go creeping out into the hall in just a t-shirt, and there was no way I was going to pull on Parrish's clothes again. They'd no doubt soaked up some of the blood from the hospital gown and I hoped never to see that bit of fabric ever again.

I did, however, pull on the sneakers. They were comfortable and a good fit.

In the days I had stayed at the manse, I'd not explored more than my own suite and the dining hall. After using Layne's en suite bath, I eased out into the main house to have a better look around.

Several maids bustled about, vacuuming and dusting. They smiled but didn't speak. That was fine by me. I wasn't sure I was ready to break my silence, either. At least not without coffee.

It was the thought of a nice warm cup of Java in a quiet room somewhere that drove me down an unexplored hallway, and landed me in a room with floor to ceiling books.

I'd never seen a library that big in a house before. An oak staircase curled upward to a second floor, and the entire room was glossed in a patina that smelled of varnish and wood. The carpet had a soft, short pile that my feet scuffed along as I wandered the breadth of the room, peeking into the tiny alcoves that housed plants and statues.

I felt like I'd been transported to Alexandria. Softly lit wall sconces lined the walls in strategic places, illuminating the book spines. So many books, and so many of them looked very old. My mother's grimoire didn't look as old as some of those books.

I froze with my finger tracing the letters on one spine. Someone had come into the room behind me. I felt like I'd been caught stealing and spun around with a book in my hand that I quickly put behind my back as Layne's father entered the library.

He didn't notice me at first and was running his hand through his peppered hair. Even this early in the morning, all disheveled and exhausted looking, he still cut a powerful image, one that made my knees weak. I had no trouble believing Parrish's comment that young women threw themselves at him.

"Good morning," I said, because I didn't want to surprise him with me standing there.

My voice seemed to startle him. He hesitated before a smile ghosted itself onto his face.

"Brie," he said. "How lovely to see you."

The warmth in his voice was unmistakable. Maybe he felt ashamed of chasing his son's girlfriend. I was inclined to forget the disastrous dinner and smiled at him in return. He shoved his hands in his trousers and I noted wrinkles made them look crumpled. No doubt he'd been out carousing all night with one of those daddy-issue women.

His gaze flicked to me and for a moment, I thought I saw confusion and embarrassment at my attire, but he recovered quickly. "I'm glad you're well enough for them to release you. What are you doing up at this hour? I presume you spent the night in your suite."

I pushed the book back onto the shelf behind me and yanked up the sweat pants.

"It's nice to see you too," I said. "I sort of ran off a while back and didn't thank you for your hospitality." I had to do something with my hands besides wringing them in front of my waist, so I crossed my arms over my chest.

He shrugged off his jacket and discarded it on the ladder-back chair next to a table that held a decanter of booze and three glasses. If the movement had been any more cliché, I'd have thought I was watching a daytime soap opera.

"Don't think twice about it. That's not our first rodeo together, Layne and I." Almost absently, he plucked one of the glasses from the table.

"Little early for booze," I said, trying to sound teasing instead of judgmental.

"Is it?" he said, checking his watch. "I suppose if you're just getting up instead of just going to bed, it might be." He turned a dazzling smile on me, one that crinkled up the corners of his eyes. "But point taken, nonetheless." He leaned out into the hall and called out to the maid vacuuming to brew a pot of coffee.

When he turned his gaze back to me, it was filled with quiet expectancy. Not sure what he wanted, I fidgeted, running my hand over the bookshelf and then pulling it back to my waist. He watched me in quiet study until he finally said, "You look spent, Brie."

Not tired. Not sad or anxious. Spent. It seemed I wasn't the only one who had a keen eye.

"I'm still not feeling the best," I confessed. "The hospital wasn't as restful as you'd think."

"Several days in a near coma wears a mind out even as it restores the body. I'm sorry you were so unwell."

I gave him a tight smile. "My fault," I said without wanting to divulge any more. I wasn't sure how much Layne had told him and I certainly wasn't going to fill him in on a black coven trying to kill me. Alpha of a wolf shifter pack or not, there was no way the man would want me in his house if he thought I was putting his property in danger. If anyone was to tell him, it should be Layne.

When the maid appeared in the doorway, he took the carafe and two mugs from her with a short bow of thanks. She dropped her eyes but not before I saw the look of possession in them and the quick grazing glance she sent my way. Seems Papa wolf was schlepping the help. I tried not to giggle, electing to pad over to the sofa.

He poured black, steaming coffee into two mugs and, with a raised eyebrow, indicated the jug of creamer a second woman placed next to a bowl of sugar on the table. I shook my head and curled my legs up beneath me.

"You look spent too," I said and pushed up the sleeves of the sweatshirt, feeling a bit too hot for some reason. Damn that alpha energy.

He approached the sofa with both mugs and passed me one, making sure to offer me the handle instead of the bowl so I wouldn't burn myself. "Even a werewolf gets tired when the woman he is wooing is insatiable."

I nearly choked at the bald admission. "Please," I said. "I'd rather not hear."

Owen slid his gaze over my bare arms and let it trail to my throat. "A man needs to find solace somewhere," he said. "But I'll spare you the details." He tugged at his shirt, pulling open several buttons. He looked rumpled and spent. Just the way you might expect a man to look who has been busy knocking boots with a nymphomaniac.

"I need to talk to you anyway," he said.

The tone of his voice was enough to make me pull my legs out from beneath me and sit straighter in the seat. I held onto the mug with both hands.

"Doesn't sound good," I said.

"It isn't."

CHAPTER TWENTY-ONE

INSTEAD OF EASING MY curiosity, Owen plucked his phone from his trouser pocket and dialed silently while I watched with a suspicious stare. After a brief moment, when I presumed the extension rang on the other end, he looked at me, speaking into the phone.

"I'd like to book the penthouse suite. It's Owen Garder." Silence for a moment and he pasted a smile on his face the way a customer service rep is told to do. "Yes. That one will be fine. The young woman will pick the keys up at the front desk and you can charge it to me as usual."

He thanked the person and tapped his phone again, and when I tried to ask what he was doing, he shushed me with a single finger before dialing again.

"I need you out front," he said into the phone. "It may be awhile, so keep the car running. You'll know where to take her when she comes out."

There was no polite signoff this time. He merely tapped the end button and slipped his phone back into his pocket as he spun to face me.

"What was that?" I asked.

"I've arranged a room for you."

"A room? Why?" I didn't want to say that Layne had invited me here, because it was Owen's property. He was alpha. If he didn't want me here, I couldn't very well stay. But I did have my own home. Granted, I doubted it was very safe at the moment, but if I had to, I'd go there.

He strode across the room and put both hands on the back of the sofa, spread a foot apart, leaving me in between, staring up at him. It was uncomfortable, and it gave him an advantage that I didn't like, so I stood. He had no choice but to pull his hands back to his sides.

I didn't want to feel trapped there, and I did feel trapped. Standing, though I was tired, seemed much better. Even if I was way too close to his face. Even if the smell of him was curling around me like a flame around a log. Awkward as it was, I stood my ground.

His eyebrow raised half an inch. He probably knew what I was doing, but he didn't comment on it. Instead, he chose to answer my question.

"I don't think you should go home," he said. "So I've arranged a room and a ride for you at the Suites."

The Suites was a top end hotel that catered to the elite from all over the world. If he was sending me there, this had to be bad. The atmosphere in the library shifted. I could almost feel the change in temperature. I knew at once what was happening. Despite the friendly facade, the teasing and flirtation, he hadn't forgotten I'd turned him down.

I fell backward onto the cushions, defeated. "You're kicking me out."

He resumed his earlier stance, with his hands on either side of me, trapping me again, but he took the time to lift one just long enough to stroke my cheek with the backs of his fingers. His skin was rough, as though he'd been chafing them against stone.

"Quite the contrary," he murmured in a voice that sounded thick and throaty. "You'll decide to leave all on your own. I've merely made it easy for you to depart and arranged a safe place for you to stay once you do decide it's the right thing to do."

I pulled his hand away and narrowed my gaze at him. "Meaning you're going to threaten me until I 'decide' it's a good idea to leave."

His smile was thin and fake looking. "Do I look like the sort of man to threaten a woman?"

"I think you are used to getting what you want and that I haven't just rolled over to your desires irks you."

He chuckled. "You are beautiful, Brie, and I would have loved to have met you before Layne, but no. I'm not that upset you chose my son instead of me." He paused, his head cocked, listening to something I couldn't hear. "A fact he'll appreciate, I'm sure," he said.

A sound at the door made me startle. Owen never so much as flinched, which meant he'd heard Layne long before I'd seen him standing in the doorway. Instead of retreating, as a guilty man might, Owen remained where he was, with one hand planted on the sofa back, his body centered over mine. Languid. Casual. As though the show of dominance was a happenstance and not deliberate.

Layne's expression revealed nothing, either. I looked from one to the other, trying to read the body language between them, wondering who would be the first to move. I hoped it would be Owen. I had the feeling if Layne gave in first, he'd have lost something more crucial than a moment of contest.

In the end, the maid was the one to break the tension. She eased her way past Layne to bring in another white mug and Layne moved to let her by. Owen pushed off the sofa about the same instant, and I let go a long breath.

"Is it always like this?" I said, fanning myself and getting to my feet to go to Layne. "I mean, the pheromones. Sheesh. It's rank in here with them. It must be very difficult for you both, but it's murder on the rest of us."

Layne circled my waist with his arm and I passed him my mug of coffee as I leaned into him. He took it and eyed his father over the rim.

"It's only this way when my father wants to prove something to me. Which he doesn't need to do." He took a slow drink of the coffee that had been too hot for me to sip at. I watched his throat muscles move as he emptied the cup.

He didn't wait for Owen's response. Instead, he took charge of the conversation.

"There's another pack in town," he said.

Owen's gaze narrowed and his shoulders tensed. "Another pack?"

Layne set the mug down on the table. "I think the alpha is making soldiers."

Owen sat on the sofa I'd vacated. He man-spread his knees and hung between them, his hands clasped together. "You think they are planning a takeover?"

Layne pursed his lips. "I don't know what they are after, but they are aiding and abetting a black coven."

"The one in the news?" he looked directly at me. Something moved in his eyes, a swirl of yellow and gold, and then it was gone.

Layne hugged me against him. "Yes, the one in the news, but not one that Brie is part of."

"No good can come from messing with witches, Layne," Owen said in a stern voice. "I've told you this. Witches will be the death of you." He cursed then and stood up to pace the room. The way he prowled without touching a single thing, just holding his shoulders tight and his fists clenched at his sides, belied the controlled tone of his speech as he went on. "I've told you before, Layne, witches always go black. Eventually, given enough time, they need more power or want more power and to get it, they will do things best kept in the shadows." He spun to face Layne. "You don't know the things I know, the things I've seen."

"Dad," Layne said. "Careful."

Owen's gaze swung to mine and for a moment, something flickered in his gaze. Under any other conditions, I would have thought it was rage but here and now, I had to guess it was worry. "You've not told her everything, then."

The fingers on my shoulder tightened for a short moment, then relaxed. "She knows we are pack."

Owen's jaw seesawed once before he got it under control. He crossed his arms over his chests. The fists opened and splayed across his forearms. More relaxed.

"I know my place," Layne said softly. "Pack secrets are yours to tell."

Owen leaned back and crossed one leg over the other as he looked me over. He indicated with a gesture that I might want to sit but I didn't. He didn't control me, and it was time to show him that unlike his pack, I still had my own mind.

Owen shoved his hands in his pockets. He looked older in that instant, like a rumpled old man who had lost something but couldn't remember what it even was. He held up his finger as he pulled out his phone, indicating we should wait. He spoke almost absent-mindedly as his fingers ran over the surface, typing.

"You're too enamored of this witch," he said and pressed the screen with a final touch. "Wolves make mistakes when they are too involved."

"Brie is not a mistake," Layne said, but Owen waved the hot declaration aside. I thought for a moment that

Layne would try to press the point, but someone down the hall screamed and both men stood at rigid attention.

"Go," Owen said and Layne was off like a shot. He left the smell of sleep-sweat and mint in his wake, and it took me several seconds to realize I was cringing in the corner. The sound of the scream and the response put the hairs up on the back of my neck.

Owen, however, turned to me with a conspiratorial smile. "He'll be busy for a few moments," he said. "Which gives us time to talk. You mentioned you thought our dominance would make our relationship difficult. I think you should understand that the truth is that we're both alphas," he said in a cool voice. "By all rights, he should have his own pack. But he won't leave. Like a lazy twenty something, he refuses to leave the nest. He chooses to stay, despite all advice he should move against me."

"I'd say you were lucky, then."

Owen smiled. "Yes. I am very fortunate. This has been his pack for more than a century, and I don't want him to leave any more than he does."

I blinked stupidly. "A hundred years?"

That's when he grinned, a strangely delighted grin, as though he'd just discovered a secret. "So he didn't tell you everything." He watched me a little too intently. "You're shaking," he said, as his nostrils flared. "You have the scent of a cornered rabbit who has given a hard chase."

I wasn't sure I liked his analogy. It felt a little too predatory.

Eventually, he sat down and I did my best not to feel cornered by how close he was. As usual, my immediate response was to strike out.

"Well," I prodded. "You arranged for him to rescue someone from a spider so you could get me alone. So what is it?"

He laid his arm over the back of the sofa, I thought as a way to connect himself to me in some way. I squirmed into the arm on my side, just out of reach of those long fingers. If he noticed, he didn't make a big deal of it. He cleared his throat and crossed his leg over the other. A casual movement, except he couldn't seem to keep his foot still.

"Layne never told you about our life spans," he said. It wasn't a question. I imagine he expected Layne to say nothing about the pack at all, and in truth he hadn't.

"He hasn't told me much."

"I'm not sure that makes me happy or not," he said. "I would have expected him to remain loyal to the pack, but to bring someone into our world without preparing them is unconscionable."

"You're not pleased with him."

"On the contrary. I'm very proud of him. He's my son. My only son. He'll be alpha if he can hold his own against the factions that are trying to break us apart."

I narrowed my gaze at him. Something was off, but I couldn't quite put my finger on it. Maybe it was his off-hand suggestion that there was trouble brewing in the pack. It seemed a good way to distract me from the things he didn't want me to ask. And if he'd rather talk about some sort of unrest, that could only mean he didn't want me to know more about Layne.

That decided me.

"You said Layne has been in the pack for a century." I hitched into the cushion. He hadn't just said it, he'd dropped it like he wanted me to pick it up. Well, so I would play.

He dropped his foot back down on the floor. "I did."

"But you didn't say how long you have been in the pack."

"It's my pack," he said. "I've been in it for as long as it has existed."

It wasn't an answer. I pulled around me the knowledge that Layne wanted me to know these things. That alone emboldened me.

"What is it Layne wanted you to tell me?"

He sighed. "Layne would want me to tell you things that don't matter. Wouldn't you really want to know the things he doesn't know? Things that mean his life and death?"

CHAPTER TWENTY-TWO

"YOU'RE THREATENED BY HIM," I said, realizing it as suddenly as that. "That's why you came on to me in my shop. That's why you sent me to the lingerie shop to buy something to please you. You want to undermine him every way you can. It's why you interfere with every relationship he has."

He seesawed his hand in the air. "You're half right. I don't interfere in every relationship. Just the ones that can damage him. The ones that threaten him."

I snorted, a most unladylike sound that made him raise an eyebrow.

"You're a piece of work, trying to make it sound like you're the good guy. The loving father." I started to get up, tired of the games he was playing, but he put his hand on my arm, not coiling his fingers around my forearm although he could easily do that by the size of his hands, but just resting it there in a manner that indicated he could and would hold me back if he had to.

"Wolves are doting of their offspring," he said, a threat in his voice.

I looked down at his hand on my arm. "And threatening to everyone else, it seems."

He withdrew his hand and smoothed it over the seat of the sofa. "Brie," he said in a mollifying tone. "Please sit. I'll come clean, but it's a long story. One I'd like to have finished before he returns."

Something in his face bade me sit back down. I pulled my legs up beneath me, facing him with my back against the opposite arm of the sofa.

"Alright," I said. "Whatever it is that's so damn secret you choose to keep it from him, please do tell me."

He smiled, a thin thing that he managed to make look victorious even beneath the insulting tone I'd used.

"Layne's mother and I split up when he was ten. She took him from me. She took him and she ran with him as though I was some monster."

I squirmed on the couch but said nothing.

"She knew what I was," he said. "It was no surprise. I think she was fine with me being a monster, but she didn't want that for Layne. I think she was afraid I'd turn him when he became of age."

"But you did," I said. "You did turn him."

He shrugged with one shoulder. "He was my only child. A son. I wanted him with me. Of course I turned him. But he wasn't forced. I would never do that to my own blood. It was his choice. One he made in his early twenties. He had a few years to think it over."

I brought to mind Layne's face. He looked older than a man in his twenties, so at least I knew they aged. Owen himself had some salt in the pepper of his hair.

"So he chose to be what he is," I said. "How can that be some secret?"

He leaned back into the sofa arm on his side and picked at his trousers. "Layne's choice isn't the issue," he said. "It was his mother. She was the problem."

"Blame it all on the women," I said. "Sounds about right coming from a misogynist."

He raised one eyebrow. "I told you I love women. That's not misogynistic."

I might argue with that, but it wasn't the time. "Go on, then. What was the problem with his mother?"

"She was a witch," he said. He waited for a full heartbeat before he added to the statement. "By the end, she was a black witch."

"A black witch." My hands flew to my chest, where the runes still ached.

"Yes. One of the witches my pack was guardians for."

My stomach felt all knotted. "He did tell me his pack was once guardians for a coven," I said out loud and caught myself. I'd just told Owen Layne hadn't told me anything about his pack. I hurried to cover up for him. "I mean, I kind of had him backed in a corner. But that's it. That's all he's told me."

He waved the point away. "No matter," he said. "Not anymore. What matters is what that legacy has brought to him. You know, I asked him to go away on a business trip some weeks ago."

I nodded.

"I sent him on a research errand. One that didn't bear much fruit, to be honest, but one that got him out of the way while I did my own work here. You see, his mother and her coven thought of us as dogs. As property. Pets of a sort, who were there to do their bidding. I thought she loved me." He closed his eyes in remembrance. "She was quite beautiful. Celtic looks. Fiery in bed and out. I was smitten. I thought she was my mate."

"I'm guessing she thought otherwise."

He opened his eyes and looked at me. "She had her reasons for seducing me. They don't matter. What does is the result. Layne." He pushed himself off the sofa and paced to the table near the door, where he poured another drink and upended it without offering one to me. He stood there for a full moment before he spun on his heel.

"She cursed him," he said. "When he left her to come to me, she was furious. She wanted to punish us both. Me for turning him and him for becoming something she thought of as lesser."

I pulled my feet out from beneath my butt and dropped them to the floor. Watching Owen's face, I could see he was telling the truth. There was too much anguish in his shoulders, too much yellow behind his eyes to indicate falsehood.

"Layne doesn't know, does he?" I said, realizing it the moment my feet touched down. Something in the way Owen's posture closed off, his shoulders rounded, was a clear indicator of a man keeping a secret.

"You're keeping it from him."

He peered over his shoulder through the door before laying his hand on the knob and closing it softly.

"Layne knows he's cursed," he said. "How else would I get him to go on a research errand and leave behind a job he loves during a time when the woman he fancies is involved in a series of horrible murders?"

"I'm not involved in murders," I said hotly. "I'm a victim of all that shit."

"You know what I mean." He crossed the room, dropping his voice. "Layne believes he is cursed to lose every woman he cares for, but the truth is much, much worse."

Something twisted in my chest, hard enough for me to gasp.

"Yes, as bad as that," he said. "You see, that bitch of a witch cared so little for her son once he became were, that she used her black power to curse him. Her own son." His voice was ragged, and I knew just how much he hated his wife in that moment, how much he loved Layne. It was heartening at least to see a side of him that put him in a positive light instead of the dark color I'd painted him with.

"That's terrible," I murmured.

A bark of bitter laughter escaped him. "Terrible is an understatement."

He dragged a hand over his head in an echo of a gesture I'd seen Layne make a dozen times. They looked very much alike in that moment and my heart chirped. But for Layne, I could easily have fallen for Owen. I saw in him in that instant, what other women must have seen, what drew them to him the way Parrish indicated. He had charisma but he had something else. There was a vulnerability in his feelings for Layne that made him attractive.

"How understated?" I asked, almost afraid to hear the answer.

He pinned me with a direct look. "It's both terrible and apt, coming from a witch as black-hearted as she. It's almost fairytale cliché. She cursed him to fall in love with a witch."

All of a sudden, the comments Parrish made about Layne and Owen and witches came flooding back. I squirmed in my seat. "Doesn't seem so bad, really."

"No?" he asked. "Not on the surface. But the witch he will fall in love with will not know her own power. And that power will be the death of him."

My knees went weak. Damn good thing I was sitting down. My throat went tight as he reached out to touch my hand.

"That witch is you, Brie," he said.

CHAPTER TWENTY-THREE

I WOULD BE THE death of Layne. A man I realized I was in love with. I blinked at Owen stupidly for several moments before the final horrible words came out of his mouth.

"You have to leave him," Owen said. "For his sake. If you love him, you'll walk away."

I tried not to clutch at the sofa arm, but I was aware my nails were digging in. "That's why you've been wooing the women he dates," I said through the tightness that had begun to make my throat ache.

"Think about it, Brie," he said, glancing at the door again. I thought he wanted to be sure Layne wasn't about to enter. "If the power that kills him comes from a witch who doesn't even know she's a witch, then how can he protect himself?"

"He can't," I murmured. "He'd never know until it was too late."

Owen leaned forward, brushing the backs of his fingers against my cheek. "You're the one. All these years, I've tried to keep him from falling in love. I left him his dalliances because a man needs such things, but I acted quickly to lure the women away with whatever means I had to do so. I'm not ashamed to admit that. I used my sex the way a harlot does if I had to. I bribed them. I did whatever needed to be done and I'd do it over and over again for him. I never knew who would be the witch that would kill him. Some of them were easy. They were nothing but trollops and money grabbers. I paid them to leave him alone. But the ones he liked, the ones I knew he would eventually commit to, I used all the power I had as alpha to pull them apart."

"You'd rather he hates you than die?" I guessed.

"He hates what I do, but he doesn't hate me. I'm his father, and I'm his alpha. I can sense it. Just as I can sense how he feels about you. You're different. Had I known I'd be so certain about the one, I'd never have bothered before. I would have saved him that torture."

His fingers trailed to my shoulder, where he gripped me gently. "This time, after you, he may well hate me, and yes, I'm willing to live with that if it will protect him. I'd hoped for a few more decades before that happened. But it's here. The moment when he could lose everything is right here. It's in front of me. I can't protect him from you, Brie."

I nodded with my throat clogged by a sob that I refused to let escape. I didn't trust my voice anyway. I knew he was right. I felt it in my marrow. The power was too much for me, and I knew Layne would do what he could to protect me from it. But what would that do to him in the end? I had no doubts the magic that I couldn't control, that took such a toll on me, would eventually be his end.

"What should I do?" I said as the dread and grief climbed my spine. "It's already gone too far." I felt the mad blush rising from my chest but I didn't care.

"I think you are smart enough to figure out a way to do it," he said with a shrug. "I tried to help you out, but now...well, you're on your own now that you've come straight out and told me to go to Hell." His smile was a faint imitation of humor and sadness mixed.

"So you're going to let me do all the heavy lifting, is that it?" I asked.

He didn't have to nod. I felt sick in the pit of my stomach because I knew he was right. The opportunity for Owen to shoulder the burden had passed. I heard Layne on the other side of the door. He was grumbling about mice and silly girls. I looked at Owen.

"So what did Layne want you to tell me? What was he going to say that he thought was yours to tell?"

Owen clasped both hands behind his neck and stretched. "It's a secret how long we live. Most packs guard that secret like they guard their lives." When his hands came away, he shook them out at his sides. "Layne is over a hundred years old," he said. "And he's young."

I remembered the comment earlier about Parrish and Zach having a hundred years of history between them, but I never expected the possibility of more than a century. I felt like someone had clobbered me. "A hundred?" I thought back to the moments when Parrish had inferred she'd been born in the seventies and Layne had changed the subject. "And Parrish" I asked.

He made a thoughtful noise. "Our newest pack member," he said. "Yes. She is probably the same age. No one really knows except Parrish and she refuses to say anything about her life during the years before her change. If anyone knows anything about her, it's Layne." He said this as though he disapproved and was put out that she wouldn't tell him.

But I thought it was more. I thought that maybe while Owen was her official alpha, Parrish accepted Layne as her true leader, and I was sure Owen sensed it too.

It rankled, I bet, that Parrish had confided her past in Layne but wouldn't give more to the real pack alpha. I didn't know much about pack politics, but I was willing to bet that was as unusual as having a female shifter in the first place.

I was about to ask how old Owen was when Layne entered. White dust sprinkled through his hair and he was running his hands through it, shaking it out.

"Saw a mouse," he growled. "She said it was in the flour. I couldn't smell a thing and was on my hands and knees, poking into the pantry when she dropped the canister on me."

Owen muttered a similar echo to Layne's, a sympathetic echo about mice and silly girls, but I saw his face. He'd ordered the cook or whoever to invent the mouse so he could have me alone. Now that I knew why, the day seemed far less rosy. I watched Layne fluffing the dust from his hair with a dreadful longing.

After a few moments, he seemed stratified and came toward me. The directness in his face made my heart hurt. Tears welled in my eyes, and I know he saw them because confusion crested across his features.

"Are you alright, Brie?" he asked, and his eyes flitted to Owen as he extended his hand to mine. Suspicious of his father as usual. Rightly so, it seemed.

I swallowed hard, and I stepped away, out of reach.

"I don't think so," I said and tried to screw a look of disapproval and betrayal on my face. I'd do what Owen asked, but I wasn't about to shoulder the burden alone.

Layne's eyebrows shot up. "What happened?"

I took another step backward and toward Owen. "Nothing happened, but I have to come clean. I can't lie to you anymore."

I pointed at Owen and then pulled my hand back when I saw my finger shaking. My mouth went dry, and I started to shake all over. Good. It would look much more convincing.

He shot a glance at his father, his expression confused and betrayed. "What did you do to her?"

Owen put his hands up in surrender. "Nothing, I swear."

When he sent me a raking look, I knew he was furious. The sizzle of yellow in his gaze revealed how he felt about me in that moment, but I didn't care. If he wanted me to leave Layne, he'd have to suffer the leaving.

"Please, Owen," I said. "It's time to tell the truth."

Layne tried to take my arm, but I pulled away again, shaking him off with a trembling hand.

"Don't," I said, putting all the pain of what I knew I had to do into my voice. I pulled out every bit of drama skill I'd acquired over the years of playing a charlatan. All that practice had been for this moment. I couldn't blow it, and yet, I didn't think I would. My pain was real.

"If you touch me, it will make this difficult, and I really have to tell you."

I swung my gaze to Layne's, but this time I hugged myself, tucking my hands beneath my armpits so they wouldn't give me away. Body language is very powerful, even if a person isn't well-versed in following cues consciously. I knew if I let my hands do what they would, they would reach out for him, and in that moment, his body would know what mine was telling him. That I didn't want to leave. That I wanted to hold him and cling to him and never let go.

His shoulders sagged. The look on his face might as well have been a hot branding iron. It hurt just as much to see the pain there. The anger.

"Brie," he said. "What's wrong?"

I hung my head, knowing what guilt looked like. He'd know too, and I had to give him what he needed to see.

I had to look authentic. More than any other time in my life, I needed to look real.

"I slept with your father," I said, peering up at him from beneath my lashes the way I would if I really had done that awful thing. Owen choked and clutched at the wall.

Layne, however, went completely white-faced. I hurried on, hating the look in his face as much as if I was truly guilty. I supposed that would help. I wanted to get rid of that expression.

"It was before we...it was...before."

There. That sounded real. But if he asked me I wouldn't be able to come up with a date or a time. But of course he wouldn't ask. He'd have the lingerie. He'd know I went to the same shop Owen sent all his women. He'd seen us together in the hallway. Every earmark of betrayal was right beneath his nose and he'd believe his own senses.

I felt shell-shocked, even though it had been my decision. My legs were weak. I tried to force myself to move, but I stumbled into the sofa.

Layne's hand shot out so quick I didn't have time to dodge it. He caught me before I fell. His face was filled with pain and anguish. His hand on my wrist was hot but gentle. The way his fingers curled around my wrist, I knew he was testing my pulse. I knew the way it raced wouldn't lie to him. He'd feel it hammering against my skin and presume the guilt and anguish of confession instead of the pain of hurting him.

When I looked into his eyes, they were yellow and hooded. Anger. Anger and something much, much more dangerous: hurt.

"Why?" Layne said, and I supposed that was the one thing he'd want to know. Not when. With betrayal on the line, when I had done this to him didn't matter.

What mattered was whether I loved Owen. Whether I preferred the elder to the younger.

Because he expected the betrayal, I realized. And that's what hurt the most. Not just that he expected a woman to prefer his father, but that I would. I couldn't imagine the wounds in his psyche after years, maybe decades, of his father torturing him that way. But I understood, at least, why Owen did it. It was hard to feel anger at him when I was doing the exact same thing. For Layne. To save him.

That's what love was, right? Sacrifice?

"I know I hurt you," I said into his face. "I never meant to."

He pulled his hand away and shoved it into his pocks as though touching me had burned him. "I should have known."

I made a show of gathering my dignity and stood my ground, shifting sand though it was. I'd made my decision. I'd already traveled too far down the road in the few seconds to stop now. There was nothing but to make it look as authentic as I could. I was aware of Owen's look of shock, his fidgeting as he watched it unfold. At least it was a good sign that I was convincing.

Owen looked at me with a curled lip. He might have wanted this, but he didn't want it this way. Well, too bad. I wasn't shouldering this blame alone.

"I'll leave then," I murmured and without waiting for either man to respond, I fled to gather my cell phone. I'd have to leave wearing his clothes. His smell was all over me.

He dogged my heels the way a beaten dog followed its master. I felt his pain like it was my pain. And it was. I was holding back a flood of tears by the time I laid my hand on my phone. The wallet case had spilled out a few things, including the photo of my mother and I shoved it all back inside.

It took several gulping swallows to cement a blockade the tears battered against. I knew if I spoke, they'd break through the barrier, and so I said nothing. He said nothing. He just watched me with yellow eyes and a rigid spine. His fists curled together against his sides, but he didn't try to stop me.

I pushed past him and fled down the hallway to the exit. If I didn't get out in the next few seconds, I was going to lose it. I grabbed the doorknob and yanked the door open. The cold from outside burned my eyes. They stung as though the air was made of acid.

"Why, Brie?" Layne said from behind me in a soft, pleading voice.

I couldn't look at him. Just couldn't. If I did, I'd collapse right there in front of him and confess the whole shoddy mess of truth. I didn't want that for him. The risk was too great. I'd rather hurt him and suffer myself than for him to end up dead because of me.

I heard him move behind me in my hesitation. He was so close I could feel his breath across the top of my hair. The heat from his chest bore into my back. The smell of him, of mint and musk wrapped around me. In my mind's eye, I was pressed against him again in that storage closet, the troubles nothing but a pale memory. I had to bite down on the sob that tried to escape.

He didn't touch me, but he was close enough he could have snaked his arm around my waist and pulled me against his chest. He wouldn't, though. I'd made sure of that.

I managed to flee before the tears fell. I knew when I stepped out into the early morning light and leaned against the door to catch my breath that he was still standing there on the other side.

And I had the feeling that even if I'd done it to save his life, I'd just killed him.

Chapter Twenty-Four

A FIRST ON-SITE CREW was already waiting for me at my shop when Owen's driver pulled next to the curb. The white van was surrounded by several workers drinking coffee from paper cups, the steam billowing in the air around them.

Dread climbed my spine as I reached for the handle. I'd known coming back would be tough, but I didn't expect to have to face all of this right away. I'd secretly hoped the mess of Scarlett's attack would already be cleared away.

"Thanks," I said to the driver, and he mumbled a *no problem* over his shoulder without turning around. I climbed out into the cool air, pulling Layne's sweat shirt tighter around my throat.

I approached my storefront with trepidation. Claws of frigid breeze fingered their way up the back of my borrowed shirt and jacket, but it wasn't the cold that made me shiver.

The supervisor met me with a scowl and a cigar that stunk like weed.

"You the owner?" he asked and then without waiting for an answer, jabbed the tip of his cigar in the direction of his workers. "They been waiting a half hour already. That's going on the bill."

I nodded mutely as I scanned the men loitering around the van. One of them took a long drag off a homemade cigarette before tossing it on the sidewalk. He stretched lazily, with his arms over his head, then starting unloading equipment and coveralls from the back.

"How long do you think it will take?" I asked the supervisor.

He used his coffee cup to point at the side of my storefront. "Depends," he said. "Man that ordered the cleanup said it was a murder we're cleaning away. So blood, brains, feces. That sort of thing can take a while. Was it inside?"

I winced at his description. "She didn't die here," I said, feeling like I had to correct him. "There's some blood, but none of the other things you mention." I clutched my stomach, remembering that I'd not eaten. The coffee wafting over his lid was making me sick.

"Well, then, maybe an hour. But like I said, I'll be putting the extra half hour on the bill."

"Of course," I said. "Make sure you bring it inside when you're finished."

"No ma'am," he said. "Bill goes straight to Owen Garder. He made sure I understood that when he called to get us to clean up the mess."

Mess. What a way to describe a woman's dying moments. The headache in the back of my skull that I'd developed in the car on the way over threatened to move to the front. All I could manage in response was to point him to the back alley where Scarlett had lain halfway over my threshold.

I didn't bother to wait for them to suit up. Rather, I rounded the shop to look for the spare key I kept hidden beneath a loose shingle so I could get into my own shop.

What met me when I swung the door open made me sink into the nearest chair. The investigators had upturned or overturned or opened everything. I thought of my old Buddha urn and genuflected at the thought that I'd long ago dumped the magic mushroom grind.

I decided a change of clothes was what I needed to attack the insurmountable task. I headed for my back storage room with a concerted effort not to look around me.

I was standing in front of the storage closet door when the full force of memory crashed down on me. Inside, with the fragrance of cinnamon and laundry detergent, Layne and I had rescued each other from the horror of the night. We had found bliss in a blitz of awfulness.

My thighs ached with the memory of strain as I held him against me, hooking my ankle around his waist.

My fingers touched down on the wood of the door and I closed my eyes in recall. My chest grew tight. A buzz of electricity streaked down my arm. When my mouth went dry and my knees sagged, I knew the panic attack for what it was and let myself slip to the floor. With legs curled sideways, I sat there with my hand on the door, gasping for breath.

"For fuck sake," said Parrish's familiar voice. "Was he that bad a lay?"

I dropped my head back to see her standing over me. Whatever she saw on my face made her curse again, and she dropped to her knees to gather me beneath her arm. I was shaking.

"My clothes," I said in a tight voice as I gestured toward the door. "I wanted to change...." I let the rest of it trail away because she knew as well as I did what had happened in that closet and I was willing to bet she understood my hesitation.

I wanted to get up and run away but my legs were as strong as room temperature butter. Instead, I contented myself with pressing my face into her armpit because it was the only part of her I could reach. Safe there, I wept softly.

"He's dead to me," she said. "If he's making you cry like that, I swear I'll use his larynx for a harmonica."

"Not him," I managed to get out. "It's not his fault."

She went quiet for a long moment and then said. "No, it isn't his fault. It's mine. I know that. I'm to blame for this whole goddamn mess."

I pulled away from her to lean against the wall so I could see her better. Her hair was plaited into two braids that tucked just behind her ear. The jean coat she wore had cream colored Sherpa wool lining the inside and it peeked out at the collar. She looked as beautiful as always.

"It's my fault," I said. "No one else's."

"But I introduced you to Honey," she said and I realized what had brought her to the shop in the first place. She'd seen Layne already. She knew we were broken up. How much else she knew I wasn't sure.

"Honey tricked you," I said, curling my legs beneath me. "I don't think she's quite sane, either."

Parrish dropped her bottom to the floor and leaned against the closet door. "I'm still sorry."

"There's no need." I took a deep breath, and surprised it came easily, took another. The trembling eased. Mercifully, the panic started to peel away like the tide from a beach.

She stretched her legs out in front of her and touched my knee with the toe of her boot. "If it's any consolation, she screwed me too, although not in the Biblical sense, more's the pity. Because of that bitch I had to spend a whole day with Doctor Good-for-Nothing."

I tittered, happy to laugh. "I'm sure he enjoyed it as well."

"Too much," she said. "Bastard rode me hard."

I lifted an eyebrow. "I didn't think you swung that way."

"Hardy Har," she said humorlessly. "Glad to see your teeth are still sharp, even if your bite is blunted."

I grinned, even happier to be distracted. "How did that go, anyway?"

"You mean after he made me dismember the prick Farrel and carry his parts in a suitcase to Papa Garder's office? Just peachy. Layne's dad ordered me to inciner-ate him at the pack crematorium."

So that was where Owen had been all night. Not with a woman like he'd said. I was beginning to think there was more to Owen Garder than he let on.

"You saw him last night, I'm guessing," I said.

She nodded. "I thought he'd want to use the body to figure out who turned him, but nope. Wanted him gone. Said his alpha already felt the pain of his death. He'd come looking for the killer in his own good time. No need to hunt him down. He'd come to us."

"Alphas can do that?"

"Beats me," she said. "All that alpha shit is a happy mystery to me." She looked down at her thumbnail, where the violet polish had chipped along the sides. "I'm not great at toeing the line. I figured he'd regret the decision, so I kept a few...things."

She scratched at the chip in her color. "I've been collecting quite a few things lately, to be honest." She chuckled. "Figure I'll open a museum of the macabre if I end up losing my job over all this."

"Like Margaret's Museum," I said, and she gave me a queer look. I waved it away because she'd not get the reference. Besides, I recognized the fake lightness in her voice. She'd hate losing her job.

"So," I said. "What other things are you collecting?" I tried for an equal amount of levity, but it came out too tense.

She smiled broadly, playing into the moment as she leaned forward. "All the best things, really. Things all typical girls dream about. Blood samples from the knife you gave Layne, Cuttings from Scarlett's shirt. That prick Farrel's purple dick head."

"Parrish," I said, aghast.

She waved away my agitation. "I was kidding about that last thing. I wouldn't have that even if it was bronzed and tied to a strap on. But not about the others. I've been doing some digging too," she said. "Come on." She pushed herself to her feet and extended a hand to me. "I've got some news that should cheer you up."

"I could use a bit of cheer," I said and let her yank me to my feet.

She looked me over and then gave me a gentle shove toward the shop proper. "You go wash up," she said. "I'll brave the dark recesses of the make-shift boudoir and wrestle from its depths a decent change of clothes for yon damsel."

I glowered at her. "I hate that term," I said, but I was grateful for the lightheartedness, and I was relieved she was going to do the things I couldn't face.

"You prefer stinky?" she asked. "Because that term fits too."

I tossed her an F-you with my finger and laughed. It did feel good to laugh. It eased the tension that threatened to shut down my throat altogether. "I have a wicker chest toward the back. I keep linens and under-wear and a couple of dresses in it." I headed off toward the front of the shop, but paused after a few steps to lean backward and catch her attention.

"I know how many pairs of panties I have in there," I said. "So don't even think about stealing any."

She poked her head back out through the door. "Actually, I was thinking about leaving a pair for you." She grinned.

"Don't tell me that sort of thing gets you laid," I said. "Because I don't even want to know the kind of chicks who would fall for that."

She leaned against the door frame, one ankle hooked over the other. "Actually, my kind of chick doesn't wear any."

I threw my hands up. "I surrender," I said. "I can't out-quip you. I'm going to the bathroom and running some water."

"Make it hot," she said as she disappeared back into the storage room. "Because, girl, you're gonna have to burn off those cooties."

The momentary distraction of Parrish's good humor evaporated when I reached the other end of the apothecary galley to see into the shop. It was just as ransacked as when I'd come in, not that I expected any different. I just had forgotten how bad it was.

I plowed through the store toward the bathroom, choosing to ignore it all, and ran hot water in the sink until the narrow mirror fogged up. Parrish found me there and tossed a shirt-dress and pair of lace panties at me. There were no shoes, so I kept the sneakers on.

She followed the change of clothes up with a towel and black facecloth, then went back into the shop, leaving me alone to make myself feel human again.

When I exited the bathroom, after holding the warm, wet cloth to my cheeks to pinken them up, and freshly dressed with a smear of red lipstick on that I'd found in the soap basket, she had picked up most of the tossed and discarded items from the floor and put them onto the shelves.

"Some of this mess was from that bastard, Kenny," she growled. "I should have torn his throat out when I had the chance."

"You know it was him?" I said, and she nodded.

"Layne told me when you were in the hospital. Sent me a bunch of things to test because he didn't trust anyone else to get it one hundred percent right. Kind of like an extra layer of protection. He has a touch of bit O.C.D. does our Layne.

"This coming from a woman who taps her car roof multiple times before she gets in."

"Four," she said. "It has to be four. Anyway, they picked the prick up last evening. My guess is he'll be playing bitch to some big dog in jail for a while." She picked up a candle from the floor and set it on the shelf with a host of other candles. "I might even pay a couple of hoodlums to do just that." She planted her hands on her hips as she surveyed the shop. "Now. Let's get this mess straightened away. I have something to show you."

"I thought you were going to show me now."

She laid a hand on her chest, aghast. "And leave this place looking like this? I wouldn't be able to concentrate."

She had me there. I didn't think I'd be able to either. It took at least an hour with her help to get things back to some semblance of normal and by the time we were done, the supervisor from the cleanup crew rang his way through the front door to tell me they had washed off the alleyway pavement and bleached the lintel of my back door.

I thanked him and passed him a candle from the nearest shelf. Patchouli or something equally mystic smelling. All of them had my logo stamped on the bottom and I figured he'd re-gift it to someone who might actually decide to return to the shop for something.

Parrish was staring at me when I closed the door behind him.

"What was he doing here?" she said.

I jerked my thumb in the direction of the doorway. "Him? He owns that First on Site company."

"Oh, I know what he does," Parrish said. "He's the alpha's cleanup crew. Why was he here?"

"To clean up the blood. Remember?"

She closed the distance between us, and opened the door to peer out. A brisk wind fingered its way in past her, cold enough to make me rub my arms.

"Odd," she said. "He only uses them for pack stuff."

"I'm sure he just wanted to thank me," I said, and she canted her head at me.

Closing the door, she narrowed her gaze at me.

"What does he want to thank you for, exactly?" she asked. "Because I've only ever seen them appear when Owen has had someone killed."

Chapter
Twenty-Five

I WAS BEGINNING TO think I was cursed. The shitty news just kept coming. My hands scrabbled to find a chair, and touching down on the armrest of one, I sank into it.

"Killed," I said. "You said Owen had people killed."

She seesawed her hand back and forth. "Not for a long time, years, really, but yes. Wolves who turn badly, who can't be controlled or who turn on others without his consent." She avoided my eye as she said it and there was an odd note of memory in her voice. "Sometimes they need to be euthanized for the good of all. But it's been a while since anyone has been turned. No need for the cleaning crew, so they hire themselves out."

"I see," I said, although I didn't. Not really. The thought that such a thing could go on undetected by the police was a foreign concept. Except, here we were with a black coven roaming around sacrificing other witches, and they didn't seem to feel the need to solve the crimes. Or maybe that was why Layne was on the force. Maybe he was the one assigned. Maybe he was the one who found the 'motives and suspects' and Owen took care of them.

"I think I'm beginning to understand a lot," I murmured.

She toed my foot with her boot before rounding the counter to peer at me from over the surface. "So why Owen would want to thank you by sending his cleaner hoodlums to wash up a little blood that could easily have been sprayed into the gutter?"

I ignored the term hoodlums. Mostly because I didn't want to think about what other organizations they might need to clean up after.

"Well?" she prodded.

I picked at the arm of the chair. "He and I came to an agreement," I said. "One that benefited us both."

"And Layne, too, I'm guessing." She ducked behind the counter and came up with a thick folder of papers and a cardboard covered book far too big to be read like a novel.

That last was interesting enough to get me out of my chair. "What's that?"

"First, the favor," she said with her hand planted atop the cardboard cover.

The papers that stuck out from the edge looked like newsprint. I reached for the corner and she swatted my hand away.

I sighed. "You know what the favor is," I said. "You saw me bawling my eyes out in there." I jerked my thumb in the direction of my closet.

"He made you break up with Layne, didn't he?" she said. "Fucking bastard. I have no idea what his problem is with Layne's dates. It's like he doesn't want him to be happy or something. And witches? Don't even go there."

I looked away, glancing at the manila folder she'd brought. That last hit too close to home. "Maybe he had enough of them after the pack was made to guard a coven of witches intent on studying the black arts."

"Maybe," she said. "That was before my time."

"You mean before the 1800s?" I said with a raised eyebrow.

She canted her head at me, curious, but made no comment, just flipped open the cardboard book, spreading the pages out to at least two feet across the counter. Then she plopped the folder on top.

"These are a few printouts of online newspapers from the early 90s when the city started toying with a blog format." She pushed it to the side of the open book. "And this beauty is a record of newspapers from the 1950s. One year in the 50s, to be exact."

"They let you check this out?"

"I know the librarian."

I made a noncommittal sound, and she chuckled beneath her breath. "At any rate, I found something interesting. You'd be surprised what they keep in the archives."

"Things like?"

She curled her nails across her palm and studied her thumbnail. "Things like the name of the man who died in front of the hotel when you and Layne were at the charity dinner."

"Sweet Jesus," I said. "The shade man. You found him."

She looked up at me. "Don't let your boobies get all sweaty. I said it gave a name. A name. John Smith. Obviously fake, but it did lead me to a few old newspaper clippings from the fifties."

At that, she made a big show of thumbing through a couple of pages to open to a spread that looked immediately to me like a bunch of photos I'd seen in my mother's trunk.

All the pictures in the spread showed the same building. My building. Dated from a summer day in 1953. And in one of them, four people stood in a cluster in front of the doorstep I had redecorated from an old, boarding house style to an upscale psychic shop.

I leaned in to get a better look at the people in the photo. It was blurry and panned out so far as to see the entire building, since that was the real subject of the photo, but I could swear the woman in the middle was my mother.

I gasped out loud and Parrish slammed her hand on the book. "I knew it," she said. "It's him, isn't it?"

If I hadn't been sure at first glance, when she opened the folder, it was to a page that was a cleaner crop of the photo, zoomed in to a blurry, but larger picture of my mother, my father, and the shade man.

"John Smith," she said, pointing to the caption.

She apparently didn't realize the connection of the others in the picture. I swallowed, not sure what to make of it all. My mother didn't merely look exactly the same as she had in the photo Smith had pressed into my hand in the basement where Farrel had jailed me. She looked the same as the photo in the trunk, the same as the photo I kept on my fireplace. She looked exactly the same as she had when I was six.

"He's a werewolf," she said with her finger tapping Smith's face. "He has to be to look the same after all these years."

I studied the picture. "My mother looks the same," I said, pointing to her in the photo. "Exactly the same."

"She was a witch, right? I don't know any witches who have managed to hold back age. Maybe she was a shifter too."

I squinted as I ran my palm over the photos. "Maybe they found the fountain of youth," I said. "Maybe that's what all this is about." I thought about the other women Parrish had examined when the coven had them killed. "Those others were sacrificed and they were just as young. You know. You saw them. You have them in your morgue."

I tapped the photo several times, landing once on each of the figures in turn. "My mother. The lingerie clerk said she hadn't changed in all the years she'd lived next door. Smith very clearly looked the same on your examination table as he does in this photo. My father died when I was six, but he looked just like this picture. And this woman, this woman you had on your table as well. Does she look any different to you?"

"Werewolves."

"You sound pretty sure."

"I've told you, I haven't met a witch who didn't age. They are mortal." She patted me on the back. "Sorry, Brie, but you will end up with crepe skin, wrinkles deep enough to sink a battleship in, and sagging boobs you can tie into a bow." She dropped her gaze to my chest. "And judging by the size of the girls, that bow will likely be a belt."

I subconsciously tucked my arms beneath my chest, weighing the amount of sag I already owned.

I pursed my lips. I knew I was onto something. "We've been chasing this black coven for months and haven't ever figured out what they are after. What if they've found a way to keep from aging? What if my mother knew the secret, the magic that it took to do so? What if that was why they wanted her? I overheard her say as much into the phone when I was a kid. She said it's my power. You can't have it."

She crossed her arms and chewed on her bottom lip, considering. "It's possible, I suppose."

"Think about it," I prodded. "Why would you invoke black magic? What goal could possibly be worth taking another's life for?"

She shrugged. "Greed. Passion. Money. All the regulars."

"You've been hanging out with Layne too long." I squatted down behind the counter to find my mother's grimoire. "I'm right. I know it. Honey is too vain and too stupid to want more than to remain pretty forever."

"Oh way to go, Brie, remind the gay werewolf that she sicked a black witch on her best friend."

I looked up at her. "I'm your bestie?"

She kicked me in the stomach with the toe of her boot. "This gay chick doesn't use such flowery language."

I mumbled that she'd have used the word if I'd not used it first and she crouched down with me. "What did you say?"

"Nothing." I rummaged through the shelf, expecting the grimoire to be where I'd left it when Layne had told me I needed to leave the shop. "Where is the damn thing?"

She ran her hands over the ephemera and stray candles and bags. "What are we looking for?"

"My mother's grimoire. I wasn't allowed to take it or my appointment book, remember? It should be here."

I had begun to pull everything off the shelf when the sound of frantic knocking caught my attention. Someone was at the front door of the shop and they were in a mad rush to get in.

"Fuck," I said, my hand frozen atop a pillar candle with a big chip in the bottom. "Do you think it's Kenny?"

"You tell me," she rasped. "You're the psychic." Then she popped up like her legs were made of springs. "Holy fucking Mother Mary," she said.

"It's him, isn't it?" I said, dropping to my hands and knees even though no one could see me. I grappled at the hem of her jeans. "Get down. He'll see you."

She peered down at me with a patronizing look. "I wish it was the little prick. But it's not him. It's some chick. And she's seen me already."

The knocking came faster now that whoever was outside had spotted Parrish. I started to get to my feet so I could peer over the counter, but Parrish's hand came down on the top of my head.

"Hold on, cowgirl," she said. "You best prepare yourself for this ride."

Irritated, I pulled her hand off my head and gripped the lip of the counter. The banging intensified, and I used the purchase of my fingers on the counter to pull myself up despite the increasing pressure of Parrish's palm on my head trying to keep me out of sight.

"Seriously?" I said as I finally dodged sideways and got out from beneath her hold. "If it isn't Kenny, then it's someone who needs help."

"You might not want to help this one," she said.

When I popped up to a full stand and looked toward the door, I understood what her hesitation had been.

The woman at the door looked exactly like me.

And she was bleeding.

Chapter Twenty-Six

Blood does odd things to a gal's psyche. As used to it as we are, it immediately ties a knot in the stomach. Blood meant pain and hurt and death, and if a woman was bleeding and pounding on the door to get in, you run to help.

I ran for the door, all but tripping over my own feet in my haste to reach it. Parrish didn't give in to the instinct. Instead, she ambled behind me, casually strolling, her footfalls a steady rhythm behind me that indicated she might not want to look concerned, but she was definitely sticking close to me. I imagined she didn't plan to let something happen to me again on her watch.

The woman's face had a large smear of red, like a handprint on her cheek, and her fist was covered in blood. She left multiple splotches of the fluid on the window of my door.

I had my hand on the knob when Parrish laid her hand over mine, keeping me from yanking the door open.

"Wait," she said, and the command in her voice was something I didn't dare disobey. She turned from me to the door and raised her voice. "We're closed," she said and tapped the sign.

"I need help," the woman said. "Someone is following me." She looked over her shoulder in a frantic move that had me pushing Parrish's hand from mine and twisting the knob. She sent me a frustrated look that I ignored. After all, the woman needed help.

"Come in," I said, sweeping my arm across the air between us. "Hurry. Get inside."

She breezed in and Parrish slammed the door behind her and twisted the lock on the door. I took in the ragged, heaving chest of my doppelgänger and immediately went tongue-tied. She was a perfect match right down to the hair. Hers might have even been the same length, except I couldn't see it beneath the slouch beanie she wore. That too, had blood on it.

"You're bleeding," Parrish said even as she surreptitiously pushed me aside, out of reach.

The woman stared at Parrish as though she'd spoken a foreign language. "Bleeding?"

That seemed to break Parrish's calm. She closed the distance between herself and the stranger in the time it took me to blink and had grabbed the hat from her head. She used it to wipe the girl's cheek and stuffed the hat in her hands.

"Bleeding," she said and lifted the woman's hands to eye level. "See?"

"He must have cut me," the girl said and lifted her gaze to mine. I knew the instant I saw the glazed look in her eyes that it was no good trying to get anything coherent out of her.

"She's in shock," I said to Parrish. "Look at her."

Parrish made a grumbling sound, and she remained between us, her shoulders knotted together.

"Who is *he*?" she asked the woman.

The woman shook her head. "I have no idea." She wrung the hat in her hands and started to shuffle side to side. I noted her sneakers were dirty. She looked dirty all over, to be honest. There was a raggedness about her clothing. Her hair, now that it was out from beneath the hat, looked greasy. Even as I noted all these things, the smell started to permeate the air. I coughed.

Parrish noticed it all at the same time. "Are you high?"

"High?" the girl asked, the dimness of her expression sparking for just one moment before it went out again. "No. I haven't used in days. Not since...not since he started following me."

Parrish took the girl by the arm. She was younger than me, I could see, now that the shock of seeing her had worn off. Maybe by at least ten years. I waited for Parrish to settle her in the armchair nearest the door before I pulled up one of the stools. I sat on it with one leg dangling. I'd had too many weird things happen in the last few weeks to leave caution to the wind. Parrish's hesitation reminded me we couldn't let down our guard.

I leaned between my knees, elbows on my thighs. "What's your name, honey," I said and Parrish gave me a nasty look that I returned before reaching across to touch the girl on the knee. "What should we call you?"

"Trisha," she said. "Trish."

"Well, Trish, tell us what happened. Start from the beginning."

Trish fell back against the chair, flopping into the cushions. "At first, I thought I was hallucinating. It happens sometimes, you know?"

I nodded. I did know. I'd banked on it in my early days as a psychic. "What did you see?"

Parrish snorted. "Apparently, she's still seeing it."

I shushed her. "Trish, what was it."

Trish bore into me with black eyes that looked nothing like mine. At least, that was different. I don't know why it relieved me, but it did. "Do you believe in were-wolves?" she said, and I thought I heard Parrish choke.

I shot her a warning look. "Do you?" I asked Trish.

She laughed without humor. "I do now. Fuck." She ran her hand through her hair and got her fingers tangled there for several seconds before she gave up and yanked them free. A mat of hair stuck out from her temple.

"Is that who you think is following you?"

She dropped her head into her hands and laid her elbows on her knees. "I swear, I saw him change right in front of me. He's been hanging around for days. I just thought he was some other homeless addict looking for a place to sleep. I have a cozy little squat in an old school. It's not much, but it keeps me out of the weather. I tell others about it for a fee."

"Drugs?" Parrish asked.

She swung her gaze to the shifter. "Does it matter?"

Parrish shrugged. "Just trying to lay down the circumstances. If you're high, no wonder you're seeing things."

The girl spread her hands wide. "You mean like all this blood?" she laughed again. "Are you hallucinating too? Are you on crack?"

She started getting agitated. I had to shut Parrish down before things got out of hand.

"Trish," I said, drawing her attention from Parrish. "Who did that to you?"

"I don't know, that's the thing. He started showing up a couple weeks back and then started coming around a bit more. Handsome guy. Older. But this morning he just changed. Right there in front of me. One minute he was this handsome older guy, the next his back started popping and his bones came right out of his skin for fuck sake. He grew fur."

She said this last in a pitch so high it might have cracked the window. I laid my hand on her shoulder. "It doesn't matter if what you saw is real or not. It matters what he did to you. And why. Parrish can help. She has connections to law enforcement."

"Fuck no," the girl jumped to her feet. "I didn't do nothing."

I held my hands out, calming her, putting a soothing note in my voice. "I know, I know. No one is going to arrest you. We want to help. What did he do?"

"He fucking bit me is what he did," she yelled. "He pinned me down and he bit me."

Parrish's face went white. "Sweet Jesus."

Trish licked her lips. "If it was Jesus, lady, I'd have been sanctified by all this blood." Another manic laugh escaped her. "This is my blood, and this is my body. I was a preacher's kid. I thought I was seeing a demon." She looked down at her hands before rubbing her neck again. The movement drew my eye, and it was only when she scratched at a wound that was much smaller than it had been when she'd entered, one with a rapidly healing bruise.

"Parrish," I said.

"Yeah," she responded. "I know." She stood up from her chair and crouched in front of the girl. "This just happened to you, didn't it? Outside. That's why you were running. It's why you came to this shop."

The girl's eye, less glazed over now, more bright than a few moments before. "He told me to come here. He told me if I wanted to live, I'd come here and ask for help. You can help me, right?"

Trish blink once at Parrish, a slow one that ended with a glassy-eyed stare that said whoever was home inside had turned off the lights.

I watched Parrish's shoulders tense. "I might not be able to help you," Parrish said. "But I can kill the bastard who turned you."

She sprung to her feet and headed to the door.

I got up and followed her, not sure I wanted to be left alone with a woman I knew had been bitten by a werewolf. Turned, Parrish said. I wasn't sure what that meant or how long it would take.

"Where are you going?" I asked.

"Like I said. It's him. The alpha who turned Farrel." She was already at the door. "Stay here with her. Order a bunch of hamburgers, pizza, anything. Just make it lots. I'll be back."

She sent one final glance toward the girl. "Fledgling wolves can't turn a human, so she won't be able to turn you. Not yet at least."

At that, she disappeared around the side of the building and I was left to stare at the street. The lamps had come on up and down the sidewalks and only a few people loitered around the shops.

Behind me, Trish moaned, drawing my attention. I turned to see her with her head in her hands. "My head hurts so much. It's like someone is dragging their nails along my brain."

"I'll get you some ibuprofen," I heard myself say and started for the bathroom. I kept a few over-the-counter painkillers in there for my monthly migraines.

I was rummaging through the cabinet when I heard her behind me. I spun on my heel with a bottle clutched in my grip. She stood in the doorway of the bathroom.

"I don't feel so well."

I couldn't imagine she did feel well. She had started to sweat. Perspiration was rolling off her temples, soaking her hat. The fringe of her hair released droplets that fell into her eyes and made her blink rapidly. In the few short minutes it had taken for Parrish to leave us and me to search for pain meds, her condition had worsened. Her pallor had gone a sickly gray. Lips that had been full and a lush pink when she'd entered my shop now looked white edged and flesh toned.

"I don't think ibuprofen is going to cut it," she groaned.

A second later, her eyebrow twitched and then she just collapsed like an empty bag to the floor. Her head connected with the door frame with such a loud crack, I thought she might have been shot until she slid the rest of the way to the floor and her eyes rolled back.

I needed 911. She needed 911. I ran for my phone, not sure where I'd left it, just that I knew I had to get to it. Stepping over her in my haste, I thought of nothing but getting her an ambulance. That changed the moment I felt fingers wrap around my ankle.

With that leg immobile and the momentum I'd put into sprinting for the phone, my body couldn't respond quick enough to keep the inevitable from happening. I went down with a thud that rattled my teeth.

Looking back, I saw her roll over onto her stomach and catch my eye. Behind her gaze was that same bright yellow I recognized in Farrel. I knew the instant her intention ran across her face.

The bitch was going to bite me.

Like fuck, I thought. I kicked hard with my free foot, driving the heel of Parrish's sneaker forward first and striking her on the chin. The runner made a thwacking sound when it connected. I felt something give way. The howl of pain she let go drowned out that of the sharp snap of bone.

I expected her to let go, but she only tightened her grip. Her other hand came down on my shin and by god if she didn't start to crawl over me, dragging her body along mine in slow, dogged tugs. For such a slight thing, she weighed a ton. Like a hundred pounds of muscle had claimed her in the last few seconds. If she made it all the way atop me, I was going to be pressed to death.

I tried to crab walk backwards but she dragged me toward her.

Right about then was the time I felt Parrish's hands on my shoulder. Strong hands with long, narrow fingers.

"Lock her in," she said. "Once I pull you free, lock her in."

One hard yank and my leg finally slid free of Trish's grip. She snarled at me and the animalistic look to her features put the fear of god in me. She wasn't changed, nor was she turning. She just looked feral.

"She's not going to make it," Parrish said as she kicked at Trish's shoulder with her boot, shoving her so hard backward that the girl pitched awkwardly sideways before flailing out with her legs. She cleared the threshold and skidded into the wastebasket, knocking tissue paper all over the floor.

Parrish slammed the door. "Get something to block her in there."

In a blind panic, I stumbled to my feet and swung around, panning my shop for something heavy enough to block the door, and seeing nothing, even if it was right in front of me.

"Brie," Parrish said. "I can hold the door for a long while, but I'm going to get pretty pissy if I miss my dinner."

Meaning hurry the hell up. Sounds from inside the bathroom indicated Trish had managed to get up and start pounding on the door. Parrish didn't look as though she was having trouble keeping it closed, but her boots were braced pretty good against the floor.

But the trouble with finding anything heavy enough to hold the door closed would also be too heavy for me to move. I closed my eyes, removing any extra sensory input so my brain could let what few synapses that were firing work to my advantage.

Parrish spat out some comment about it not being the time for a nap, but I ignored her. I shut out the sounds of frustrated pounding and imagined my shop in my mind's eye. I roamed it mentally, sorting through all the things I knew were placed around the building. I imagined myself trying to secure the door.

The bathroom was close enough to the counter and the stairs that led to the second floor that I should be able to tie the handle closed.

I had a length of rope left over from when I'd hired a handyman to clean the chimney and he'd tied himself off. That was in the storage closet, I thought. Back behind a toolbox on one of the shelves.

I retrieved it without thinking about Layne until I was tying one end to the bannister of the stairs. Chalk one up for the newly turned werewolf, she had probably just reset my memories of the place. Next time I needed to go in there, I knew I'd think about this terrifying incident before that with Layne.

I pulled the rope tight and Parrish helped me tie it around the knob.

We stepped back tentatively, both our gazes pinned to the door.

"Where did you learn to tie knots like that?" I said to her as the knob rattled ineffectively. The door moved a quarter inch but never opened.

Parrish planted her hands on her hips. "BDSM 101. Class one: how to keep your lover frustrated."

"Do we call Owen?" I asked her.

She let go a long, thoughtful sigh. "I think so. She won't be able to fully make the transition till the full moon, and until then, she might be a bit unreliable.

I hate to leave her in his hands if she's going to be a masher, but we also can't let her go to her alpha." She pulled her cell from her pocket.

I watched the knob try to twist. "Why is that?"

"Because if she's a masher, she'll kill everyone she sees. We put them down when we can."

A sick, clammy feeling shivered over me at the thought, and it was worse because she looked so much like me. It felt like I was on the chopping block right with her. But that wasn't the question I wanted answered.

"No," I said. "Why can't you let her go to her alpha?"

Parrish was dialing her phone. "Because at this stage, he's the only one who can remove the magic. And we need her exactly as she is."

Chapter
Twenty-Seven

Needing a werewolf was about as horrible as it sounded. Parrish thought Owen might be able to use her to track down the alpha who made her, but the problem was the longer Trish went without her cure, the more likely it would be she'd become fully were.

"The real problem is she's not going to be a good were," Parrish mused aloud. "At least not at first. A lot of people will die before that happens. And not in a pleasant way."

I gave her a long look and she shrugged. "I just know, OK?"

I'd have to take her word for it, but I did not want to see her suffer much longer.

"If Owen gets her to track to her alpha, will he force the reversal?"

It took a long time for Parrish to answer. "If there's time left, he might. Then again, he might just put her down." There was a tightness in her voice that bothered me.

"Maybe call Layne then," I said. "He's alpha, right? Surely he can do the same thing as Owen."

She grinned. "I thought you might say that."

Layne arrived after Trish seemed to have slumped against the door, having exhausted herself with repeated barrages against it. I was surprised my makeshift barricade worked. Trish, for her part, took to growling softly.

A flash of mental image shot through me, of her panting like a caged animal, her face—so like mine—taken over by a monster's facade. It felt too personal, but even if it didn't, I wouldn't want that to happen to her. It made me uncomfortable to think I'd consider her a monster when I knew perfectly well that didn't have to happen. Parrish and Layne and Owen were all perfectly human in their emotions and socializations. This girl didn't have to become a monster.

And yet...Parrish had said she might be a masher. That didn't sound encouraging.

By the time Parrish pulled out her phone and swiped to read a message, I knew there would be no hope for the girl inside. It had taken too long to get help, and judging by how fast she had transformed in the few moments she'd been in the front of the shop, I doubted anyone could do anything for her now.

"It's taking too long," I murmured, watching the door as the girl within renewed her efforts to escape. Parrish rolled her eyes at me and left to go to the shop door.

Layne came back with her, walking ahead at a brisk pace. I heard them talking softly as they approached, Parrish no doubt filling him in with the details I knew he'd be asking for.

He didn't look at me as he approached. His body language was all over the place and hard to read. I guessed he was consciously making an effort to keep himself in check but was struggling with it. Bully for him. I started trembling the moment I caught sight of him. I hoped he wasn't as good at reading body language as he was of controlling it.

"You said you didn't find the alpha?" he said to Parrish as he tested the rope that had by now begun to slacken with the repeated shouldering of the door from the inside.

"My guess is he attacked her quickly then took cover."

"Coward," Layne spat out. "You said she indicated he sent her here to ask for help?"

"Crafty bastard," Parrish said.

Layne laid his hand on the door and I faced Parrish, not sure I could stand to watch him.

"Why crafty?" I asked her.

"Because he wanted to freak you out."

I stared hard at the door over her shoulder, noting the way it kept gaining space in the rope to open wider with each thrust from inside. "Mission accomplished."

Layne made to yank open the door and Parrish backed me up a step, walking into me so I would move. She held her hands out at her sides, keeping me from scooting around her or the girl from reaching me if she lunged.

I expected Trish to rush him, but she just stood there, staring into Layne's eyes. Submissive. Obedient.

"Damn that freaks me out every damn time," Parrish said.

Layne extended his hand. The air swelled with energy. Parrish went to her knees, head bowed. Her movement left Layne and Trish in my full view.

The fledgling shifter took Layne's hand, her own head bowed submissively. I watched as he led her from the shop and out the front door without a single word. Only when the door closed behind him did something pop in the air and the vacuum of energy let go.

"He should be pack alpha," Parrish said and I noted there were tears in her eyes.

"Was it like that for you?" I said, realizing right then that she'd not seen me in Trish, but herself.

She turned amber eyes on me, swept me with a long, penetrating glance. "He was the only one who could stop me," she said in a soft voice. "Any other alpha, including Owen, would have killed me."

She directed her gaze to the door as though she couldn't stop herself from searching for Layne. I didn't blame her. I felt the same way. After a long while, she blew out a long sigh and stood, shaking out her legs.

"What say I bring you back to your hotel? It's already nearly dinner and Layne is going to be a while with that one. If you didn't smell like a rotten peach, I'd take you out for pizza."

I ran my hand through my hair. "I do stink. I can smell myself."

"Adrenaline sweat," she said. "It has an aroma all its own. But after a shower and a good night's sleep, you'll feel better." She looked around the shop we'd managed to put nearly to rights. "We'll tackle the rest in the morning."

I didn't argue. I had no energy or desire to anyway. "Just let me get a few things," I said, and started to gather up the photos and ephemera we'd been combing through when Trish had banged on the door. I'd order a pizza for myself and run through the papers again to see what jumped out at me.

I was happy to get into her car, and both of us were too tired to speak, so I locked up the shop while she stood to the side keeping her eye on the street. She did her usual tapping of the roof and steering wheel before turning on the ignition, and we remained silent the entire ride.

I spent the time perusing the hotel website and looking at photos. I had to give it to Owen. He didn't scrimp on the amenities. The photos showed me a suite posher than I'd ever dreamed. With a white marble walk in hot tub that resembled a Roman bath as much as it did a contemporary one, the suite took up half the floor.

A bank of windows offered a view of the city and the ocean on its outer edges. I'd be able to watch ships and pleasure boats come into harbor from the tub. The private terrace outside was lit up with solar panels that shed a warm glow over the potted plants that climbed the railings. If I cared to pull out a heavy blanket, I could lounge on one of the cushioned settees with a glass of wine. At least, that's what the website said. I probably wouldn't do more than spread my mother's papers across the coffee table and slurp coffee till I was glassy eyed.

I climbed out and shot her a reassuring smile as I pulled the books and folders against my chest.

"Come by for coffee in the morning," I said. "We'll go over all this together tomorrow while Layne does whatever he has to do. It'll keep your mind off her." By her, I knew she'd understand I meant the new werewolf. I had the feeling the girl's transformation had affected her more than she was letting on.

She nodded and I knew she was glad of the distraction. Whatever was running through her memory, it wasn't pleasant.

I slung my hip against the door, shoving it closed with a thunk. One more half smile in her direction and she pulled out of her parking space, leaving me to cart the load to my room alone. That she hadn't offered to help was one more indication she was mightily bothered by what had happened.

No matter. I could manage it by myself. In truth, I looked forward to a little time by myself anyway. And the distraction of all the papers and photos would be a good way to keep my mind off Layne.

There were more important things going on than love life troubles. Without me in his life, Layne had a better chance of staying alive. I'd just keep telling myself that until I convinced my heart to let go.

I stopped at the desk for the keycard and then got all the way to the elevators before I saw the black dog again. Abbi. That's what I'd named her when I'd had to speak of her to Scarlett. We were alone next to the bank of elevators, and Abbi shuffled her front paws without moving forward. Testing me, I suppose.

"I see you," I said with my heart in my throat. "What horrible thing are you portending now?"

Abbi's jaw moved in a silent bark. She looked better than she had in my hospital room. More solid.

She got with me into the elevator and we rode it to the top floor, and stood next to me while I set the books down to dig for my key card.

That was when she bit down on my leg, not hard, just enough to get my attention.

She barked. Loudly. Loud enough that I jumped.

"I'm going as fast as I can," I told her. Damn thing probably wanted me out of the hallway and into the safety of the room. I felt the same sort of urgency, to be honest. The hair on the back of neck was prickling. And when I got inside, maybe I'd hop into that big tub. Bubbles galore. A glass of wine just in reach. Maybe I'd order from room service and have a decadent meal.

But that's not what happened. I pressed the card against the lock and it buzzed. A little green light lit up and disappeared. I gave the door a shove with my hip as I leaned down to pick up the books.

And someone grabbed my arm from inside.

Chapter Twenty-Eight

MY SCREAM WAS SMOTHERED long before I managed to get it out as a rough and stinking palm pressed down on my mouth. Someone dragged me inside the hotel room, and I kicked madly. A man's hand, I thought and I knew I was right when he gripped me tight against his chest and his beard abraded the back of my neck as I struggled. Fetid breath washed over me. I gagged beneath his palm.

He growled low in his throat, much the same as Trish had done and for a second, I froze as I processed what that might mean. Hadn't she said both her and her boyfriend had been attacked?

The thought that I was in the hands of another were-wolf, one who might be what Parrish called a masher, made me buck and arch against him to no avail. Sucker was strong.

He hoisted me at least a foot from the floor as I tried to connect his instep with my foot. Dangling, I kicked backward, hoping to strike his shin.

I missed and my foot went between his legs instead, meeting air and putting him off kilter for a second. In the instant, I thought I might have gained enough distraction to yank free but his hold was a vise that bit into my stomach where he held me and made me gag where his palm held my mouth.

A movement to my left, where the main part of the suite held a sofa and various chairs and tables, indicated we were not alone in the room.

"Put her down," said a female voice that made my skin crawl the moment I heard the bright and cheery but so very wrong timbre.

Honey. She'd drawn the blackout curtains. The only light that played over the suite came from the flicker of dozens of black candles.

I recognized the smell of sulfur. There was the faint underlay of rosemary or thyme. Garlic, too.

Shadows moved in the space as the rustle of clothing whispered against skin.

"I said let her go," Honey said and the werewolf did just that. I immediately streaked for the door. I was mere feet away. Surely I could escape before either of them had time to react.

But she had already planned for my escape. Even as I reached for the doorknob, it glowed red with a heat that radiated to several inches away. I stopped just in time to avoid burning my hands.

"Nice," I said and swung around to face the darkness.

Now that my vision was starting to accustom to the dark, I could make out several more shapes. Twelve of them to be exact, not counting the werewolf who sort of sagged into the shadows around him like an automaton turned off for the night. The stink that came from him in waves was enough to make me want to retch.

If Honey smelled him, she made no comment as she approached me. She wore a dark cloak and hood but the details of her face were still clear even if somewhat shadowed. Where the smudges of dark struck her face on an angle, she looked ugly and hard.

"I was afraid you'd miss your home-coming," she said. "We've been waiting for you."

I stood straighter. "How did you get in here?"

She tittered a laughter that sounded like bells that had lost their tuning. "How else? We have a key."

"We," I said. "Meaning all your crazy coven."

"Not crazy. Committed."

I backed up another step, hoping the doorknob had gone cold again or that I could at least find something to wrap my hand in as I grabbed hold of it. While I stood stupidly staring at nothing, my brain working overtime but going nowhere, Honey advanced.

"You aren't thinking of leaving yet are you? We haven't even started."

The werewolf-in-waiting slid behind me, barring my retreat. With his movement, the rankness of his clothes and unwashed skin swept over me. I gagged.

"You might have made him shower first," I said to Honey. "I mean, I'm sure whatever plans you have, you can't want to do it with all this awful stench." I made a show of waving my hands as though to remove the stink from the air.

"You won't have to worry about it for long," she said.

The words put a cold claw around my heart. Whether or not I wanted to, I stepped backward into the stinking smell of the homeless addict. Instinct is terrible that way. What is a bit of stink to the very real possibility that I might be dead in a few moments.

"What is it exactly you plan to do with me?"

Fortunately, the fledgling werewolf didn't wrap his arms around me again. He merely let me sink into his filthiness. I scanned the room in the candlelight to see what was behind Honey besides the lurking witches who were covered head to toe in cloaks and hoods. Just like they'd been in my vision back in the basement.

Honey flicked her wrist, tossing the sleeve back off her wrist as though she was tossing away my comment. The movement caught the glow of the nearest candle and revealed a host of runes running up her arm.

My mouth went dry as I saw them. They looked very familiar. Except hers looked drawn on in blood. Whose blood, I didn't want to imagine. The witches behind her began to hum very low. The air vibrated.

I scrabbled behind me, trying to feel around the living zombie. "I saw you all in that basement. I saw all your fucking revolting faces."

She laughed at that. "Did you now? And just why didn't you report me to Parrish when you met me? Is it because I wasn't there or because you didn't really see us at all?"

The humming grew louder, a distraction, I thought, as she advanced on me. Why she hadn't already ordered the addict to grab me, I couldn't know. I just prayed whatever signal she was waiting for would come too late.

My fingers met the hardness of wood and plaster.

She extended her hand. "Come now, Brie. It's useless to fight your destiny even if that destiny calls you to our service. You can't leave. You saw the power we drew from the sacrifices. The reaper. The wolves we've called to our bidding."

"Wolves," I said with a snort. "Sick, homeless addicts. I'd say your powers are pretty pathetic if that's all you can do. And if you're the leader of the coven, then they really are shit out of luck. Whatever it is you want, you won't get it. I won't let you. Layne won't let you."

The humming all but halted.

"What we want," she said with a note of bitterness that told me my barb had struck home. "What we want is to finish the spell we began nearly three decades ago. The spell we've been working at for over eighty years."

I looked at her then, as the candlelight swam over her face. She looked haggard. The crags in her face came and went like a kaleidoscope playing over her expression. Her hand when it reached for me was wrinkled and crepey.

"You're dying," I said in a breath of realization. "You're all dying." I cast my glance at the coven as they eddied into a circle. Each one took their place beside a pillared candle and lit it with the same fragrant stick of incense that they passed one to the other.

The circle they'd drawn on the marble floor looked like it had been etched with tar. My mind knew the name of the fluid but it didn't want to admit what it was. In the dark, the only thing that lost its creepiness instead of gaining it was the color of blood.

"We've been waiting a long time, searched for all the right ingredients," Honey said. "All we need now is you."

"Fuck you," I said as she confirmed my fears. "Are you so arrogant that you think you can touch me without consequence?"

I lifted my chin as my fingers found the door handle finally. The wolf shifter even leaned just a bit to the side, as though he was fighting whatever spell that forced him to do Honey's bidding. "Do you really think Layne or Parrish don't know I'm here? Your DNA will be all over the place."

I jerked my chin toward their casting circle. The witches had halted in place and laid their hands each over the others' much like I would have customers do at a séance.

"Oh, darlin'," she said. "Do you really think we are without allies? Layne is tending to a very sick, very familiar looking and newly turned werewolf. He'll be busy for quite some time with the doppelganger. A feat, I must admit, was my doing. A bit of hair. A few nail clippings. The magic isn't difficult, really, and the glamor should remain in place as long as we renew it. And when the love spell kicks in—courtesy of one of our members—he'll forget about you quite quickly. After all, there won't be any body for him to find or grieve. As far as he's concerned, you've already broken his heart. He'll be dying to heal it and when you close up shop and leave town, he'll find a way to get over your little love affair."

I choked at the words as I reached behind me. I had to get out. I couldn't let this, whatever it was, happen.

My hand clutched at the knob. Mercifully, it was cold as the steel it was made of. I twisted and it released. I almost sobbed in relief. It took those seconds for me to process what she'd said.

"How do you know we broke up?"

A thousand things ran through my mind in that instant. Parrish. Parrish knew. Layne knew. Owen knew.

Owen. Knew.

"Sweet Jesus," I said. "It's been Owen all along. That rat bastard."

"I'm sure he has his reasons," she said. "The least of which, a vow he took four hundred years ago to protect our coven and do its bidding. But whatever those reasons are, it enabled us to bind him to us again. Wolves," she said with a snort. "So deathly afraid to be rogue. To be without purpose."

Putting aside the thought that Owen was centuries old, I concentrated on what the witch was really saying.

"Owen was Farrel's alpha," I said, trying to add it all together so that if I did get out of this mess, I could finger every fucking black-hearted bitch in this room.

He'd known I'd gone to the lingerie store; in fact, he'd picked the store out for me. No wonder Layne or Parrish hadn't detected a new pack scent. They were in the same pack.

Owen had bitten the addict. He'd sent the young girl to my shop, probably knowing I'd call Layne. He'd probably even demanded the coven find him a replacement for me so Layne wouldn't be heartbroken.

So he wouldn't look for me.

I sincerely doubted there was a curse on Layne at all. Unless you counted having a prick for a father. That would most surely be a horrible curse.

I shoved my hip sideways, fetching into the addict and moving him far enough to get both hands on the knob.

A bark of command from Honey and he had me by the waist. The door opened as I yanked and he pulled. The mouth of the opening yawned for me. The tongue of the hallway spread itself before me.

I was close. So damn close.

But I was losing ground and purchase as the addict tugged me back into the room. A shadow caught my eye by the elevator. A big shadow. A shadow I knew Honey was afraid of. Abbi.

I just couldn't understand why the dog hadn't just appeared in the room with me the way she usually did. Why did she wait outside like a creature of bone and blood. Why did she look as though she was waiting for something?

As it spotted me, the dog padded forward, tongue lolling out. It looked like it was grinning. The intelligence in its eye caught me off guard.

Behind me, the witches had begun to chant. Honey lifted her hand and pointed something at me. I recognized the blade I'd given to Layne, the one John Smith had used on Farrel.

"Come now, daughter of Hecate. It's time to meet your destiny."

"I'll meet your fucking face with my fist," I said, knowing it was fake bravado. I was terrified. My heart raced so fast that I was sucking air loudly.

The circle began chanting, dropping their heads back. The flames of the candles lengthened and rose to sharp peaks as their incantations rose to the air.

I wasn't sure what kind of spell they were casting until the addict behind me started walking me toward Honey. I was pushed along with him, bucking and fighting him to no avail. For a spindly fellow, he'd grown muscle much like his girlfriend had. His hold on me didn't leave me much room to struggle, but struggle I did, and when he couldn't get his feet to move past my frantic kicks, he hefted me over his shoulder.

She stepped aside to let him lead me closer to the circle.

Things went faster then. I screamed and Honey chuckled. The scent of sulfur rose around me, and I understood how a coven had been able to cloak themselves against witnesses as they performed their heinous acts. They'd used their magic to hide in plain sight.

And now, that magic was going to take my life.

CHAPTER TWENTY-NINE

IN THE NEXT MOMENT, blue light exploded over the room. The choking smell of sulfur caught in my throat. I couldn't breathe. I felt like I was drowning on dry land.

When I woke inside the casting circle, I knew I'd passed out. Evidently, I'd not struggled hard enough and the werewolf had maneuvered me. I lay on my right side, my ribs feeling like they'd taken too large an inhale.

I faced three witches from the coven whose faces were lifted slightly upward as though they were calling to God in benediction. Each of them had shed their cloaks and hoods and stood as naked as Adam. I imagined if these women, with sagging bellies and unbound hair were nude, then the rest of the coven was as well.

I didn't relish taking in any more menopausal hips and thighs. Even at my distance, the candlelight wasn't kind to the cellulite. If I wasn't sure of what would happen if I closed my eyes, I'd have squeezed them shut on the sagging skin.

Chanting rose around me, swelling and letting go with a cadence that had a musical lilt. The air was electric enough for the hairs to raise on my arms.

That was when I realized I was naked too. Damned addict had even pulled off Parrish's runners. I strained to see over my shoulder, counting the bodies that stood together in communal preparation. Yes. They were all there. Bathed in the glow of a hundred candles, their skin appeared intermittently smooth and wrinkled. The men, both of them, were bald and the light reflected off their pates and made the sheen of perspiration appear golden.

It was ungodly hot in the room. Someone had cranked the heat up way too high for the hotel to be pleased when they got the utility bill. If the bastards were cold maybe they should have kept the damn cloaks on. No one wanted to see untrimmed bush and pendulous nads. At least, I didn't. I was pretty sure I would have nightmares about aging now that I'd got such a good precognitive peek.

Using my hands, I scuttled an inch or so sideways, trying to be inconspicuous and not draw attention to my movements. The werewolf had to be there somewhere. I couldn't imagine him being let off so easily so soon.

I caught sight of him where he'd been when I last saw him. He stood near the door, a silent, sullen automaton robbed of all life. Poor, hopeless bastard.

It took me several more seconds to notice that the witches hadn't just dumped me in the middle of their casting circle. They'd prepared. Beside me, just out of reach was my amulet and my mother's grimoire.

Each of them rested in their own, smaller circle. The white outline that went round them would be salt, no doubt. That was an easy deduction. It was the small, roundish pile of dirt atop the grimoire that took a bit more deduction.

But a gal brought up by a witch enthralled with death knew what it was when she looked it over. Grave dirt. I knew from my Sunday strolls through the graveyard with mother dearest that the substance had its own powers akin to death magic. And death magic was very powerful indeed.

Whose grave it had come from I couldn't guess, but I knew it would be from someone that mattered to this coven. Maybe one of the sacrificial psychic's graves, or Smith's. I supposed any of them would provide the voltage the coven would need to ramp up their magic.

Having gotten a good look around, I tried to get up. But I couldn't manage more than a cross legged sitting posture.

The chanting grew louder, a level that should have awoken the inhabitants of the other half of the penthouse. So, they'd managed a cloaking spell as well. Yelling for help would be useless.

Bully for them, the bitches.

"What do you want with me?" I said, and when no one answered, I shouted it.

No one broke ranks or paused or got thrown off rhythm whatsoever. Each witch kept up the chanting. The only difference seemed to be that they sped up, as though they were afraid they'd get distracted. Maybe magic was much like the *Exorcist*, and they needed to quicken the pace to outsmart the devil or whoever the hell it was they were conjuring.

Satanists. I thought of Honey and my lip curled back at the newspaper clippings she'd been oh so excited to show me. It took several moments of sitting there watching the nearest witch to recognize any of the words. Hecate came through, I thought, except they pronounced it heck-a-tee. The others were Latin phrases I recalled from several spells I'd studied on Wicca blogs. I just wasn't well-versed enough to know what they were meant.

"Whatever you are doing, it's a waste of time," I said to the nearest witch, an older woman with sagging breasts.

"You'll just kill me for nothing. No one is coming. No goddess. No god. No devil." I forced a laugh because I was deathly afraid, and fear held its own power as well. I didn't want them to know how terrified I was. I didn't want to add to their wicked magic.

Someone moved in the circle behind me. I knew it by the breeze that moved across my skin, teasing the fine hairs on the back of my neck. I craned to look over my shoulder and saw Honey's face. Her hair was unbound and she'd pulled the weight of it over one shoulder. It reached the crest of her left breast. The nipple below it was swollen and large.

It wasn't her nudity that had me gaping at her, but the knife in her grip that she held onto in entirely the wrong way. Instead of the blade pointing out, she had it in a stabbing position.

"Fucked if I'll let you just kill me without a fight," I said to her.

"I'm to be first," she crowed. "Even though I'm the most naive to the coven, I found you. I get to be first."

Had she been a man, she'd have thumped her chest. As it was she tossed her hair. A lock of it swept across those full lips Parrish had so wanted to kiss.

"You'll be the first to have my fist crammed down your throat if you touch me," I said even though I knew as well as she did it was an empty threat. She didn't dignify my weak bravado with a response.

Unafraid, she stepped closer, her bare feet, slim and showing the remnants of a summer tan. She was a thong wearer, or flip-flops. The triangular strips over her instep were thin.

I cringed as she drew close, folding over to protect my belly from her attack. My mind raced but nothing worthy of escape took root as a plan within it. I waited helplessly as she approached until she stood inches from my reach.

She lifted her face to the ceiling. A hum went through the coven.

"Hecate, goddess of witchcraft, of the moon, and the night. Lady of Death, Crone mother, you who have power over the sky, the earth and sea, we are here on the waning moon as is your favor. We wait at the crossroads as is your affinity. We wait with beast and sacrifice and your blood as is your desire. We take from you all those things that you are. We take your immortality. We take your gifts. With this last sacrifice we bind your daughter to our blood. Her blood will power our magic. This ritual sanctifies our intention. You must obey. Hear us."

"Hear us," the coven repeated.

"Hear us," Honey said again.

I snorted loud enough to make Honey level her gaze at me. Her eyes were pupil-filled. She watched me as she drew the incantation out again in perfectly enunciated syllables. She extended her hand toward the door, and to my consternation, the young werewolf jerked to life.

He walked, wooden-legged and stiff to the circle. As he nudged up against the two men, they lifted their arms over his head, using their forearms to shove him toward Honey.

The young addict fell to his knees in front of her and tilted his head back, arching his throat in her direction.

She laid the blade against his throat as she intoned the words once more and I knew with both relief and dread that she was going to kill the addict and not me. The relief was short lived as I really registered that she was going to cut his throat right there in front of me.

"Seriously," I said, pleased I'd managed to put so much sarcasm in it to hide the fear. "That's going to be hard to clean. I'd rethink slitting his throat if I were you."

She flicked her gaze over me with a ghostly smile. The fledgling werewolf reached, mutely, for the handle and held it firm against his own throat. Honey released the knife to his care and touched him on the top of the head, laying her palm on his filthy hair as if it were a benediction.

"One of our own guardians," she intoned. "His magic will seal the ritual and add to our power when we most need it."

Then, the coven began to chant louder. Honey joined them, her breasts lifting as she raised her arms over her head.

The blade caught the light from a nearby candle as it glinted against the poor man's neck. I thought I heard him make a sound of protest as he wrenched his hand away. The knife clattered to the tiled floor. He swung wide eyes to mine and shuddered.

He suffered a moment of clarity. No doubt he was terrified. I reached for him, not sure what to do. But he was an innocent in all this. I had to do something even if all I could do was let him see compassion in my face.

Honey dropped to her knees, still chanting. She touched his forehead and his face went expressionless again. He retrieved the knife from the floor and stared up at Honey.

"Don't," I said, lunging for him. "Don't do this. Don't let them win."

My words didn't matter. He was deaf to them. He ran the sharp edge of the blade over his own wrist, cutting lengthwise all the way to the elbow.

A spurt of blood sprayed over Honey's stomach. Drops flew at me. They landed hot and cooled quickly.

My stomach could take no more. I folded over and threw up bile and water. My nose burned from the acidity. My gallbladder spasmed. I coughed out the last, with my palms on either side of my knees. With great effort, I managed to untuck my legs and stretch them out behind me to ease the numbness. Pins and needles immediately jolted through my feet.

I panted, chest heaving as I tried to swallow down the adrenaline that was pumping through me. I caught sight of the grimoire just inches from the fledging's body. He'd slumped onto his side, his eyes staring at me. I gagged on another rise of bile.

An eerie hush fell over the coven, one that was pregnant with tension. They waited for something to happen. Whatever they had invoked with that spell, whatever they hoped for, they weren't sure they'd achieved it.

I prayed it hadn't. I knew I wasn't just there for decoration. They'd abducted me for a reason and I was pretty sure it would be the climax of their spell. If forcing a fledgling werewolf to commit suicide was any indication, my own fate didn't seem too rosy.

I had to get to the grimoire. I had to get the amulet. That amulet could cloak me. I'd seen the grimoire blast magic at their reaper.

Either one would do, pig, I thought and tittered helplessly, manically, at the old movie reference.

I tried to claw my way toward the amulet since it was closest. Honey's bare foot came down on the floor between me and the stone.

She crouched to lift the amulet from its circle and the gem crackled and sizzled with energy as it met her fingers. I'd never seen it do that before.

That couldn't possibly be a good sign.

"Blood of Hecate, Bone of Hecate," she murmured as she turned her gaze to me. The words weren't a chant or an incantation, just thoughts spoken aloud in a musing way. "We own you."

A crack of lightening bloomed in the room at her words, a silent jolt of power that raised the hair off my head. Looking around, I saw it also lifted each witch's hair as well. Even the werewolf's hair rose from his scalp as he lay bleeding onto the marble. It stood straight up in the air, greasy and heavy looking.

I pulled my knees to my chest and hugged them tight. Despite the warmth of the room, my entire body broke out in goosebumps. A roar shredded the room, then mutated to a high pitched scream.

"She's coming," Honey said in a breathless voice. I had the feeling it wasn't what she expected. "Sweet Magic, she's coming."

She raked me with her gaze and grabbed the knife from the wolf's dead grip. "You," she said in a snarl that was reminiscent of a predator in a cage. "What did you do?"

I blinked stupidly at her. I hadn't had time to do a single thing. "Whatever it is, you did it."

I tried to get up again as she stormed the few steps toward me. Her hand was raised, the blood from the knife pooling onto her wrist as she aimed it at me.

She barked out a few incantations as the knife jabbed downward. I braced for impact, my arms flung over my throat. But whatever spell she'd tossed out ahead of her met with a blast of air that pulled my hair forward as though a gust of wind had swept over us both.

The blade yanked itself from her hand and flew toward the wall behind her. It struck an invisible barrier at the edge of the circle and fell.

The sound of it striking the tiles echoed like a gun shot.

The next I knew, Smith stood in the circle with Honey, the werewolf, and me. Every candle in the room went out as though blown dead with a single breath.

And yet, I could see clearly as if the room had been flooded with light. Smith's face was contorted in rage. Honey swung around, surprised, blinded in the darkness.

Whatever she'd been expecting it wasn't this. The circle hiccupped through its incantation before stalling altogether.

It didn't take long to figure out that none of the coven could see either. Whether they were in the dark because the candles had been snuffed or they'd been blinded by magic, I couldn't know. I just knew I saw everything as if it was day and they acted as though they couldn't make out a blessed thing.

One of them, a male witch leaned into the circle as though he was trying to make out something in the shadows. It was only when he spoke that I realized he was aiming for Honey.

"What have you done, you stupid bitch," he said as he yanked his hand from beneath his partner. Something popped in the air, as though a cord had been yanked out of a socket. "You've brought her right to us."

Honey took a step sideways, her hands out in front of her, trying to feel her way around. She panned her feet back and forth, searching for the knife, no doubt. She felt around the air in front of her chest, reaching out with those long, painted nails.

Smith watched her with amusement, closing the distance to her in a few steps slowly and deliberately. As Honey froze, sensing someone was near, he canted his head back and forth, studying her. Her chest rose and fell in spasms. One of the other witches started whimpering. Not Honey. Young and naive to the coven she might be, but she held her ground.

"We bind you," she intoned. "With our sacrifice and your own relics, we bind you here. You are mine to command. Your magic is gone, crone. We own it."

She threw her shoulders back, but I could see she was afraid. So could Smith.

"You dare test me, witch, after what I did to your lapdog wolf?"

Honey didn't budge but her breath hitched. I could see it in the way her chest hiccupped. The chanting grew faster, almost manic.

"You are ours to command," she said again, this time more uncertain. "We have your bones. We have your blood. We have your daughter." At this, she pointed at me. "With her blood we will own your immortality."

Smith grinned with an unearthly smile that sent a tremor through me.

And that's when everything went to shit.

CHAPTER THIRTY

EVERY CANDLE IN THE suite came to life with an explosion of light so bright it made the coven members rush to shield their eyes. Several of them let go gasps of surprise. Honey jumped backwards as she saw how close to her Smith stood.

The effect was that the coven dropped their circle of power. Before Honey could ward herself, Smith had grabbed her by the throat. A waddle of double chin that hadn't been there moments earlier waggled over his fist.

I crawled onto my hands and knees, intending to test the spell. If it was broken, I should be able to get up and move. And if I could move, I was going to hightail it out of there and leave the witches to their own ends. Smith included.

I managed to get to my feet. Like a fool, I hesitated for just one second and that instant was the one when Honey shouted a word of power. In response, Smith let go her throat in a jerking motion. He reeled backward as though he'd been struck.

When he stumbled against one of the men, the warlock grabbed him by the shoulders and heaved him back toward Honey with a thrust that came from every muscle. He fell on his hands and rolled over, hurt, I thought.

The coven recovered. One by one they began re-linking their hands over one another's. I sped for the nearest break, knowing if they closed the circle before I made it to the perimeter I'd be trapped inside.

I didn't make more than a single step. They closed the circle swiftly, efficiently. Witches who had done this sort of thing a thousand times before. The chanting rose afresh. Even more manic this time. As though their lives depended on it.

Maybe their lives did.

A force pressed against me, an elastic sort of wall I couldn't break through long before I reached the outer edge. My heart hammered against my ribs, sending pain up to my throat. A buzzing jolt raced down my arm. Dizziness washed over me.

Great. Another panic attack. Such perfect, perfect timing.

I stood facing a woman I recognized from the basement where Farrel had held me captive. Her gaze flicked over me as I stared at her, then they unfocused and stared over my shoulder. Her voice was all I could hear.

"Let me go," I said to her. "You don't have to do this." I clutched at my arm, praying it wasn't a heart attack. "You're killing me."

I thought she flinched but I couldn't be sure. Maybe she didn't want to be there. Maybe she had as much choice as I did.

"Help me," I rasped. "Help and I'll make sure the police know you are a friend."

She blinked. I thought she might relent, but then her chanting sped up in time with the others. She closed her eyes against me.

She'd seen something over my shoulder. Something that made her change her mind.

I grit my teeth against the pain in my arm. I forced myself to take long, intentional breaths as I spun in place. I could pass out later, maybe even die later, but I would not let these black-hearted bitches use me.

What met my gaze when I did turn around, explained the witch's hesitance. Honey advanced on Smith and in that instant, I knew she owned the power of the circle. There could be no defection. Not now.

Smith lay with his elbows on the floor, supporting him as he struggled to get up. I called out to him, shouting at him to get up.

By the time she was a foot away he had stood. I blinked at him. He didn't look weak and hurt at all. I'd thought he was afraid as he'd lain there, a victim of the coven. Now I knew he'd been biding his time. His arms hung limply at his sides, casual, unafraid. He looked strong.

"You have no power here," Honey said to him.

He cocked his head to the side, thoughtfully as he studied her.

"You might think that," he said, "but we have your wolf's magic."

At first, Honey snorted. "That wolf is dead," she said but even as the statement exited her mouth, her expression shifted. A light went on somewhere in the recesses of her memory and she didn't like what she saw. "The cop," she said. "Your familiar ate his magic."

A slow smile spread over Smith's face. "We left his body for the mortals to claim," he said. "It didn't belong to us. Magic belongs to us, though, so we took it back. And it was most welcome. You weakened us with your spells. But we have power now. Your werewolf was a gift." His expression hardened as he narrowed his gaze at her, accusatory. "We will use it well."

At that, he smiled and it looked just as wrong on a human face as it did before. It made me shudder. I backed up a step.

The magic of the circle pushed back, as if it thought I was trying to escape. I rebounded like a rubber ball and went down to my knees.

"Your coven hounded us for years, seeking our power, using our guise of humanity against me. Remember, witch. We are Hecate. We are magic's master. You will pay for your mistake. You and all your brethren."

Someone in the coven cursed and I had the feeling it was directed at Honey. Haughty or stupid to the last, she threw her shoulders back, defiant. Her moment of hesitation had ended.

"Use Farrel's magic if you can," she said. "It won't be enough. You're nothing but a shade anymore. The rest of them are foolish to be afraid of you now." Honey sent Smith a smarmy grin as she swatted her hand in the direction of her coven peers. "You can't resist us. Not now. We stripped you of your power. We drained it. That dog's magic is nothing against that of the entire coven."

"Is that what you think, witch?" he said and without waiting for Honey or the coven to respond he inclined his head toward the hotel room door. "We come. Be afraid."

I felt the air in the room squeeze, and it was so intense, my hands flew to my head, cupping my ears just because I wasn't sure my skull could contain the pressure of it. As one, the entire coven gasped, no doubt sensing the same thing. They struggled to hold their own, to keep from doing the same as me and breaking their circle.

Even Honey stumbled as she fought the instinct of her own body to protect her head, but she regained her footing quickly. She stood firm, her feet planted. Her fists were curled at her sides, her arms ramrod straight from effort.

A moment later, the black dog was there in the room with us. It drew every eye as it gathered the shadows of the room around itself and gained corporeality. Its head was low as it took in the circle. Its eyes glowed red. A sound came from its throat that sounded like no noise I'd ever heard come from a dog's throat.

My bladder spasmed with the want to release every ounce of fluid it held as the low rumble of noise carried across the room. The physiological response to dump everything unnecessary to give speed to my flight. But I couldn't flee. I was stuck there, watching with grim fascination, held fast by the magic.

"We are one," Smith said as he regarded the dog. "We are at once inside and outside the circle." He lifted his arms to the air the way a referee might before dropping a flag. "We are here. Be afraid, witch."

The arm came down, and at his words, the dog leaped.

Honey threw out her hand in a defensive gesture. She let go a shriek as the dog landed in the circle. It swung its huge head, taking in the entire coven with a sweeping glance.

I curled into a tight ball, trying to make myself as small and unnoticeable as I possibly could. I'd seen what that beast could do to human flesh. I didn't plan on being an unfortunate casualty the way Farrel had been.

Two witches from the coven dropped their hands and made to flee the circle, but their partners grabbed them by the wrist and held them firm. Someone muttered it was too late to run. Even I could see the terror in their faces. All of their faces. All I could think was if these black witches were afraid, then I should be terrified.

I dove for the dead werewolf, thinking he might be the best shield I had. I cringed there beside the dead body like a coward, and feeling sick at the same time for knowing I had no choice. If I wanted to live, I needed to let fear protect me.

Smith dropped to a crouch next to the beast and whispered in the dog's ear. That seemed to be the signal to the coven to rally their magic once more. As one, they shouted. The witches who had tried to flee shouted the loudest. Probably fear. Maybe out of instinct.

I recognized a spell when I heard it and this one came as the last syllable died. A sizzling blue light opened up in front of each witch's chest and joined them together like a chain. The whole of the room lit with a blue glow.

Honey thrust her hands out in front of her, an antenna of sorts. The light streaked toward her and gathered there as it let go the rest of the coven. Whatever they were gathering it was going to be a shitload of awful. Even Smith seemed to know it.

"Hide, daughter," he said and I took it to mean me, and I took it to mean right away.

I did my best to pull the cold body over me, fighting off the nausea that threatened to have me puking my guts up helplessly. He was already stiff, his blood already cold and sticky. Bile rose to my throat and I swallowed and swallowed convulsively to keep it down.

An ear-splitting crack rent the air and the whole of my body came alive with gooseflesh. The poor dead addict bounced atop me twice, coming down on my ribs with a sickening thud. A gust of breath escaped my lungs, leaving them burning for want of air. I'd be lucky if I hadn't cracked a rib.

I peered out from beneath the addict's shoulder to see the light Honey had gathered surrounding Smith in a macabre sort of bubble wrap. The dog strained to get at Honey's throat. She only managed to hold it back by that electric light that tethered her to the coven's magic.

I thought the coven might actually win the battle.

Then, Smith took a wide stance and opened his arms. Honey's expression of arrogance faltered.

At once, the magic pulled taut as it pulled itself free of the coven. As it snaked across the circumference of the circle, it gathered between Smith's outstretched arms as though it belonged there.

The vacuum the magic left in its wake also left Honey vulnerable, and from my spot beneath the dead boy, I could see she knew it. She threw up her arms to cover her face just as the dog leaped for her.

The magic crackled and snapped like a live wire. The voices of the coven rose. Candles around the room flickered and went out. I stuffed my fist into my mouth to keep from screaming as the dog landed with its paws flat on her chest.

She fell backwards.

In my mind's eye, I saw the moment with Farrel all over again. I imagined the tearing of flesh and the sound of thick jowls moving around blood and tissue. I sobbed at the memory and at the knowledge that this was going to happen again. That I was going to see it all over again if I didn't close my damn eyes.

Honey was a black witch, but my humanity couldn't take the thought of her dying that way. In horror.

But even as I stared, unable to hide my eyes from the sight, something shifted. Smith faltered, just a bit. The magic wavered. Honey managed to roll out of the way of the dog.

"Fucking hell," I said because I knew what it meant even though I couldn't possibly understand how she'd managed it.

Smith was losing power. Honey had been right. Farrel's magic hadn't been enough to sustain him for long. The detective hadn't been a werewolf for long. He hadn't built up centuries of power.

Honey rolled toward the knife and came up with it like a warrior, with it in her hand. Her lunge coiled the muscles in her legs.

She swung her gaze around the inside of the circle, and then she saw me.

I squeaked out my surprise and fear and ducked beneath the werewolf again, praying, praying something would distract her.

I saw her bare foot the instant before she swiped downward at me. Too late, I rolled to avoid it. At first, I thought I had managed to get away, but when I put my palm down on the floor, it slid across the marble. I left a smear of viscous fluid behind. In her attack, she'd managed to cut my arm.

"Bitch," I screamed at her and looked up in just enough time to catch Honey's wrist as she dropped the knife again.

That one instant gave Smith time to hurl himself across the circle at me.

"The runes, daughter," he said.

The runes. The knife.

I knew what I had to do. With both hands, I grappled for the handle. The coven's incantations all around me filled my ears and I'd long become deaf to the words or what they meant. If they were attempting to send power to Honey, it wouldn't be long before she attacked me with more than just a blade.

I was fighting for my life and I knew it. That alone gave me strength I didn't expect to possess. The pure frenzy of adrenaline put steel in my muscles. If my arm hurt where she cut it, I didn't feel it.

I rolled when I got my hands on her wrist and I twisted. Hard.

The knife clattered to the floor.

She went for it.

My legs were still stuck beneath the werewolf. She was going to reach the knife before I could grab it. She was right there. Right within reach of me.

Only one thought came to mind. I yelled as loud as I could. Straight into her ear right about the same time I jabbed at her face with stiff fingers.

Her hands went up instinctively to protect her hearing, and I felt the squishiness of her eye on my index finger as I met my target. My stomach recoiled at the sensation. She howled. Reeled back.

I took the instant her pain gave me to grab the knife. Fight magic with magic. I knew Smith didn't have enough. And the dog, harbinger of every awful thing that had happened to me in the last months, had disappeared again.

It was up to me to stop this.

I needed more magic than an incidental cut in the arm would allow. I needed intentional magic. I needed the ritual of doing it to myself, of bringing the blood and calling to the power with intent. I needed to call to my magic.

I took a deep breath and drew the sharp end of the blade across the runes. The pain made me gasp. I almost couldn't finish. I faltered.

Then, I caught Smith's gaze, and I could swear the corners of his eyes crinkled as he watched me. I took a sharp breath and finished the cut. Words erupted from me that I knew were incantations of power, even if I'd not studied the languages of ritual. My voice warbled at first, but it gained strength as the words left me. I was ready. The ritual was complete. Now, I could call to the magic with intention, and whatever came of it, would be the best I could do.

At the same moment my palm landed on the marks on my chest, so did Smith's. His palm was frigid, like the touch of death. But it was firm and confident. No hesitation within him as he did the same thing he'd done to me back in that basement where Farrel had held me prisoner, waiting for the coven's leisure. He'd channeled my magic then, and he did it now as we faced off with the circle.

As his palm touched down, that coldness spread within me. It burned, that cold. It drained me. I felt something coiled deep in my marrow, then circling my body like blood drawing to my solar plexus and it hurt, dammit. It really hurt.

I thought I saw Scarlett standing in the shadows, mouthing the words at me. "Don't forget."

As I looked up, hoping my awkward ritual was enough, I caught sight of a faint red glow that began to expand within the circle. It radiated energy like a forest fire and we were at its center. Honey and the coven threw their heads back, crying out as one.

Something pushed back at us. A force that felt like a nudge. Testing.

Smith held one hand out toward the circle, then. From his palm, that stream of red light spun a web of energy around the two of us. A shield, I thought. He was using the magic stored in my blood to buffer the power coming at us.

Because I didn't know how to control the power, didn't know how to use it, he was doing the work for me.

But there was more. With each pulse of energy that struck us from Honey and the coven, my insides twisted and writhed, and concentrated itself into that red beam.

Smith was fighting back. We were fighting back.

And we were winning.

Each member of the coven wavered in and out of focus. One by one, they screamed in pain. Honey called out to them, ordering them to be strong. To hold the circle.

"More, daughter," Smith said, and I gave it. I surrendered to the magic, letting it suffuse me with an electric buzz that felt like fire ants were chewing on my skin from inside trying to get out.

One of the witches, the one I'd begged to help me, let go a scream that pierced my ears and then combusted. The flame consumed her so fast, she turned to ash in seconds. Then another followed suit and another.

And all the while, Smith directed my magic. One by one, my power railed at the coven, and one by one, they turned to ash, the years or decades or centuries catching up to them at last. Six witches and one warlock fell before I knew I could offer no more.

I was too mortal to contain all that power. And in the end, my mortality failed it.

But the circle had fallen. My breath was coming in short hiccups. My lungs burned and whatever energy I had left in me wasn't even enough to follow Honey with my eyes as she lunged for the amulet and grimoire.

Smith screeched a most unholy sound when Honey's hands touched down on the objects. He was most mightily pissed, and from the bond that streamed energy between us, I felt is desolation at losing them to her care.

Even so, he didn't falter. He held his palm to my chest as Honey and the remains of the coven threw up one final spell, tossing a word of protection into the air like confetti. He kept his palm on my skin as though to break connection would make him crumble the way so many of the coven had. I didn't fight him. The magic needed a channel.

The last thing I saw as the coven broke ranks finally and began to flee the room, was sparks falling from the web, raining down on us. It was beautiful, the kind of thing you saw when you were dying.

I didn't even question the whisper in my ear as I closed my eyes. It sounded like an angel's voice calling me home. Softly feminine, it held a note of pride that made my heart swell.

"Well done, daughter," she said. "You did well."

It didn't matter that she said I did well; the verb sounded like *died*. I tended to agree with her. I did die well.

I nodded mutely, letting the rest of her words flow over me because none of them mattered. I'd made a choice to meet my maker to stop the coven. Wherever they'd fled to, for however long it would be before they re-surfaced, they were hobbled now. My magic had done that. My magic, my ritual, and my determination.

But my magic was too strong for one mortal, and I'd let it loose anyway. Now, I would pay the price.

***

Someone was shaking me awake. A cold blast of air made me shiver as my eyes fluttered open and then closed again. The scratchy heaviness of wool cascaded over my skin. The weight pressed me further into the floor.

"Brie," Parrish said. "Brie, thank Baby Jesus's balls, you're alive."

I peeled open my eyelids. The room was empty. Gone, was the coven and all its accouterments. I still lay on the floor but the werewolf was gone. So too was the amulet and grimoire, the piles of dust and cloaked hoods. While the air smelled faintly of scorched wax, every remnant of candles and sulfur had been cleaned away.

I was alone in the hotel room as though nothing had happened. Except for me being naked and weak, I might have thought I'd dreamed the whole thing.

"I called 911," Parrish said in a rush. "They're on their way. Thank god for that dog of yours, It fucking Lassie'd the hell of out me until I followed it here. Damn fucking ridiculous thing driving down the streets watching for a black dog running like the blazes in the dark." She laughed nervously. "But I did it. Steve Mac Queen and Lassie movies all rolled into this one butchy chick."

She was tying a tourniquet around my arm as she spoke. "I don't know what's worse, this arm or that chest but as God is my witness I'm going to fucking kick your ass if you live through this you stupid fucking awful bitch."

"I love you too," I mumbled.

"Shut up," she said. "You can't afford to waste energy talking." Then she hollered over her shoulder for whoever was pounding on the door to get the hell in here quick before she returned to tightening what looked like a silk scarf around my bicep.

"I remember," I said.

"What's that?" She shifted as a paramedic fell to his knees beside her, giving him room.

"I remember. What Scarlett said. I remember."

She scrambled over my torso to the side where the paramedics were already pulling out masks and bandages.

I tried to hold her gaze but she was so fuzzy, it was giving me a headache. "She said I need to find her."

"Find who?"

"My mother." I closed my eyes. I was so tired. Dying was such exhausting business. "She's lost. The coven broke her and she's lost. She needs to be put back together."

Parrish's cool palm laid itself down on my forehead and I rolled into it, enjoying the feel of comfort it gave me. The smell of her shampoo and deodorant was a relief. I could go to my grave with her comforting fragrance enveloping me.

"Tell me you'll find her," I said as I gripped her hand. "Tell me you'll help."

Parrish leaned down, brushing aside a lock of hair. "Help her yourself," she muttered. "Stay alive you fucking bitch and help her yourself."

"Promise," I said and she looked down at me with pity and grief, mourning me already, I knew. "Promise me you'll find her and put her together again."

"Girl, if Humpty Dumpty needs the king's horses and the King's men, then by Jesus we'll both gather the pieces. But I think you better get dressed first."

I tried to send her a smile to reassure her as the paramedic pulled a mask over my face. She was a good friend. I was grateful she'd been in my life. She'd try to keep me here with her humor and her will, but there were other forces at play. Stronger forces than her will and my mortal body.

Her promise was all I needed to give me courage to let go. She and Layne would find my mother. They'd discover a way to bring the goddess back to her true, tri-faceted self, and she'd make the coven pay for what they did to her.

I'd done my part. I'd done my best.

My mother had said she was proud of me. My mother, the goddess Hecate. She'd done what she could for me, protected me all these years by putting her essence into the vessels she had at hand. A man who loved her. A familiar she created from the spirits of all those creatures she'd sacrificed, giving them life eternal. A daughter who carried her blood. Those were the things Scarlett had whispered to me in the dark hours of her death.

That my mother loved me.

And that was all I needed to face what lay ahead. That sense of belonging was a caress across my forehead that remained there as they hoisted me onto a stretcher. It stayed there as they wheeled me into the hallway, and then to the elevator. It held me close as they wheeled me into the ambulance.

I held onto it just as tightly, afraid for a moment, that I'd not be brave enough to face what came, but then I caught sight of a smudge of shadow, hulking into the corner of the ambulance.

The dog. Abbi. Harbinger of all awful things. But harbinger also of life. She always kept me safe in the end, no matter what awaited me.

And I let my eyes close with the sense that everything was going to be alright.

-The End...for now-